WITCH WAY TO SPELLBINDER BAY

A Spellbinder Bay Cozy Paranormal Mystery - Book One

SAM SHORT

www.samshortauthor.com

ISBN: 9781980635116

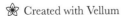 Created with Vellum

Also by Sam Short

For Katie. My very own magical lady.

Chapter 1

*M*illie peered through the grimy window at the old brick wall beyond. She pressed the phone closer to her ear as her lips formed the lie. "It's a wonderful view," she said. "The river is sparkling below me, and I can see right across London."

"It sounds lovely, Millie," said her surrogate aunt, her voice remarkably clear for somebody who was on the other side of the world. "We're so proud of you! Who'd have thought that our Millie would be a successful model, living in a London penthouse! Your mum would be grinning from ear to ear if she could see you now!"

If her Mum could have seen her now, Millie was certain that pride would have been the last thing she'd feel. Disappointment maybe. Pity definitely.

Chipped crockery rattled on the dirty sink in the corner of the room, and the light-shade swayed a little on the dirty white cord which attached it to the ceiling. She'd concluded that not only was her apartment a hovel, but that it was also situated directly above one of the underground tube-train lines which crisscrossed the bowels of the city.

Millie craned her neck to watch the polished shoes of people trudging along the pavement above her — the owners no doubt on their way to a glamorous city job, and not condemned to another long day in a damp subterranean apartment, watching daytime TV and worrying about how the rent would be paid next week.

"It's not all glitz and glamour, Aunty Hannah," said Millie, cringing as the long fleshy tail of a city rat slithered behind the plant pot outside the window. The plant in the pot had been long dead when she'd been forced to take residence in the apartment — probably a victim of engine fumes and a lack of sunlight. She supposed the plant was better off dead. Living below street level with hardly a beam of natural light, and traffic passing by all day and most of the night, was not a pleasant set of circumstances to live in. Not at all. Even for a plant.

Aunty Hannah continued. "You know you could have come with us, sweetheart. Australia is such a beautiful place, and I promised your mother I'd treat you like my own daughter. I promised her I'd look after you for as long as you wanted and needed me to." She paused and cleared her throat. "I know you know, but I just want to hear you say it one more time… you do know you could have come with us, don't you, Millie?"

"Of course I know," said Millie. She also knew that not going to Australia was turning out to be one of the worse decisions she'd ever made.

"And you know you're always welcome to come over if things don't work out for you? As long as I own a roof, there will always be a bed available beneath it for you, sweetie."

"Thank you," said Millie, wiping a finger through the dust on the once white windowsill. "Thank you for everything you've ever done for me."

Aunty Hannah coughed, and Millie guessed she was crying. She'd always been a woman who wore her heart on her sleeve, and for a moment Millie thought about telling her the truth. She thought about telling her mother's best friend that her move to London had been based on a con. A con that had seen her spend most of her savings on expensive headshots which would never get her a modelling job, and a con that had seen the promise of sharing a penthouse with two other girls, turn into the soul-destroying reality of living like a hermit in a damp and dingy flat. She swallowed. "I love you, Aunty Hannah."

"And I love you, Millie Thorn. I'm so glad you're happy, and I can't wait to see your photograph on the cover of Cosmo! I always said you were pretty. From day one, when I visited your mother in the hospital when you were born. I said, 'she's going to be a stunner, that one. You mark my words!' It's those big brown eyes of yours… they're beautiful."

It wasn't her slightly crooked nose then, or the cleft in her chin that could sometimes resemble the buttocks of an overweight builder, if the light caught it just right, that made her beautiful. No — it was just her eyes. Her best feature. The only feature people ever mentioned.

She'd been a fool. She knew as much. She was pretty, yes… but model material? Arguably not. She could admit that to herself. How she'd ever fallen for the lies of a woman who'd approached her on a social media site, offering her a contract purely on the basis of a few photographs, was beyond her.

Being a model had never been an ambition of hers, and she put the fact that she'd jumped at the chance down to the turmoil which was going on in her life at the time. She had been taken off guard. She had been taken for a fool.

However she looked at it, she'd fallen for the woman's lies — and instead of jet-setting across the world with her surrogate family, Millie had moved to London and become the victim of a sleazy scam.

Millie frowned. "Forget Cosmo and things like that," she said, conjuring up a feasible way to prevent her aunt from scouring the pages of fashion magazines in the hope of seeing pictures of her. "I'm just doing small stuff for now. Adverts for local companies and things like that. Who knows where that will take me."

"It'll take you far, my darling," said Aunt Hannah. "I'm certain of that." She paused. "Listen, sweetheart… I feel so rude… it's lovely to hear your voice, but we're in different time zones. I really must get off the phone now. I know you probably haven't had lunch yet, but it's time for me to go to bed."

"Of course," said Millie, the sound of crockery rattling from behind her once more. "Goodnight, Aunty Hannah, and pass on my love to Uncle James and Peter."

"Peter is fast asleep, but I'll tell him in the morning when I'm struggling to dress him for school. I'll tell James you send your love when I go to bed. Goodnight, Millie the model!"

Millie held the phone to her ear even after the call had ended. Wishing there was still another human on the other end. Wishing that she had somebody to talk to.

LYING ON A LUMPY MATTRESS AND WATCHING TV AT three o'clock in the afternoon was an activity Millie had never anticipated herself taking part in. She sighed. She'd look for work again tomorrow. Surely there must be one job in the whole of London which would pay a semi-unskilled person, as she liked to think of herself, enough money to pay the rent on a hovel.

In the small Welsh valley village she'd lived in with Aunt Hannah, she could have rented a three-bedroom house for the same amount she was paying to live in a slum. That bird had flown, though. Aunt Hannah had sold her home in the valleys, and Millie had no reason to return to Wales.

She'd need a plan. And she'd need it quickly. Her bank account was running on fumes, and she had nobody she could call on to borrow their sofa to sleep on for one night, let alone until she managed to get on her feet again.

She knew Aunt Hannah would pay for a plane ticket to Australia if she discovered Millie was struggling, but that was not an option. Not yet. Not while a sliver of pride remained within her dying soul.

She reached for her phone and grimaced as a static shock sparked from her fingertip. She'd been suffering a lot of static shocks recently and had put it down to the build-up of energy in the cheap nylon carpet which ran out of worn thread an inch away from each of the paint peeling walls.

Her phone felt good in her hand. A lifeline to the outside world, and the only luxury she reluctantly paid for. She opened Google and searched for jobs within five miles of her postcode. That seemed like a reasonable distance to walk each day until she'd earned enough to pay the rent and afford a bus trip twice a day.

Movement caught her eye, and Millie glanced to the left as a shadow passed the window. The sharp knock on the front door startled her. The landlord had explained that the tall iron gate set in the fence on the pavement, which opened onto steps leading down to the flat, had rusted shut years before. Millie had been forced to use the door at the rear of the building, which led off the narrow corridor outside the tiny bathroom. The door which opened onto the rat-infested rubbish strewn alleyway beyond. She'd attempted to open the gate, but it was as the landlord had told her — impenetrable due to age and weather.

Nobody should have been able to open the gate, and nobody should be knocking the door. Millie only opened it an inch or two when she wanted a little fresh air blowing into the room — and she always checked for rats first.

Even the most eager of cold-calling salespeople gave up reaching the door when they realised the gate was firmly shut in place, and the landlord had never visited, even when she'd begged him to fix the leaking water pipe which was turning one corner of the room into a thriving environment for mildew. He'd use the back door anyway.

Then it dawned on her — the police. They must have finally got around to investigating the scam she'd been a victim of. She'd reported it three weeks ago, but it seemed that losing all her savings to a con-woman masquerading as a modelling agent was near the bottom of the priority crime list. Maybe they'd forced the gate open in their eagerness to finally solve a low priority crime.

Millie climbed off the bed and ran a hand through her hair, tidying it the best she could. She opened the front door, which protested with a grumbling creak, and stared in wonder at the man who looked up at her.

"Miss Millie Thorn," he said. A statement rather than a question.

Millie managed to draw her gaze away from the man's colourful three-piece suit, a watch chain hanging from the pocket of the red waistcoat, and focused on his eyes — magnified by thick lenses set in circular gold metal frames. "How did you get through the gate?" she asked.

The man looked over his shoulder and stared at the gate, which stood wide open. "I pushed it, Miss Thorn. As one does with a standard gate." He turned his attention back to Millie, bringing his battered leather briefcase close to his chest. "Now, I think I should come in. We have a lot to discuss, and I need to be on a small island off the coast of Scotland before the full moon tonight. Time is of the essence," he insisted, taking a quick step towards the doorway.

Millie put a hand on the door-frame, using her arm as a barrier. "Wait right there!" she demanded. "I'm not about to just let you into my flat. I don't know who you are, or what you want. Are you a policeman?"

The man didn't look tall enough to be a policeman, although Millie knew height restrictions surrounding police recruitment had been lifted years ago. He seemed older than retirement age, too.

There was more, though… something Millie could

only refer to as an aura — a concept she'd never considered as being real. He simply didn't *feel* like a policeman.

"Golly gosh, no," said the man, attempting to peer past Millie, who moved to block his view. "I'm not a policeman. I'm Mister Henry Pinkerton. I'm here to change your life, Millie Thorn." He crouched to peer beneath Millie's arm at the interior of the flat, turning his short nose up at the sight. "For the better, it would seem. Let me in, Miss Thorn."

Despite not knowing the man, and despite being the recent victim of a scam, Millie surprised herself. She stood aside, not understanding why she trusted the little man, but aware that her own mind was fighting against her willingness to allow a complete stranger into her home.

The sensation in her head was not too far removed from the feeling she'd had when she'd tried cannabis for the first time… calm, but slightly confused. She was a little peckish, too.

"Shall I sit here?" said Mister Pinkerton, pointing at the only seat in the room.

Millie closed the door, rubbing her forehead. She blinked three times. "Yes, please. Sit down. Erm… why did I invite you in?"

"Because I asked you to," said Mister Pinkerton, opening his briefcase and retrieving an old black leather journal from within. "Take a seat on the bed, Millie. Let's begin."

Millie lowered herself onto the edge of the mattress, her head beginning to clear. "I don't understand why I let you in."

"I can be persuasive," said Mister Pinkerton, flicking through the yellow pages of the journal. "Here we are," he said, studying the page he'd paused on. "Millie Thorn, born on the twenty-fourth of December, nineteen-ninety-three. A Christmas baby. That makes you twenty-four years old."

"The fact that you have my date of birth written down in that book makes me nervous. What do you want, Mister Pinkerton?"

The little man smiled. "Henry, please."

Millie raised an eyebrow. "Okay. What the hell are you doing here, Henry? I don't know why I let you in, but I'm just about ready to throw you out."

Henry looked up from his book. "I'm no threat to you, Millie. You must be able to sense that?"

Millie narrowed her eyes. The man was small and certainly nearing seventy years of age. She imagined she'd be able to fight him off if he did become a physical threat, but Henry was right — Millie did sense that he was no threat to her. "Strangely, yes, I do sense I can trust you," she admitted.

"Strangely?" asked Henry, peering over his glasses.

"I'm not the best judge of character," explained Millie. "Recent events would pay testament to that statement," she added.

Henry took a fountain pen from his breast pocket and put nib to paper. "Curious," he said, taking notes. "The recent event you're referring to is the unfortunate incident involving the woman who tricked you out of your savings, promising you a job as a…" He studied the page again and smiled. "…model?"

"Why the pause and the smile?" said Millie. "Are you inferring I'm not model material? And how on earth do you know about that, anyway?"

Henry tilted his head, his eyes inquisitive as he

stared at Millie. "No. I'm not inferring anything. Not at all. I'm surprised you'd want to be a model. That's all."

"You're acting as if you know me," said Millie. "You don't know what I want or don't want in life. How could you? Just why are you here, Mister Pinkerton? And why do you have notes about me in that book of yours? How did you know that I was conned? Tell me right now, or I'm going to have to insist you leave. And then I'm going to phone the police."

Henry glanced upwards as the light-shade swayed on its cord, and looked to the left as crockery rattled on the sink. "Impressive," he said. "Could you do that once more for me, please?"

Millie took an exasperated breath. "I'm going to have to insist you leave. And then I'm going to phone the police," she repeated.

Henry shook his head. "No. I don't want you to do *that* again. I want you to make the crockery rattle and the light-shade swing again, please. If you'd be so kind."

Millie stood up, anger rising with her. "Are you here to make fun of me? I'm not in control of the London Underground train timetable, and if I was, I'd make the next train that passes beneath us rattle you right off that chair and out into the street."

Henry removed his glasses and gave a gentle smile. "There are no train tunnels beneath this street, Millie. You made those things move. You're beginning to discover who you are, and what you can do."

Unease swelled in Millie's stomach, and her mouth dried. She wanted him to go. "The only thing I'm beginning to discover is that you're more than a little strange, Mister Pinkerton," she snapped. "And I'd really like you to leave."

Henry put the journal in his briefcase, snapping the metal latches closed. He stood up. "I don't wish to make you feel uneasy, Millie," he said. "That's the last thing I want to do to you. I'll leave, but would you just do one last thing for me, please?" He reached inside his jacket and retrieved something from an interior pocket. He offered the small square of card to Millie, being sure to remain at a respectable arm's length. "Would you look at this photograph and tell me how it makes you feel?"

"Really?" said Millie.

"It would be very helpful," said Henry, "and if you still want me to leave after you've looked, I promise you'll never see me again."

Millie sighed. She glanced at the photograph between Mister Pinkerton's podgy thumb and finger. The woman was upside down, but Millie could still tell that the face portrayed was friendly. She gave Mister Pinkerton a stare which she hoped conveyed her impatience, and snatched the photo from his loose grasp.

As her skin made contact with the glossy coating, Millie's legs buckled beneath her, and with her mind calming, she lowered herself back onto the bed. "Oh," was all she could mutter. "Oh. Wow."

Chapter 2

"*H*ow do you feel, Millie?" asked Henry, sitting down and opening his journal once more.

Millie attempted to answer, but no words came. She ran a finger over the face in the picture, tracing the wrinkles in the elderly lady's face with her nail. The woman's eyes matched the obvious sincerity of her smile, and Millie could have remained sitting on the edge of her lumpy mattress staring at the stranger's face until she was forced to move.

Henry did the forcing. He leaned forward and plucked the photograph from Millie's hand. "How do you feel, Millie?" he repeated, his voice soft.

Millie shook her head and put a hand over her chest. "I'm... I'm not sure," she muttered. "I think I feel... fulfilled. I think I feel whole."

Henry scratched some notes in his book. "Like you belong?"

Millie gave a slow nod of her head. "Yes. I feel like I belong."

"Good," said Henry. "And I'm assuming that the last few weeks have been the lowest point of your life so far. Since your mother died, of course."

Whatever trance Millie had been under began to break, and she straightened her back. "How do you know about my mother?"

Henry gazed at the page before him. "She passed away after a long illness. You were ten, and your mother's best friend took you on as her own. You had no other family, and Hannah didn't want to see you end up in the care of the state."

Millie closed her eyes to prevent tears. "Yes," she said.

"Open your eyes and look at me, Millie," said Henry.

Millie did as he asked, her vision swimming with moisture.

"The last year has been hard on you, hasn't it, Millie?" asked Henry. "Your boyfriend cheated on you with the girl you called your best friend, even though you both disliked each other. The village you lived in was small, though, and friends were hard to come by. You tolerated each other in order to feel normal, in order to pretend you each had a friend. You loved your boyfriend, though." Henry studied the page. "It says here that it was real love. On your behalf anyway, not so much on his. He'd always had his eye on your friend. He used you to get nearer to her."

"How could those things be written on that page?" said Millie. "I don't understand."

Henry ignored the question. "You stayed in Britain to be with him when your aunt and uncle moved abroad, and when he left you for your friend, you had to move away from the village. You couldn't remain and be reminded about the betrayal every time you saw them together."

The strong urge to confront had abandoned Millie. The emotions she'd experienced when she'd held the photograph had been too comforting. She wanted answers, and would allow Henry to get to them in his own time — however much hurt he insisted on dredging up from her past. She gave a small nod. "Yes. That's right."

"Having moved into your boyfriend's flat when your aunt moved overseas, you had nowhere to live when your boyfriend asked you to leave. You rented a room in a nearby bed and breakfast and searched for jobs, but being under-skilled due to leaving school with no qualifications, jobs were hard to come by in such a small village.

"You posted on internet forums further afield, and just as you were about to admit to your aunt that the boy she'd warned you about had let you down, and ask her if you could move to Australia to be with her, you were contacted by a woman offering you what seemed like an answer to all your prayers."

"She said she'd seen my post on a forum and clicked on my Facebook page," said Millie. "She said I had just the sort of face she was looking for."

"People like *her* send messages to thousands of people — hoping to find somebody like *you*," said Henry.

"Like me?"

"Vulnerable," said Henry. "She took advantage of a vulnerable person. You didn't want to admit to your aunt what a terrible mistake you'd made by staying in

Britain for a boy who betrayed you, so you jumped at the chance of moving to London to live a life of what you thought would be luxury. You were taken in by a con woman while you were down on your luck. You won't be the last young person to do so."

"I suppose so," said Millie.

Henry wrote another note in the book, and peered at Millie. "So, I'll ask you again. Having spent all your savings, and not knowing where next week's rent is coming from, would you say that the last few weeks have been the lowest point of your life since the death of your mother?"

Millie slumped lower. "I'd say so."

"Good," said Henry.

"Good?" *That seemed cruel.*

Henry smiled. "It means you're ready, Millie Thorn. It means you're ready to fulfil your purpose in life. It means your powers are beginning to flourish. That's why I'm here. The reaction you had to Esmeralda proves beyond doubt that after the challenges life has put in your way, you're ready to belong again."

"Esmeralda?"

"The wit—" Henry cleared his throat. "The lady in the photograph."

Millie pressed the soles of her feet into the thin carpet and took a long breath. When she considered herself grounded enough, she stared into Henry's eyes. "What exactly is happening here?" she said. "What are you telling me? What are you *trying* to tell me?"

Henry closed his book and slid it into his briefcase. "My job isn't to explain anything to you, Millie. My job is to make you think, and when that's been achieved, which I consider to be the case, my next job is to invite you to find out more — to find out why I have all this information about you. To find out why I think you can make light-shades swing and crockery rattle, and to find out why that photograph had such an effect on you. There's a great deal for you to find out, Millie. The question is, are you intrigued enough to want to know more?"

"I need answers," said Millie. "I have a lot of questions, but I don't know which one to ask first."

Henry tugged on the watch chain in his pocket, retrieving a small silver timepiece. He opened it with one hand and glanced at it. With a concerned frown, he snapped it shut. "I'm afraid my time with you is over for the moment. I have to be in Scotland before the full moon rises, or one small island community is going to have a memorable night. A night that won't be forgotten for a very long time indeed."

"You don't have the time," said Millie. "You can't get to Scotland before nightfall. Even by plane. And what *is* going to happen if you don't get there before the moon rises?"

Henry laughed. "Oh, I'll be there on time," he said. "And it's better that I don't tell you why I must be there." He reached inside his jacket and pulled out a plain brown envelope. He placed it on the seat as he stood up. "You'll find the first piece of the puzzle in there," he said. "Open it when I've gone."

"What is it?" said Millie.

"An invitation of sorts." He took a step towards the door. "It's been a pleasure meeting you, Millie Thorn, and now I must go and meet another young person like you. Our paths will cross again soon, I hope, but for now, I bid you farewell."

Millie watched as Henry opened the front door, his briefcase in hand and a smile on his face. "Good-bye," she said, too confused to offer more.

She sat still for a few minutes after the door had closed, staring at the envelope on the seat. It seemed quite thick for a simple invitation, and Millie fought against the urge to rip it open. She knew in her soul that when she opened it there would be no going back.

There were already too many unanswered questions boring into her mind, another might send her over the edge. She'd leave the envelope until the morning, by which time her brain would have had the time to process the strange events which had already occurred.

She got to her feet, her legs a little wobbly, as if she'd been spiked with drugs, and opened the door. She stamped her feet to scare away any rats, and climbed the moss-covered steps which led to the gate. The metal felt cold against her palm as she took a firm grasp of the gate and gave it a tug. It was as she'd expected. The gate remained firmly rusted shut. There was no way such a small man as Henry Pinkerton could have forced it open. She'd seen it with her own two eyes, though. The gate *had* been open when Henry had stood on the doorstep.

Overcome with sudden fatigue, Millie trudged back into the flat, and even though darkness was still an hour away, she lay on the bed, fully clothed, and quickly fell into a deep uninterrupted sleep.

SHE WOKE TO THE LOUD RUMBLE OF TRAFFIC OUTSIDE and rubbed her head. Her phone told her it was half-past-nine in the morning. It also told her she had missed two calls.

Had she drunk alcohol last night? She didn't think so. She couldn't really afford to. Wine was too expensive for somebody struggling to pay their rent. She sat up on the bed and scanned the room for empty bottles. No, she'd not been drunk. So why the hangover?

Her eye caught the envelope on the seat, and it all came rushing back. That hadn't been real. Surely?

"It can't be," she muttered to the empty room.

Henry Pinkerton *had* been in her flat, though. If she took a deep sniff of the air she could still smell the aroma of old books and leather which had hung in the air around him. He must have drugged her. He must have used a sophisticated drug which was administered through skin contact, or through the air as an aerosol. That was the only logical reason for the strange events of the previous day and the relentless throbbing in her head.

Millie remained on her bed, studying the envelope with suspicion. Did the envelope contain traces of a drug, too? If she touched it would she experience another strange incident like the day before?

She considered phoning the police. Maybe they could give her a drug test. Henry Pinkerton was an easy man to describe, and he would have been picked up on one of the numerous CCTV cameras which lined the streets of London. It would be simple to track him down.

But she didn't feel like any harm had come to her. She didn't feel like Henry had committed a crime against her. Without being able to put a finger on why,

Millie simply knew that Henry had meant her no malice.

Then she remembered how calm she'd felt when she'd studied the photograph of the elderly lady… Esmeralda. Even repeating the name in her head stirred Millie's emotions gently, and the more she recalled the kind face of the smiling woman, the more confident she felt about the envelope. She had to open it.

She swung her legs off the bed, and crossed the room, approaching the envelope on the seat with caution, as if it might have a life of its own. It didn't of course, and as Millie stared down at the plain brown package, the more curious she became about its contents.

Taking a deep breath, she picked it up. It had a little weight, and as she pressed the package between her fingers, she guessed what made up the familiar shape of the contents.

"Money?" she whispered.

She opened the envelope gingerly, peeking inside as she folded back the flap. The scent of wealth rose to her nostrils, and Millie stared in awe at the wad of banknotes. Twenty-pound notes. Lots of them.

There was something else, too. The familiar colour of a train ticket, and a folded piece of paper tucked alongside the money.

Millie withdrew the money and placed it on the side-board. The wad was thick, and the notes were crisp and new. She placed the train ticket next to the money without checking the details, and unfolded the piece of paper. A note. Handwritten in neat curling letters, and written using real ink from a real pen, not a cheap ballpoint.

The note was short and precise.

Dear Miss Thorn,
I trust my visit was not too inconvenient to you, and I thank you for allowing me the time to speak with you.
The fact that you are reading this note means that our meeting went well, and you are ready to learn more about yourself and your rich heritage.
Please use the money for the purposes of your choice. It is yours and comes to you unconditionally.
Should, as I hope you will, wish to learn more, please use the train ticket. It is valid for five days, and I can assure you that you will not regret taking the journey.
Should you take the trip, please rest assured that all your needs will be met.
Yours sincerely,
Henry Pinkerton.

Millie refolded the note and counted the money. A thousand pounds. Why on earth would anybody give her a thousand pounds with no strings attached? There was always a catch. If something seemed too good to be true… it usually was. She'd recently learned that the hard way.

Millie's eyes widened as a worrying thought crossed her mind. *No. It couldn't be.* Henry didn't resemble the pimps she'd seen portrayed on the TV, and surely Esmeralda wasn't a madam who ran the brothel in which Millie was to be forced to work in, under the influence of drugs.

No, it was her mind playing tricks on her. There had been something kind about Henry, he wasn't that sort of man at all, and the mere memory of Esmeralda's face told Millie she was way off the mark.

That didn't mean she was about to accept the money and use a train ticket which would take her to heavens knows where — for a reason she didn't mildly understand — let alone fully understand.

No. She would put the money aside and not touch a penny of it. Henry might come back for it if he realised that Millie wasn't about to jump on a train and leave whatever semblance of a life she had behind — because a strange little man had turned up unannounced and left her a wad of cash. *No way!*

She slid the money back into the envelope and tucked the unread train ticket alongside it. She reached for the note, and drew her hand protectively against her body. The paper had moved! No, not *moved* — slid, towards her. With intent.

She glanced at the window. It remained firmly shut, and she could feel no breeze. The paper had moved on its own. She was certain of it.

She stepped backwards. The note was no longer merely moving — it was unfurling, as if an invisible hand was preparing it for reading.

With narrowed eyes, she stared at the note. Her heart thudded hard against the wall of her chest as she read it. *No*. She had to be wrong. *It was impossible.*

There they were, though. Words which she was convinced hadn't been written when she'd first read the note. A single sentence written in a neat hand at the bottom of the page. She lifted the note, touching it with care. Nervous of it. She read the newly materialised words.

P.S Before you make any rash decisions about not leaving London behind, you should listen to the two voice messages on your phone.

With trembling fingers, she slid the note back into the envelope. *Those words hadn't been there before.*

She grabbed her phone. The two missed calls were still displayed on the screen, and a further notification told her she had voice messages. She dialled the message service, waiting to hear Henry's voice, and wondering how he'd acquired her phone number, and what it was he had to say to her.

A minute later she placed the phone on the sideboard and took a seat, her legs suddenly wobbly. How could Henry have known? Had he hacked her message service? No, that was impossible. And anyway, the appearance of the fresh words on the note was far more unnerving than a potential phone hacking incident.

She re-ran the voice messages through her mind. One from the police telling her the investigation into the con-woman had been put on the back boiler for the time being, due to the lack of any leads, and the second message from her landlord, telling her the building she lived in had been classed as unsafe for human habitation. Millie was to vacate the premises by the following morning.

Millie believed the universe had plans for people. She didn't believe in a higher power, but she believed that when a person received signs, they should take heed of them.

She took a steadying breath and reached for the envelope. The train ticket felt cold between her fingers, and as she studied the destination name, the same coldness ran through her veins.

Chapter 3

a s the train left the urban landscape behind and chugged through the countryside, heading for the south coast of England, Millie allowed herself a smile. She glanced at her ticket. The destination name seemed a lot less sinister when read against the moving backdrop of rolling hills and a bright blue sky than it had in a dingy basement flat.

Anyway, she'd Googled it. Of course she had. She wasn't *that* stupid. *Spellbinder Bay* seemed like a normal small coastal town. A tourist destination in the summer, and a regular fishing town all year round. Google had informed her that the town had acquired its name because of the abundance of a certain species of seaweed which flourished in the bay, a seaweed which had gained the nickname *Spellbinder* from silly myths and legends of the past. Myths which revolved around warty old women using the seaweed to toss in their cauldrons, along with toad's legs and the eyes of newts.

The abundant seaweed had been said to possess

magical qualities, and the name Spellbinder Bay had stuck.

It was as good a name as any she supposed, and not nearly as awkward as a lot of English town and village names were, such as Bell End, or Shitterton. There were far worse place names in England to have your mail sent to than Spellbinder Bay, and it was probably the perfect name for attracting tourists to the town.

Millie gazed at the passing scenery. She knew that what she was doing would be considered stupid and dangerous by many people. If she'd had friends or family in Britain to speak to, she'd probably have allowed herself to be talked out of it, but here she was nonetheless — twenty minutes away from a town she'd never heard of before, with a thousand pounds she hadn't earned tucked away in her small suitcase, along with her meagre wardrobe and the few personal keep-sakes she owned.

The more Millie had thought about Henry's visit, and the things he'd said to her, the more intrigued she'd become. She didn't believe in the supernatural, but even she had to admit that whatever trickery Henry had used to almost convince her of its existence, had been good.

The magically appearing words on the letter had probably been written in some form of invisible ink which was activated by light when removed from the envelope. Clever.

How Henry had known she'd receive two voice messages was a mystery, but with the ever-increasing flaws in modern technology and its security, not a total impossibility.

The opening of the gate was an easier mystery to

solve. Henry was stronger than he looked. It had to be that simple. Millie had known plenty of ex-miners in the village she'd lived in in Wales. Small elderly men who, to the eye, looked weak, but after decades of arduous underground work were far stronger than they appeared to be.

With hindsight, she was sure Henry hadn't drugged her either. The reaction she'd had to the photograph, and the ease in which she'd allowed Henry into her flat must have been down to suggestive language. She'd seen celebrity illusionists like Derren Brown do it on the TV. All it took was a few trigger words and a persuasive personality.

It was the information about her that Henry had possessed which had unnerved Millie the most, and she *had* to find out why, and how, he'd known so much about her life.

There was *something* wrong with the whole situation, but Millie was as sure as she could be that she was in no danger.

To make herself feel safer, she'd contacted the Spellbinder Bay police station to let them know she was arriving. The policeman on the other end of the phone had enquired as to why Millie had felt the need to explain her impending arrival to him, but even when Millie had failed to give him a reasonable explanation, he'd still promised to fulfil the unorthodox request Millie had made of him. He would telephone her on the evening of her arrival to make sure she was safe. He probably thought she was a little mad, but that didn't bother her.

As the train rounded the base of a forested hill, Millie caught her first glimpse of the sea, peeking through a distant valley. Her spirits lifted. She was on her way to a seaside town, and she didn't know why. It was an adventure, and anything would be better than one more day beneath a pavement in London.

A young child smiled as he peeked through the gap in the seats in front of her, and Millie pulled her funniest face, eliciting a giggle from the child who stuck his tongue out at her in friendly retaliation.

When the child's mother had dragged him back into his seat, citing safety concerns, of which Millie was sure the child had no concept, she pressed her head against the glass in the rattling window and watched the scenery zoom by, wondering what life had in store for her in Spellbinder Bay.

"MILLIE THORN?"

"Erm… yes, how did you know?" Millie said.

The lady looked Millie up and down. "You're just as Henry described. Long brown hair and stout of build."

"Stout of build?" said Millie, staring down at herself. Her thighs did seem a little wide in her tight jeans, but that was probably caused by the angle she was viewing them from.

Admittedly her bras *had* begun to feel a little tighter on her back since she'd spent most of her days in her London flat doing nothing and eating too many pot-noodles, but *stout of build* seemed to Millie like an insult which would have been used in the Victorian era. "That doesn't sound very nice, and anyway… how did Henry know I was arriving today. I didn't tell anybody."

The lady waited until the train had pulled away, its

roaring diesel engine echoing through the surrounding hills. "I didn't ask him, and I don't care. I don't really want to be picking people up from the train station on a Monday afternoon. I've got far more important things to be doing than babysitting new arrivals."

Millie bristled. "And I don't require a babysitter," she said. "I didn't ask to be greeted at the station. Just tell me where I can find Henry Pinkerton, and I'll look after myself. I don't want to keep you from *important things*."

The lady peered at Millie from beneath her short greying hair and pulled her knitted floral cardigan tighter around her chest. "Just pick up your suitcase and follow me, young lady. I'm not in the mood for argie-bargy with a young upstart today. I've had my daily disagreement, and let me tell you... Albert Salmon won't be calling me a *nosy old bint* again. Not after the flea I put in his oversized hairy ear." She turned on the spot and scurried towards the car-park, where a lone yellow car sat beneath a beech tree. "Quickly, now. This way."

Getting into a car with an elderly lady she'd never met was a reasonable risk to take, Millie decided. Especially after taking the major risk of leaving London behind for reasons unknown, on the request of a money gifting stranger.

She put her suitcase on the back seat as instructed, and fastened her seatbelt as the lady started the engine and pointed the little car at the narrow country lane beyond the car-park.

"Can I ask your name?" said Millie, digging her fingernails into the seat as the car veered around a blind bend. "You know mine it seems."

The old lady squinted her eyes as sunlight flooded

the car interior, and she swung the car around another tight bend. "I'm Edna Brockett, but you can call me Mrs Brockett until I deem it acceptable that you may call me by my first name."

"It's a pleasure to meet you too, Mrs Brockett," said Millie. "I have a feeling we're going to get on like a house on fire."

"Feisty and sarcastic," said Edna, a slight smile teasing her lips. "Just how I like it."

"Where are you taking me?" said Millie, more concerned about Mrs Brockett's driving skills, or lack thereof, than the fact she deemed sarcasm a positive personal trait.

"To your cottage."

Millie's stomach flipped as the car navigated a hidden dip in the road. "My cottage? What do you mean, my cottage?"

Edna Brockett laughed. "I love that dip. I've had all four wheels off the road in the past. You have to hit it just right though, at over sixty miles an hour."

Millie dug her nails deeper into the seat. "What do you mean, my cottage?" she repeated, considering whether closing her eyes would be a good idea or not. Was it better to see death arriving, or let it take you by surprise as the car you traveled in left the road and struck a tree? She decided to keep them open.

"I mean, your cottage," said Edna. "The cottage in which you shall live. The cottage which will be your home. The cottage you own."

"I don't own a cottage!" squealed Millie, as the car rounded another bend at speed.

"I don't know what Henry has or hasn't told you, Miss Millie Thorn," said Edna. "It's not my job —

and neither am I inclined — to begin explaining things to you. Reuben will no doubt be happy to explain a few details to you when I drop you off at the cottage. He likes the sound of his own voice, that one!"

"Reuben?" said Millie, her heart hammering as hedges close enough to touch zipped by on either side of the car. "Who's Reuben?"

"He's your cockatiel," said Edna. "I'm sure you'll become very *familiar* with him." The low laugh Edna gave at the end of the last sentence gave way to the harsh squeal of brakes as the car took a lurching right turn. "There's your home," said Edna, pointing through the windscreen. "Windy-dune Cottage."

Edna slowed the car to navigate the bumpy unfinished track which meandered towards the stone cottage, and Millie gazed at the turquoise sea which the lone building overlooked. "It's…stunning," she said.

"It's yours," said Edna, drawing the car to a halt and viciously lifting the handbrake. "The key is in the door. I hope you'll appreciate it."

Millie stared at Edna. "Did you say cockatiel?"

"A few sentences ago, you dizzy young girl," said Edna, leaning over Millie to open the passenger door. "Now grab your suitcase and get out of my car, if you'd be so kind. Like I said — I have more important things to be doing."

"But I don't know what's going on. I don't know —"

Edna fixed Millie with a hard stare. "Get out now, please. I have to be somewhere."

Millie stood with her suitcase at her feet, watching the little yellow car as it bumped along the track, finally vanishing as it reached the narrow lane and turned right, heading downhill towards the little town which nestled at the base of green hills and steep cliffs.

She spun slowly to face the cottage and took a deep breath of fresh salty sea air. "Wow," she said, under her breath.

Chapter 4

*W*ith tall sweeping sand dunes behind the cottage, and smaller dunes in front, which led the eye to the golden sand of the beach below, the cottage exuded beauty. The front door faced away from the ocean, and Millie imagined the rear of the building provided a beautiful view of the sea.

The soft breeze encouraged dune grasses to perform a gentle dance, and seagulls soared on the stronger winds high above the cottage, calling out to one another. Millie was no expert on buildings throughout the eras, but she guessed the thick stone walls and slate roof meant many years had passed since it had been built.

Standing alone on the windswept and rugged seafront, the cottage commanded an outstanding view, and Millie allowed her eyes to wander. Windy-dune Cottage inhabited a finger of land which curved out into the bay, forming one half of a horseshoe. The opposite point of the horseshoe, at least a mile away, was home to another lone building — far larger than the cottage — which sat atop a tall cliff.

In the centre of the horseshoe, embraced in a sweeping hug from lush green hills and winding lanes, was the town itself. Spellbinder Bay appeared colourful and beautiful. Brightly painted homes stood in streets which crisscrossed the sides of hills, and the section of town which Millie assumed would be where the shops and businesses were situated, crept almost all the way to the seafront, meeting a harbour which homed a vibrant collection of moored vessels.

Small fishing boats slid in and out of the harbour, and when the wind blew in her face it carried with it the screaming engine sounds of a speedboat which bounced over distant waves.

She licked her lips and tasted salt, a calmness creeping over her as she took in the numerous footpaths which led in all directions from the cottage. Some of the paths snaked downhill through the sand dunes, leading to the beach, and others disappeared into the dunes behind and above the cottage.

One path, wide enough for vehicles, led away from the cottage to the very end of the spit of land, where a lighthouse stood, painted in the standard stripes of red and white she'd become accustomed to from pictures and TV shows.

Millie picked her suitcase up and stared at the cottage. It wasn't hers. *It couldn't be hers.* Edna had been wrong. She must have been. She was there now though, and she could see a set of keys glinting in the sunlight as they hung in the red wooden door. A good omen. Red had always been her favourite colour.

No fences surrounded the cottage. It seemed the sand dunes and the ocean formed natural barriers, and Millie approached the door with a little unease bubbling in her stomach. *Why was she there, and what was happening?*

She knocked on the door, the sound echoing beyond, but heard no reply. Nobody came to let her in so she tested the large brass doorknob, discovering the door was unlocked. She gave it a gentle push and stepped over the threshold, placing her suitcase on the floor next to a beautiful grandfather clock.

The scent of spices greeted her nostrils, reminding her of how much she missed the baking she'd enjoyed before moving to London. Light flooded the open plan floor space, streaming through the large french-doors at the rear of the cottage, which offered a panoramic view of the ocean beyond.

A large kitchen area occupied the space near the french-doors, accessed through an arch which led from the comfortable lounge. Millie gazed upwards. There was no upstairs she realised, and two large roof windows offered more light through the slope of the roof, and no doubt a wonderful view of the stars at night.

Only one other door led off the space, tucked away to the right of the huge stone fireplace, which Millie guessed she could stand in — if she stooped just a little. A large bookcase, complete with books, lined one wall of the lounge, and the furniture appeared to be comfortable and clean.

Even though there was no evidence of a recent fire in the hearth, the cottage was warm — probably a bonus afforded by the thick stone walls. She took her jacket off, draped it over an armchair, and gazed around.

Eye catching pictures decorated walls, with consideration for their positioning, and the large television set in the corner to the left of the fireplace didn't seem out of place in the old building. Millie stepped through the lounge area and into the kitchen. The large two door oven took pride of place — a modern piece of equipment, modelled on the old Aga design — the type of oven she'd always imagined owning one day.

In the centre of the kitchen stood a hefty oak table, and Millie smiled when she spotted the fully stocked spice rack attached to a wall. Maybe one day she'd get to use them. Maybe she could use the oven to bake some welsh cakes or a spiced loaf! She missed baking. The little grill oven in the flat in London had barely had space inside for one scone, let alone a large batch.

A shudder of delight ran through her. The place was lovely! It was just how she'd have fitted it out if she'd decorated it herself!

Millie shook herself out of the daze the gorgeous cottage had put her in. *It wasn't hers.* She had to remember that. She may even be trespassing.

She felt at home, though. She couldn't explain it, but she felt that when she'd crossed the threshold, she'd crossed into a place which made her feel… safe.

She jumped in fright as a loud squawk broke the silence. "Who's a pretty boy, then! Who's a pretty boy, then!"

Millie looked around. The unmistakeable sound of a speaking bird was coming from somewhere nearby. There it was, on a small table, pushed against the wall in the lounge — the shape of a birdcage, with a black cloth draped over it. It had to be the cockatiel which Edna had spoken of.

"Reuben's a pretty boy!" came another squawk from beneath the cloth. "Reuben's a pretty boy!"

"Oh, you poor thing!" said Millie, hurrying to the cage. "Trapped in the dark!"

Millie slid the cloth from the cage and gazed at the little bird. Coal black eyes burned vivid against the bright yellow of his face, and the red dabs of colour on his cheeks gave him the appearance of a jovial and feathery clown.

"I'm a pretty boy!" squawked the bird. "Reuben's a pretty boy!"

"You are a pretty boy, Reuben," said Millie, delighted. "A very pretty boy!"

Reuben tilted his head and fixed one little eye on Millie. "Feed me," he said, his voice an octave or two lower than it had been.

Millie took a step backwards. The bird had sounded *almost* human.

The cockatiel hopped along his perch and pecked at the cage bars. "Reuben's a hungry boy!" he squawked, his voice a speaking bird's again.

"Somebody trained you well," said Millie. "You're amazing." She looked at the little silver food bowl attached to the bars of the cage. "You have food, Reuben," she soothed. "Your bowl is full of seeds."

"Not seeds! Not seeds!" screeched the cockatiel. He lowered his head and pecked at a toe which curled around his perch. "Not seeds, I beg of you, kind lady," he said, his voice low and soft.

Millie took another step backwards, her eyes wide. "You're freaking me out," she said, her voice faltering. "You're a little too well trained."

The rumble of a loud engine outside the cottage drew Millie's attention, and she turned her back on the bird. The rumbling grew louder, and Millie was sure the wood floor beneath her feet vibrated.

"What now?" said Millie, making her way to the open doorway.

The engine noise stopped as Millie reached the open door, and she stared at the motorcycle which had pulled up outside. She didn't know much about motorbikes. Nothing at all really, but she associated the shining chrome and long handlebars of the bike outside with the type of machine that a Hell's Angel would be proud to swing a leg over. The man who climbed casually from the bike and slid his helmet off, was as easy on the eye as the machine was, too. Millie straightened her back. *He was very easy on the eye.*

The stranger placed his open-faced helmet on the bike seat, and ran a hand through his stylishly messy black hair. He gazed at Millie with piercing eyes and flashed her a gleaming smile, the masculine lines of his jawbone accentuating his perfect lips. "Hi," he said, his voice as deep as the sound the bike engine had made. "I'm George."

Millie returned his smile. "I'm Millie," she said, aware she was toying with a lock of her hair.

"Hello, Millie," said George, "I like what you've done with the place." He unzipped his black leather jacket. "The red door really stands out as you approach the cottage. And the roof windows look great. It's a nice touch."

Millie raised an eyebrow. "I haven't done anything to the place. I've only been here ten minutes, and if I'm honest, I don't even know *why* I'm here."

George looked Millie up and down. "Oh. You're *that*

new. They told me you were new around here, but I didn't realise just how new they meant."

"They?" said Millie.

George flashed another smile. "It doesn't matter."

"It *sort* of matters," insisted Millie. "If you knew what had happened to me since yesterday, you'd understand."

"Yesterday?" said George, the wind moving his hair. "What happened yesterday?" He smiled, and nodded slowly. "Oh! I see! Henry said he was visiting somebody yesterday. It was you? You didn't waste much time getting here."

"What's going on, George?" said Millie, slumping against the heavy wood of the doorway. "Who is Henry, and why am I here? Am I being groomed for some sort of cult?"

George approached the cottage, and stood in front of Millie, gazing down at her with calming eyes. "You feel safe, don't you, Millie? You might feel a little confused, but I'm guessing you feel safe? Especially in the cottage?"

Millie looked at the floor. George's eyes were too mesmerising to risk staring into for too long. "Yes, but I don't know why. It's as if I'm in a dream. It's as if I *know* I'm in a dream, and when I wake up everything will be okay — although being *in* the dream is confusing, and a little scary. Nothing makes sense. Nothing. I don't even know why I came here. I'm not the sort of person to do things like this."

"Just go with it," said George. "You'll understand everything soon enough. I promise."

That was easy for him to say. Millie shrugged off his

throwaway response. "Why did you come to see me?" she asked. "Did somebody send you?"

"I didn't come to see you, actually," said George. "It's just a *very* pleasant bonus that you're here."

Millie's cheeks burned. "Oh. Why did you come then?"

George pointed at the panniers attached to the rear of his bike. "To bring Albert Salmon some supplies, and to feed Reuben. I've been looking after him for the past week, but now you're here I won't need to do *that* job anymore. Just a visit to Albert Salmon it is," said George.

"That's the second time I've heard that name today," said Millie, "and I've been here for less than an hour."

"Oh?" said George.

Millie nodded. "The lady who picked me up from the station…Edna — I mean, Mrs Brockett, mentioned him. She said she'd had a disagreement with him today."

"Edna has disagreements with everybody," said George, with a smile, "and Albert Salmon isn't the easiest of people to get along with. Most people find him disagreeable. Put those two together and you've got a tinderbox waiting to ignite. Did she say why they'd argued?"

"No, she didn't," said Millie. "Who is this Albert Salmon?"

George pointed to his right. "The old man who lives in the lighthouse," he said. "He's housebound, due to his age and the fact he has a false leg which doesn't work too well. The witc— *lady*, who used to live in this cottage looked after him, but since last week a few people have banded together to make sure he's okay. People he hasn't offended, that is."

"What happened last week?" said Millie.

"Esmeralda passed away," said George. "But now you're here, you can take over where she left off."

"Esmeralda?" said Millie, warmth washing through her as the name left her lips. "I've heard of her. She lived here?"

George cleared his throat. "Listen, Millie. I've said too much. No more questions for now, okay? Why don't you jump on the back of my bike and come and meet Albert? If you decide to stay here he'll be your closest neighbour. You may as well get to know him. I've got a spare helmet in the pannier."

Millie looked at George, and then looked at his bike. Why not? The day couldn't get any stranger, so why not intersperse the weirdness with a ride on a motorbike with a man who looked like he should be a film-star? "Okay," she agreed. "Let me get my jacket."

"Do you mind if I come in and have a look?" said George, as Millie headed inside for her coat. "It seems to have changed a lot since Esmeralda was here."

"It's changed a lot in a week?" said Millie.

"Things move quickly around here," said George, following her inside.

Millie considered questioning just how and why the cottage had been renovated so quickly after the previous owner's death, but a fresh wave of calmness and acceptance flooded her thoughts. "Oh," she said. "I see."

"It's nice here," said George, looking around. "I like what you've… I mean *they've* done with it."

"Bloodsucker!"

Millie jumped at the sudden noise. "What did he

say?" she said, spinning to face the cockatiel. "Did he say bloodsucker?"

The cockatiel studied George with bright eyes, tilted his head, and whistled.

"What did he say?" repeated Millie. "It sounded like bloodsucker."

George shrugged. "Some nonsense. He shouts gibberish all the time." He looked at the cage. "He's not the cleverest of birds."

"Tosser!" screeched Reuben, hopping on his perch and flapping his wings. "Tosser!"

"He seems clever," said Millie. "And foul-mouthed."

George grabbed Millie's jacket from the back of the armchair and handed it to her. "We should get going. If Albert doesn't get his supplies soon, Reuben's foul mouth will seem tame in comparison to what you'll hear that old man calling me."

Chapter 5

Millie clung tight to George's waist, the smell of leather in her nose as she looked over his shoulder at the track in front of them.

He'd promised to ride slowly, and he'd stuck to his promise, although Millie guessed it was because his bike was not built for the sort of track he was navigating, rather than his concern for her trepidation.

Despite her concerns, Millie found she was enjoying the ride, and was a little disappointed when they reached the lighthouse within a couple of minutes. There was always the return journey to look forward to, she decided.

Millie climbed off the bike when George brought it to a stop outside the tall building, and removed her helmet while George placed the bike on its stand and began unpacking the panniers.

"It's quite the spot to live in," said Millie, sucking in sea air. "It's beautiful."

"Albert's a lucky man," agreed George, removing his

helmet and shaking out his hair. "It was even nicer when his wife was alive. She took more pride in the lighthouse. She even had a little rose garden near the door, and the plants climbed up the wall. Albert allowed them to wither away after Betty had gone. It's a shame."

Millie craned her neck to peer up at the building. The red stripes had looked bright and clean from a distance, but up close it was a shame to see peeling paint and dirty stains.

The lighthouse occupied the very last few feet of solid land, and the curved edge nearest the ocean loomed over jagged rocks and crashing waves — so close to the ocean that sea spray spattered Millie's face when a strong gust of wind blew inland.

She wiped water from her eyes. "Does the light still work?"she asked, gazing upward, and raising her voice to compete with the roar of breaking waves.

"No. Not for a very long time," said George, a bag of supplies in each hand. "The lighthouse was taken out of service decades ago, and the light was deactivated."

Millie followed George to the steel door. The door needed to be heavy she supposed. She imagined that in a hard winter storm the building would need to resist a ferocious onslaught from tall waves and strong winds.

"Ring the bell," said George. "My hands are full."

Millie pressed the small black button set in the wall.

"Now we wait," said George. "He'll appear at the window half way up, look out to see who it is, and if we pass muster, he'll throw us a key. He's extremely security conscious for a man who lives in a fortified tower."

"Shall I press it again?" said Millie, after half a minute had passed.

"Not if you don't like swear words," said George. "He can't walk very well, but believe me, unless he's dead, he's heard the bell and will appear at that window anytime now."

Sure enough, the small window half way up the tower swung open, and a white bearded face appeared. "Who is it? If it's you, Jim Grayson, you can bugger off! I'm not letting you in! I'm fed up of people today. I've already told you, I don't even like lobster! They taste of posh socks! Dirty ones at that!"

George took a step backwards so Albert could get a clear view of him. "It's me — George! I've got some supplies for you. Didn't you hear my bike?"

"Don't infer that I'm deaf!" shouted Albert. "My ears are just fine. I was listening to music."

"He's hard of hearing," said George. "But he won't admit it."

"Where is your bike?" shouted Albert. "I can't see it!"

"Around the side, Albert, away from the sea-spray. I value my chrome fittings."

"Bloody death trap anyway," shouted Albert. "It would be better for you if the damned thing fell in the sea. Here's the key! Catch!"

Millie shouted out in pain as the heavy metal key bounced off her head.

"Who's that? Did I hear a woman's voice?" shouted Albert.

"She's standing next to me, Albert," yelled George. "Can't you see her?"

"There's nothing wrong with my eyes either, you cheeky bugger. The sun was in them! Now get inside with my supplies before I starve to death. Esmeralda used to visit me almost every day. I never once ran out of coffee when she was around. It's only been a week since she died, and I've already been forced to drink herbal tea since this morning! Ghastly stuff that it is!"

"He heard me scream well enough," said Millie, rubbing her head. "He can't be that hard of hearing."

"It *was* a loud scream," said George, dropping the bags. "Let me look at your head, you might be cut."

Millie bowed her head as George ran his fingers through her hair, parting it to check her scalp for wounds. "No. You're not cut, but you have a small bruise. You're lucky. The key's heavy."

"You're telling me," said Millie, retrieving the key from the ground at her feet.

The key slid into the lock with a clunk and Millie gave it a firm twist, unlocking the door with a clicking of mechanisms which echoed through the heavy steel.

"Come on," said George, pushing the door open with his foot. "Let's get his coffee to him. If you think he's rude now, imagine what he'll be like when the caffeine withdrawal really sets in."

As Millie stepped into the lighthouse, she envied Albert Salmon. The circular space was larger than she had imagined it would be, and the small windows offered a gentle natural light which gave the space a cosy atmosphere.

A spiral staircase rose from the centre of the room, disappearing into the wooden ceiling, and the space was filled with odds and ends. It was obviously the portion of the building used as a halfway house for coats and dirty boots. Laundry washing and drying machines were fitted next to a large chest freezer, which shimmered with a layer of condensation, and stacks of boxes reached high up the walls.

"The other floors are a lot nicer," said George. "And you should see the view from the light-room, especially when you step out onto the balcony. Not that Albert will let anyone up there these days. He stopped using the balcony when his wife died, he says it reminds him of the meals they used to share out there, under the moonlight. He wasn't always as cranky as he'll come across to you today. It seems he was once a romantic at heart."

Millie nodded, lost in the eclectic collection of pictures and ornaments which took up wall and shelf space. It reminded her of a jumble sale, and she laughed when she saw a picture of dogs playing poker. "My mum had that picture," she said, indicating it with a nod of her head.

"I think most people have a family member who once owned one of those pictures," said George, with a smile. "Come on, shut the door, Albert will accuse us of rifling through his belongings if we don't get upstairs with his stuff."

As Millie turned to close the door, she became aware of a presence towering above her. She let out a frightened shriek and took a hurried step backwards as long white teeth glinted in the light, locked in a permanent snarl.

George laughed. "It's not the nicest of things to have in your home, is it?" he said.

"It's horrific," said Millie, shocked at the size of the animal's paws. "The poor creature."

The stuffed bear stared at them indifferently through glass eyes — its body sagging a little, as if it had given up on life for a second time.

"It's seen better days," said George, prodding the beast's limp arm. "It looks like it needs re-stuffing. It stinks, too."

"Poor thing," said Millie, picking a piece of rogue stuffing from the bear's wide chest. "It needs to be laid to rest, not filled with more stuffing."

George pushed the door closed and made for the staircase. "Come on," he said. "Forget the stuffed animal. Albert will be like a bear with a sore head if he doesn't get his coffee soon."

Millie followed George up the staircase, curious about what the next floor of the lighthouse would look like. She received a pleasant surprise.

Gone was the chaos of the ground floor, replaced with a serenity of sorts, manifested through calming pictures on the walls, and minimal furniture. The spiral staircase finished its journey on the second floor, the route to the upper floors provided by a more traditional curved flight of wooden stairs, which formed a shelter for a sofa and a sideboard.

A curved bookcase followed the contours of the wall, and a high sided leather armchair served as a throne for the man who sat in it, staring sternly at his visitors.

He narrowed his eyes and looked at George over a mass of facial hair, his long unkempt white beard displaying remnants of his last meal. "You took your time getting upstairs," he said. "Looking through my stuff, were you? Do I need to check your pockets before you leave?"

George placed the bags of supplies on the floor. "No, Albert. You don't. We're not thieves." he said. "Do you need me to take your bags up to the kitchen, or can you manage?"

Albert snorted. "I can manage."

"There's coffee in there," said George, kicking one of the bags. "Bread, tins. The normal stuff."

"Milk?" snapped Albert.

"Yes, Albert. Everything you asked for," said George.

Albert shifted in his seat, the old leather creaking under his weight. "Who's this?" he said, looking Millie up and down.

Millie smiled. "I'm —"

"I didn't ask you," said Albert. He jerked a thumb at George. "I asked him."

"As polite as ever, aren't you, Albert?" said George, offering Millie a quick wink.

Millie took a step forward. "I'm Millie," she said. "It's a pleasure to meet you."

"New," said Albert.

"Pardon?" said Millie.

Albert sighed. "Are you new around here, young lady?"

"She's moved into Esmeralda's cottage, Albert," said George.

Millie shook her head. "I've not really moved in."

"So you'll be visiting me regularly, like Esmeralda did. May she rest in peace," said Albert. "You'll do, I suppose. Just be polite and don't ask too many questions, and I'll tolerate you."

Millie understood the look George gave her — *just agree, it's easier.* "That sounds reasonable," she said, applying just the right amount of scorn to each word. "Why wouldn't it?"

"Edna told Millie she'd had a disagreement with you today, Albert," said George, changing the subject.

"Nosy old bint," said Albert, teasing his moustache

between two fingers. "A gossip, too. She was here this morning, not long before Jim Grayson turned up. She wanted to know if I was going to take flowers to Betty's grave. She told me she'd been to the grave to check if I'd visited! She called me heartless! She left the door open, too — I had to struggle down the stairs to close it after her. I shouldn't have even thrown her the key! I should have left her out there, shouting. It's none of her business what I do on a day like today. "

"A day like today?" said George.

"An anniversary," said Albert, dropping his eyes. "Three years today since Betty succumbed to her injuries. Since she died. None of Edna's business, though. Nosy old bint."

"I'm sorry," said Millie, suddenly realising how small the old man seemed, lost in the size of his chair.

"None of your concern," said Albert. He dropped his eyes, and slumped a little in his seat. "It has been a difficult day, though. I went upstairs to the balcony. I only do it on Betty's birthday or… this day every year. She loved sitting up there, watching the boats."

Millie stepped closer to Albert. "I know you don't want to hear it, but I am sorry. Today can't be easy for you."

Albert swiped a gnarled finger beneath his eye. "Aye, well. That's life, as they say. It's not been a good day, though. Before Edna arrived, a tradesman turned up. I'd forgotten I'd booked him. I threw him out after twenty minutes. He was making all sorts of noise, and I wanted to sit in peace. *Then*, after Edna had buggered off, Jim Grayson turned up, accusing me of all sorts. Accusing me of things I couldn't possibly do. I hardly take my boat out anymore, and I've never liked the taste of lobster. It's a bit posh for my common taste buds. I left *him* standing outside — I wasn't about to let him into my home."

"What did he accuse you of?" said George.

"Emptying his lobster pots," said Albert. "He's got it in that thick skull of his that somebody is sneaking out in a boat and stealing his catch before he lifts the pots. I told him that he's never been the best fisherman in the bay. He's probably lost the knack. I mean… what fool would sneak out in a boat just to steal his lobsters? The man is losing his marbles!"

"Not a great day for you at all," said Millie, seeing through the old man's harsh exterior, and sneaking a glimpse of his vulnerable interior. "Is there anything I can do to make it better?"

Albert seemed to sense that his defences had dropped. He gathered them around him again. "You can both bugger off, that's what you can do. You can leave me in peace."

Millie nodded. "Okay. We'll go. Come on, George. Albert needs to be alone."

"Lock the door after you," said Albert. "That's your key now, Millie. It used to be Esmeralda's. Just use it to let yourself in when you come to visit. Can you bake?"

"Erm, yes, I can bake," said Millie, "but I probably won't be staying in Spellbinder Bay for long, Albert. I doubt I'll be around long enough to need a key to your home."

Albert waved a disinterested hand. "You'll be here long enough to do some baking, I'm sure. Nothing bland though. Don't be bringing me cakes that taste like they came from a supermarket. And no alcohol, do you hear me? None of them fancy cakes dripping with brandy, okay? I don't touch alcohol."

"Okay," said Millie. "No alcohol and no bland baking. I get it."

Albert nodded. "And make sure to lock the door when you leave. There's been a woman skulking around on the rocks outside, next to the sea. I don't trust her."

"What woman?" said George.

"I don't know, do I?" snapped Albert. "She's been here a few times. Some blonde woman. A young un'. I shouted at her to sod off, but she ignores me, and I'm too old to be scrambling over slippery rocks to chase her away. Just lock the door. No bugger could get through that. Now go on, get lost, the pair of you."

Millie gave Albert a smile. "I hope the rest of the day turns out nicer for you."

As Millie prepared to follow George down the stairs, Albert called her back, his voice low. "Millie," he said. "Did you come here on the back of his bike?"

Millie lowered her voice to match his. "Yes."

"If you want to do something for me, promise me you'll walk away from my lighthouse. What you do on the open roads is up to you, but I'd hate for something to happen on my doorstep."

Millie tilted her head. "You don't like bikes?"

"I used to love them," said Albert. He formed a fist, and rapped on the portion of his left leg below the knee. "Hear that? It's wood. Let's just say that human flesh and metal motorbikes don't go together too well when things go wrong. You'd do well to stay off motorbikes. They ruin lives."

Millie gave him a gentle smile. "I'll walk back to the

cottage. I promise. It will be nice to admire the view," she said, her voice still hushed.

The old man gave the briefest of grins. He raised his voice, his demeanour switching. "Good. Now bugger off, and be sure to lock that door," he yelled. "I don't care who turns up after you've left — I'm not letting anybody else in today!"

Chapter 6

*a*s George started the engine, he shouted to Millie. "Enjoy the walk back. I'll see you around."

"I'm not sure how long I'll be around," said Millie, her voice competing with the engine's grumble. "I don't think I'll be staying."

"Wait until the Board of Governors have spoken to you before you decide to leave," said George. "They'll explain the things you want to know."

"The Board of Governors?" yelled Millie, as George pulled away in a spray of gravel and sand. "What's that?"

"You'll find out!" shouted George, speeding away in a cloud of dust.

Millie frowned. What on earth was going on? The day before she'd been living in a basement flat, unsure of how she was going to pay the rent, and now she was about to take a scenic walk from a lighthouse, back to a beautiful seafront cottage which she'd been told she owned. She pinched her thigh. The sharp pain told her that she was indeed awake.

She checked the lighthouse door once more. It was securely locked, just as Albert had instructed. Slipping the key into her pocket, Millie began walking, watching seabirds dipping and rising on the wind, and enjoying the scent of the salty air.

She'd been walking for less than two minutes when she heard the sound. Was it a man's shout, or was it a species of seabird she'd yet to encounter? She listened, and heard it again, the sound blown on the wind from the direction of the lighthouse.

She used a hand to shield her eyes from the sun as she turned to face the lighthouse, half expecting to see Albert shouting after her, reminding her that he hated bland baking.

There it was again. A man shouting. It was unmistakable. She couldn't make out any words, but the yells conveyed an urgency which put Millie on edge.

She scanned the rocks below the lighthouse, and then allowed her eyes to travel up the walls of the tower, checking the windows for Albert's bearded face. Movement caught her eye, right at the pinnacle of the building, on the balcony which surrounded the light. The sun was bright, and too much distance stood between her and the lighthouse to make out details, but Millie was certain that the person she could see was walking backwards.

More shouting drifted on the wind, and Millie *just knew* something was very wrong. With an urgency growing within her, she began running, closing the distance between herself and the lighthouse, trying to keep her eyes on the balcony and simultaneously scan the path ahead for trip hazards. It was impossible of course, and as Millie lifted her eyes from the path, her blood ran cold.

She stopped running, a scream forming on her lips, a scream which left her mouth as quickly as the person falling from the balcony approached the rocks and waves below.

With her own scream still ringing in her ears, Millie ran again, adrenaline affording her a speed she'd never have been capable of under normal circumstances. Her breath left her in ragged gasps, and as she neared the lighthouse, heading for the spot she seen the falling person…. *she'd seen Albert*, land on, fresh movement caught her eye.

She stopped and stared at the balcony. She'd seen something. A shadow. *Someone*. She was certain. As certain as she could be. Her legs shaking, she studied the balcony but saw nothing. She had been sure, though, and as she ran towards the rocks and waves, she kept an eye on the lighthouse door, nervous that somebody would appear.

Reaching the rocks, she slowed to a cautious walk, not wanting to see what jagged rocks could do to a human body dropped on them from height, but knowing she had to look.

She peered through her fingers, staring at the rocks and waves below her, but could find no evidence of a human, dead or alive. As another huge wave crashed over the rocks, the spray wetting her legs, Millie looked further out to sea. If Albert had perished on the rocks, it was likely that powerful waves and currents had dragged him out to sea.

The water offered her no clues. White-tipped waves

rolled and collided with one another, and a few seabirds floated on the rough water, but there was no sign of a person.

With growing enthusiasm, Millie wondered if she'd imagined the whole thing. The sun had been bright, and the calls from some seabirds could have easily been mistaken for the shouts of a man.

No. She'd seen what she'd seen.

She reached for her phone. It wasn't in her pocket. Of course it wasn't. It was on the kitchen table in the cottage, where she'd left it. There was something in her pocket, though. The key Albert had given her.

The lighthouse had taken on an ominous appearance. Looming over her, its shadow reaching inland like a blackened finger, it no longer seemed as quaint as it had five minutes earlier. With growing trepidation, Millie walked around the base of the building and stared at the door.

She withdrew the key from her pocket, but didn't slide it into the lock. She'd try the bell first. Maybe Albert had thrown something off the balcony, and was enjoying a cup of coffee inside, unaware of Millie's concerns. Or maybe — hopefully, the falling object she thought she'd seen had simply been a trick of the light.

With a shaking finger, she pressed the bell, and waited. After a minute, and with no bearded face appearing at a window, she slid the key into the lock and twisted it.

The lock clunked open, and Millie pushed the heavy door. She was taking a risk. She knew as much, but common human decency spurred her on. She had to know if Albert was okay, and if somebody else *was* in the lighthouse. She'd cross that potentially dangerous bridge when she came to it.

She was assuming too much. If another person was in the lighthouse, it didn't *necessarily* mean Albert had been pushed from the balcony, although the panicked shouting did suggest that it was a sensible, and sinister, assumption to make.

Millie peered into the lighthouse and listened. The total silence added to her growing concern, and her own voice scared her as she called out. "Albert!" she shouted. "Albert?"

No answer came, and Millie stepped into the building, her heart beating a steady rhythm. She glanced around, glad that this time she was aware of the macabre bear standing to the left of the door. A crunching sound beneath her foot made her jump. It was just a few small pieces of broken glass scattered at the feet of the bear, amongst old stuffing which had fallen from the animal.

She calmed herself, ignoring the bear's mocking gaze — it was alright for him — he was over seven feet tall and already dead. He might not have been frightened by the sudden sound of crunching glass, but Millie had every right to be scared — she still had her life to preserve, and there could have been a murderer in the building.

Looking around for something to use as a weapon, she spotted a set of golf clubs, propped up against three stacked boxes. Sliding the club with the largest head out of the golf bag, and satisfied that the room was empty of other people, Millie made her way up the spiral staircase, peeping over the floor of the room above as she neared the top.

Albert's seat stood empty, and so did the room.

The weight of the makeshift weapon in her hand installed some confidence in her, and Millie made her way up the next flight of stairs, emerging into a kitchen area. A wooden partition separated the second floor into two areas, and a bath was visible through the open door in the wall.

Millie wondered why her brain would automatically jump to the fact that a bathroom next to a kitchen was not hygienic, and not to the fact that there may be somebody hiding in it. A defence mechanism of the brain, she supposed.

She looked around the kitchen. Albert's two bags of supplies sat atop a kitchen counter, but some of the groceries lay on the floor. *Maybe there had been a struggle?*

With a rush of blood pounding in her ears, Millie stepped through the door into the bathroom. She let herself breathe again. It was empty, and there was nowhere to hide.

Holding the golf club tighter, she peered up the next flight of stairs. The lighthouse had narrowed as she'd gained height, and she was certain the next floor would be the last. The light-room, as George had called it.

She was wrong. The third floor housed a small double bed and a wardrobe. The bed was too close to the floor to offer a hiding place, so she checked the wardrobe, lifting the club above her head as she opened the door at arm's length. Devoid of people, but stuffed with clothes, Millie pushed the door closed and peered up the next set of stairs.

She took them slowly, a breeze brushing over her face as she neared the top. Peeping into the space above her, she paused before taking the final three steps. The large light filled most of the space in the room, and an open door swung in the wind, the balcony rails visible beyond it.

Climbing slowly into the room, Millie sensed there was nobody there. With large glass windows making up most of the round walls of the room, she could see outside. The balcony was devoid of people, and there was nobody crouching behind the light inside the room.

She stepped onto the balcony, the height making her stomach flip, and did a full circle of the lighthouse, relaxing a little when she found herself back at the door. She was alone. *She had seen somebody else, though*. She was sure.

She looked inland, checking for somebody running away from the building. There was nobody to be seen. She was alone, but she shouldn't be. Albert should have been there, too

Millie dropped the golf club, the handle clattering on the metal grid balcony. *Albert must be dead. He had to be.*

With tears forming, Millie gazed out to sea and studied the vast sheet of moving water below her. It didn't take long, and with a sob of horror, she stepped back into the light-room. The bright red and white checks, floating further away from the safety of shore, had been all she'd needed to see. The same red and white checks of the shirt Albert had been wearing.

Tears burned her cheeks as Millie descended the stairs. She needed to find Albert's phone.

———

"It saves me having to phone you tonight, I suppose."

Millie stared at the policeman. "What?"

"I spoke to you on the phone. I promised I'd ring you to make sure you arrived safely, remember?"

"Oh, that was you?" said Millie.

The policeman nodded, continuing to write in his notebook. "I'm the only policeman in Spellbinder Bay. Address?"

"Pardon?" said Millie, staring out to sea.

"What's your address? Where do you live?" said the policeman.

"Erm. I'm not sure."

"You're not sure?"

Millie shook her head. "Put Windy-dune Cottage down. That's where I live for the moment. The very short moment."

"Oh," said the policeman. "You're one of them."

"One of who?"

The tall man, wearing black, who'd been standing nearby took a step towards Millie. "That's enough questions, Sergeant. For now. She's new. Very new."

The policeman closed his notebook. "Oh. I see. Is she under the influence?"

"No! I'm not!" snapped Millie. "I can assure you I haven't had a drop of alcohol in days!"

The tall man gave what Millie believed to be a smile of sorts, his thin lips forming a humourless slash across his face. "Now, now, Sergeant. Whether Millie is under the influence or not is of no concern to you."

The sergeant slipped his notebook into his breast pocket. "I've got all I need, anyway. It seems Albert may have fallen, or heaven forbid, jumped. It was a sad day for him today — the anniversary of his wife's death. It may have been too much for him. We'll know more when, or if, we fish his body out of the sea. There's no evidence that anybody else was here, and Millie says she locked the door after she left the lighthouse.

"Nobody could have forced their way in, and Millie is certain there was nobody in the lighthouse when she looked around." He studied Millie's face, concentrating on her eyes. "And I'm not sure that Miss Thorn should be treated as a suspect. Not until we find out what happened, anyway."

"I haven't done anything!" said Millie. "And I told you — I'm sure I saw somebody else. On the balcony!"

The tall man in black put a gentle hand on Millie's shoulder and tucked his walking cane beneath his arm. "Sergeant Spencer knows you didn't do anything, Millie. As do I. There was either an unfortunate accident or a suicide here today… *or* perhaps you did see someone on the balcony, and we're looking for a murderer. We'll get to the bottom of it, though. We always do in Spellbinder Bay."

"Or perhaps Albert is alive and well," said Sergeant Spencer. "Perhaps he went out. Perhaps Millie imagined what she thought she saw."

"Sergeant Spencer, you trust my instincts, do you not?" said the tall man.

The Sergeant nodded. "I believe I do."

"Then you'll take Millie at her word. She speaks the truth. My instincts tell me as much. Treat the information she has gleaned us with as factual, and investigate in the manner required. You can ask her more questions when she's had time to get over the shock of what she witnessed."

"Understood," said Sergeant Spencer.

Millie stared out to sea again. "Thank you… Detective?"

The tall man gave a strangled laugh, his thinning grey hair dancing in the breeze. "I'm not a detective, Millie Thorn. I'm Mister Dickinson. I'm a headmaster. The headmaster of the school I'd very much like you to attend with me when we leave this lighthouse. There are a few… people, eager to make your acquaintance."

"I don't understand," said Millie.

"What do you not understand?" said Mister Dickinson.

Millie didn't need to wrack her brains for too long. There were a lot of things she didn't understand. "Firstly, I don't understand why a policeman *and* a head-master would turn up when I reported a possible crime. A possible *murder.* And secondly, I don't understand why you want me to visit a school. There are plenty more things I don't understand, too, but I'm not in the frame of mind to ask about them."

"A trip to the school may put you in the frame of mind to ask questions, Millie. The Board of Governors welcome questions, and I think you are already familiar with one of the board. I believe he visited you just yesterday."

"Henry Pinkerton," said Millie.

"Indeed," said Mister Dickinson.

Once again, Millie didn't understand why she felt the way she did. She *shouldn't* trust a stranger. Especially a tall thin one, dressed in black, who carried an ornate walking cane. He looked every part the villain in a chil-dren's film. Trust him she did, though, and it pained her that she didn't know why. "Where is this school?" asked Millie.

Mister Dickinson lifted his stick, and using it as a pointer, aimed it across the sea, indicating the large building built on the spit of land on the other side of the bay. "Over there," he said. "On the cliff. That's Spellbinder Hall, and waiting in that building are people who can answer all the questions you can think of, Millie Thorn. Will you come with me?"

Mister Dickinson walked towards the two vehicles parked alongside the lighthouse. Sergeant Spencer had arrived in a regular police car, but Mister Dickinson had pulled up in a large black four-by-four, complete with tinted windows.

Millie looked at Sergeant Spencer, as if for advice on what she should do. The policeman shrugged. "I don't get involved in school matters," he said. "Unless I'm asked to, but you can go. You'll be perfectly safe. Probably."

Needing, and urgently wanting answers, Millie shrugged, too. She watched Mister Dickinson bending his long body as he climbed into the black vehicle, and gave the policeman a wry smile. "Well, if I go missing, you know where I went, Sergeant Spencer."

"Aye, young lady. I'll know *exactly* where you went."

Chapter 7

*T*he fact that dusk was beginning to fall didn't help the old building's image. Spellbinder Hall reared from the clifftop, its numerous chimneys and ornate roof embellishments casting long shadows over the gravel driveway and car-park. The building was old, and constructed from what Millie guessed to be local stone, the rough edges smoothed by centuries of storms and salt air.

Stone gargoyles peered down at her as Millie followed Mister Dickinson up the steps, and two granite dragons guarded the tall door, one on either side and both gazing inland.

"This way, please," said Mister Dickinson as he pushed the door open. "Welcome to Spellbinder Hall, Miss Thorn."

It was no less unnerving inside the building. As Mister Dickinson closed the heavy door behind himself, the sound echoed through the large entrance hall, making Millie shudder. If a film director ever approached Millie in the hope she could recommend a setting for a horror film, she had just the place in mind.

The chandeliers offered a dim light, which barely illuminated the wood panel walls, and the smell of old books, dust and leather hung in the air — reminding her of how Henry Pinkerton had smelt.

"There'll be plenty of time to become acquainted with the building," said Mister Dickinson. "If you decide to stay with us. For the time being, though, I'd ask that you follow me. There are people awaiting your presence."

"Okay," murmured Millie, giving a full-sized suit of armour a wide berth as she followed the headmaster. Half expecting the visor to snap open, she averted her eyes from the antique and followed Mister Dickinson up the sweeping staircase — the metal tip of his walking cane clicking on hard wood.

He turned right at the top of the stairs, and Millie trailed dutifully behind him, under the watchful glass eyes of stuffed owls, their glass case tombs lining one long wall.

The lights were no brighter than they had been downstairs, and the hairs on Millie's arms stood on end as she peered into dark crevices and corners, her eyes making sinister shapes out of simple shadows.

The homely scent of wood polish gave her a sense of safety, and as they passed a room with an open door, the Bunsen burners lining the classroom benches, and the blackboard on the wall provided her with even more security. It *was* a school after all. Not the secretive base for a murderous cult.

Mister Dickinson paused outside a closed door. "We're here. Please have an open mind when you hear what must be said, Millie," he urged. "You may find things hard to understand at first, but please know they are true."

Millie swallowed, the lump in her throat refusing to leave. "What's happening?" she asked.

Mister Dickinson chose not to answer, and opened the door, the glow from the light within the room bathing his face in orange. "This way, Miss Thorn. It gives me great pleasure to introduce you to the remainder of the Board of Directors."

Millie stepped into the room, and blinked. She was happy to smell fresh coffee, but less happy to see the three people who lined one side of a long wooden table. Oak she presumed, but perhaps mahogany. She shook thoughts of wood from her head.

What was wrong with her? Surely the species of wood used in the construction of an admittedly beautiful piece of furniture, was less important than the fact that one of the men's eyes seemed completely black, and the stern woman seated at the end of the row had been transparent when Millie had first looked at her.

No. She couldn't have been. It was the dim lighting arrangement playing tricks on her eyes. That was the only answer that made sense. *The only answer her mind would accept.*

Millie allowed her eyes to focus again. That was better. The man's eyes were perfectly normal, and the woman was as solid as the ground Millie stood on.

She scolded herself for being so silly, aware that her body didn't feel like her own. A little like the day she was forced to stand up in front of the whole school and read the poem she'd written. On that day, she was escorted from the stage by a concerned teacher and taken to the nurse, who explained Millie had probably suffered a panic attack. Millie wondered if this school had a nurse she could bother.

She took a deep breath — just as the nurse in the *normal* school had instructed all those years ago, and shrieked as something hard pressed against the back of her knees.

"Please, sit down," said Mister Dickinson from behind her.

A chair. It was a chair! How silly of her. She sat down slowly, her eyes flitting between each of the faces that stared at her. "Thank you," she managed. "It was a chair!"

The man at the centre of the table peered at her over his spectacles. "Are you okay, Millie? You remember me, don't you?"

Millie nodded enthusiastically. "Mister Pinkerton! Henry Pinkerton! I'm so happy to see you. I didn't recognise you in the gloom. It was a chair!"

Mister Dickinson took a seat on the end of the row, and Henry spoke to him in a lowered tone. "Are you sure she's under the influence? She seems very nervous. Too nervous, one might say."

"She's had a shock, Henry," said Mister Dickinson. "She visited Albert Salmon today, with George —"

"My George?" enquired the man whose eyes Millie was almost certain *had* been black.

Mister Dickinson nodded. "Yes, Fredrick. Your George. It seems he was doing his bit for the community. He took Albert some supplies. Esmeralda used to do it, you see. Albert doesn't get out much. He can't."

"How noble," said Fredrick, the sallow skin of his

cheeks covering a narrow face. "I knew he'd eventually mature. It's taken him long enough, but he's learning."

"You mentioned a shock, Headmaster," interrupted Henry. "Let's keep the conversation on track, please."

"Of course," said the headmaster. "As I was saying, George and Miss Thorn visited Albert. Miss Thorn had just taken residence in the Coven Cottage, and it seems George invited her along with him to the lighthouse."

"Coven Cottage?" said Millie, her mouth dry, and a floating sensation in her arms.

The headmaster laughed. "I'm sorry, Miss Thorn. I mean Windy-dune Cottage, of course. What was I thinking?"

"Continue," said Henry, "and please get to the point. Miss Thorn seems very agitated."

"Well," said the headmaster. "It would seem that George left the lighthouse before Millie, and young Miss Thorn was witness to a terrible incident. She saw poor Albert fall to his presumed death from the top of the lighthouse. Thinking she had seen somebody else with Albert before he fell — or was pushed, she rushed into the lighthouse with no thought for her own safety."

"Because she was under the influence?" said Henry.

"Indeed," said Mister Dickinson. "That would explain her heightened emotions at this moment in time. Some of the magic was wasted on giving her the courage to potentially confront a murderer."

"I see," said Henry. "And Albert… what's happening there?"

"Sergeant Spencer is on it," said the headmaster. "He'll need to speak to Millie and George again, of course."

Henry sighed. "Poor Albert. We'll get to the bottom of it."

The lady at the end of the table stood up. "Should I be expecting Albert?" she said. "Perhaps I should be ready to greet him if he decides to come back?"

"No, Florence," said Mister Dickinson. "His body is yet to be recovered."

Florence sat down again, and through tear-filled eyes, Millie was certain she had witnessed her become briefly transparent again.

"I see," said Florence. "Poor fellow."

"What tune is that, Millie?" said Henry. "It's nice."

Millie concentrated on his face, watching his mouth move and hearing his words, but unable to respond.

"The tune?" said Henry. "What is it, Millie?"

Millie listened. It was a nice tune, but not one she recognised. She shrugged.

"Could you stop humming it, please Millie?" said Henry. "It's nice, but very repetitive."

Millie giggled. "I'm humming!"

"You have been for a minute or two," said Henry.

"It was quite annoying," said Fredrick. "You can't carry a tune very well at all."

Millie giggled once more. She pointed a trembling finger at Florence. "That woman was see-through! Like a misty window! Or a lacy bra!"

"How rude!" said Florence. "Bras should not be spoken of in the company of men, young lady! Such talk will make them giddy!"

"She's in shock," said Henry, reaching inside his jacket. He withdrew an object familiar to Millie, and walked around the table. "Here, Millie," he said, holding it out. "Take a look at this."

Millie took the photograph from his hand, and no sooner had the card made contact with her skin, than her mind calmed. "What's happening?" she murmured.

Henry took his seat again, straightening his shirt as he made himself comfortable. "You hold onto that photograph, Millie. I want to let you into some secrets. You've already had a hard day, and I can see you're struggling to cope, so I'll give you the basic outline. If you choose to stay with us in Spellbinder Bay, all your questions will eventually be answered, and you'll feel like a part of the community. I promise."

Millie ran a finger over the photograph of Esmeralda, her heartbeat slowing, and her breathing becoming regular. "Okay," she said. "I'm ready to listen."

Henry smiled. "Just promise me one thing, Millie. Wait until we've finished until you ask any questions. It's better that way."

"I'll try my best," said Millie, studying Florence with nervous suspicion. *She'd been transparent.*

Chapter 8

a hush fell over the room, and the four people at the table all turned their eyes to Millie.

"Millie," began Henry. "You're not human. Not in the way you think you are. None of us in this room are, and neither are a lot of the population of Spellbinder Bay."

Millie sat upright. "What do you mean — I'm not human? Of course I'm human. Is this some sick joke? Is there a hidden camera? Will I be on Youtube?"

"Hold the photograph in both hands, Millie," said Henry. "It will help to calm you."

Subconsciously, she knew Henry was right, but she wasn't sure how she knew. She did as Henry asked, a peaceful acceptance washing over her as she grasped the picture in both hands.

"There," said Henry. "You look calmer."

"I feel calmer," murmured Millie. "Why?"

"The photograph is imbued with magic, Millie. Esmeralda's magic. She was a witch, you see, and before she passed over she applied some of her magic to that photograph. The magic will only work on witches who are part of the same coven she belonged to. It works well on you, Millie. It proves beyond doubt that you are the right witch to take over Esmeralda's cottage, and her place in our society."

"The magic helped you accept things," said Mister Dickinson. "Without questioning them too thoroughly."

"Why else do you think you left everything behind and jumped on a train to come to a place you'd never heard of before?" said Henry. "Only a fool would take the risks you have since yesterday… without magic guiding them along the way."

"You're under the influence," said Florence. "That's how we like to describe it."

"That's probably why you ran into the lighthouse when you thought there could be danger inside," said Mister Dickinson. "Your inhibitions have been some-what reduced since your first meeting with Henry."

"How did you open the gate, Mister Pinkerton?" said Millie. It seemed like a sensible question, but the blank faces before her told her it probably wasn't.

"Gate?" said Henry.

"The gate outside my flat. It was rusted shut."

Fredrick gave a low laugh. "The foolish girl finds out she's a witch, and is worried about rusted gates. Are we sure she's of Esmeralda's bloodline?"

"Quite sure," snapped Henry. He smiled at Millie. "I used energy, Millie. Magic, if you will. The same magic I used on you to persuade you to allow me into your flat, and the same magic I used to change the words on the note I left for you."

"Oh," said Millie. "Magic, huh?"

Henry nodded. "The same energy you tapped into

to make the light-shade swing and the crockery rattle, Millie. The energy is all around us, you see. Invisible, but accessible to those who know how to utilise it. You were able to utilise it in moments of heightened emotions."

Millie looked at the ceiling. "So why isn't the chandelier swinging now? I'd say my emotions are extremely heightened at this moment in time!"

"Magic can't be used accidentally in Spellbinder Hall, Millie. This place is a school for the paranormal. Could you imagine the disasters we would experience if the magic of inexperienced pupils was allowed to run havoc? We have tight controls in place, and preventing subliminal magic is one of them."

"Right," said Millie. "So the swinging light-shades and rattling crockery in my flat was all down to my own subliminal magic. And the money you left for me? Is that magic, too?"

"That's your money, Millie," said Henry. "It's part of your legacy. Your inheritance. You'll never want for money again, Millie. If you choose to stay. You have access to bank accounts going back centuries, money accrued by generations of witches, and passed down the bloodline. I left that cash in case you decided not to come to Spellbinder Bay. Just enough to help you through the hard times you were in."

"Oh. I see," said Millie. "I'm rich *and* a witch. It rhymes. A rich witch."

Fredrick leaned over the table and looked deep into Millie's eyes. "Are we absolutely sure, Henry. She seems very disinterested, and you did say she'd recently been conned. Surely one of Esmeralda's bloodline couldn't be conned? They'd see right through a person with ill intentions."

"I found that curious," said Henry, "but it is what it is. She's a late developer, that's all. Her powers are yet to manifest themselves. I'm sure she'll be reading thoughts before the end of the month."

"Reading thoughts?" said Millie, clinging to the photograph. "Like a mind reader?"

"Not quite," smiled Henry. "Just thoughts, and only strong ones at that. I was surprised you'd allowed yourself to be taken in by a con woman, I'd have imagined you'd have been a better judge of character. It will come with time though. It's embedded in your bloodline."

"And I'm to believe all this?" said Millie, wondering if she should make a break for the door. The photograph calmed her, of that there was no doubt, but it did nothing to reduce the anxiety bubbling in her stomach. She was scared. More scared than she'd ever been in her life. "I'm not sure I can believe it. Any of it."

"Stubborn," said Florence, her high-necked blouse keeping her petite chin raised.

"Nervous," corrected Mister Dickinson.

"Millie," said Henry. "You come from an ancient bloodline, and much like the bloodlines of human's African ancestors have been diluted over millennia, so have yours. There was once a time when — what you would call paranormal folk — roamed the Earth, free from the danger of persecution. As humans grew greater in number — as their populations exploded, and stories began to be told about people like us, our ancestors took to the shadows, our only legacy the frightening stories people tell each other — the legends and the myths."

"All based on fact," added Florence.

"And embellished with pure fiction," said Mister Dickinson.

"Many witches walk the Earth, Millie," said Henry. "But most never come to our attention. They live out their lives, aware they are different, but never knowing why."

"Some become what humans call mediums," said Mister Dickinson.

"Or fortune tellers," said Florence. "Ridiculed by some, but cherished by others."

"How did I… come to your attention?" said Millie, every muscle in her body tense.

Henry adjusted his glasses, pushing them further behind his ears. "When a witch dies, her energy is released into the world. It needs a home — a host, if you'll allow me such vulgar terminology. It searches out who it is best suited to — normally a witch with little or no family, and a witch who is finding life hard. It searches out a witch to save, a witch to bring into the fold and out of the troubles of the outside world.

"It found you, Millie; one of Esmeralda's bloodline, and a young lady going through a hard time. When the energy found such a witch, I became aware and came to find you. You were lucky, Millie. Many witches were overlooked, and they'll continue their lives as they were, miserable and unfulfilled."

"So, you're telling me I'm a witch," said Millie, her voice sounding distant to her own ears. "And I suppose you're all magical too?"

Florence smiled. "I'm not magical, dear. Not unless you call the simple transfer of energy through a wall, magic."

"I… don't know what you mean," said Millie. She closed her eyes. She knew exactly what Florence meant, she'd seen through her. Literally. She couldn't allow herself to believe it, though. She couldn't *bring* herself to believe it.

"Oh, for goodness's sake," said Fredrick. "Enough of this beating around the bush! Florence is a ghost, I'm a vampire, and Henry is… just Henry."

Millie opened her eyes slowly, afraid of what she might see. "Vampires and ghosts, too? Wonderful."

"Others too," said Florence. "The paranormal world is a rich tapestry of diversity."

"And that's good?" said Millie.

"Of course it's good!" snapped Fredrick. "Paranormal folk have helped shape the world of humans. We've given the human world a helping hand many times over! Paranormal people walk among humans in every walk of life — inventors, doctors, actors — always doing good. For the most part. There are rogues of course, but we deal with them ourselves."

"You expect me to believe that paranormal people are walking around towns and cities across Britain?" said Millie.

"The whole world," corrected Henry.

"I think I'd have noticed if that were the case," said Millie. "As would most other humans!"

Fredrick sighed. "You've already been informed that you are not, in fact, human, Millie. Not completely. I do wish you would accept that fact. As for assuming you'd notice paranormal people — you didn't notice anything untoward about George, did you? You didn't notice that he's a vampire."

"George is a vampire?" said Millie, a chill running through her. "I see."

"I turned him myself," said Fredrick, nodding. "He's one of mine."

Deep in the part of her brain which controlled logical thought, Millie knew that everything she was being told was true. The part of her brain which protected her sanity seemed to be rebelling, though. She gave Fredrick a wry grin, and giggled. "So, you have big pointy teeth? Which you use to bite people, and turn them into vampires?"

"Only if they want me to," said Fredrick. "Only if turning them is the only way to save their life, so to speak."

Millie gripped the photograph tighter, leeching as much calming energy as she could from it. "I don't believe you. I don't believe anything any of you have told me," she lied.

Fredrick slammed his fist on the table, startling Millie, and stood up. "Right! Then I shall prove it to you!"

"No, Fredrick!" said Mister Dickinson. "This is not how we do things!"

Fredrick's eyes flashed black, and Millie sucked breath in through her teeth, her whole body trembling. Inside and out.

"Please sit down, Fredrick," said Henry Pinkerton, "or I shall be forced to ask you to leave. We're dealing with a scared young witch, not somebody who wishes to ridicule you. Have some respect for her. It's been a very long time since you were brought into the paranormal fold, but you must remember how scared you were?

How hard it was to understand what had happened to you?"

Fredrick sighed, and pulling his waistcoat tighter, he sat down, his eyes normal again. "The girl needs proof. That's all I'm saying. I know she saw my eyes upon entering the room, and Florence hasn't been at all cautious about controlling her transparency. The girl knows our utterances are the truth, her mind prevents her from believing so."

"There are better ways to prove things than by you taking on your other form, Fredrick," said Mister Dickinson. "Less frightening ways."

"And as for my transparency," said Florence. "Do you have any idea how hard it is for me to appear solid? It's not my natural state, Fredrick. It's a struggle! You can be very insensitive at times, Fredrick. Very insensitive indeed!"

"Calm yourself, Florence," said Fredrick. "Have some decorum."

"You speak to me of decorum!" said Florence. "You were prepared to transform into a vampire in front of our guest. At least I have the presence of mind to make an attempt at appearing *normal* in front of the young lady! Or perhaps I should walk through a wall, or rattle a chain! That may scare her as much as you transforming into a vampire would have!"

"Enough!" said Henry, through gritted teeth. "Enough! Our aim is to provide Millie with proof that her magic is real, not proof of everything that is paranormal. That will come to her in time — naturally — the longer she lives in Spellbinder Bay." He looked to his right. "Mister Dickinson, would you be so kind as to bring Edna into the room. Millie has already met Edna, perhaps a friendly witch's face will help ease her nerves, she appears to be very shaky."

She hadn't noticed, but as Mister Dickinson stood up and left the room, Millie realised that her legs *were* shaking, and she seemed to have developed a twitch above her right eye. She took three deep breaths and concentrated on the bottle of wine, or two, she'd already promised herself she would guzzle on her return to London — which would be as soon as Millie felt well enough to stand up, leave the room, and run from the building.

So, Edna — the woman who'd collected her from the train station was a witch. How wonderful for her! She held the photograph of Esmeralda tighter, wondering how terrified she would be *without* the calming effects of the picture. She imagined she'd most certainly be in fainting territory, if not the realm of cardiac events.

Mister Dickinson was not gone for long, and Millie kept her eyes averted from the three people at the table as she waited, ignoring Florence's smiles and Fredrick's sighs.

Henry stood up as Mister Dickinson brought the new arrival into the room. "Mrs Brockett. We have a nervous witch in our midst, a witch who is finding it hard to process events. Would you be so kind as to perform some simple magic, please? Maybe seeing what she too will be capable of one day will help her understand. And help her accept her place in life."

"Why not yourself, Henry?" said Edna, staring down her nose at Millie. "You're quite capable of magical parlour tricks."

"I wanted it to come from a female, Edna," said

Henry. "Women are more adept at being reassuring, although you don't always fit that stereotype, it would seem."

Edna shrugged. "So be it, although Miss Thorn wasn't so nervous when I picked her up from the train station. She was quite full of herself!"

Millie offered Edna a smile, her mouth too dry to form words.

Edna's expression softened. "There's no need to be so nervous, Miss Thorn. Let me show you what humans refer to as a magic trick. Perhaps that will help ease those nerves."

"Perhaps," whispered Millie, aware that the door hadn't been shut as Edna had entered the room. She should make a break for it. Escape the nightmare she seemed to be trapped in, and escape to London. Escape to anywhere. Anywhere that wasn't named Spellbinder Bay.

"Look at the fireplace, Millie," said Edna. "It appears to be normal, doesn't it? A regular fireplace, don't you agree?"

It was a large fireplace, but as Edna had pointed out, it did appear normal. Millie nodded.

"Would you like to stand up and check the stonework is solid, Miss Thorn? As they do on those magic shows that are shown on television," offered Edna, warming to her role.

Millie shook her head.

Edna took a deep breath. "Okay, Miss Thorn. Keep your eyes on the fireplace."

Thinking it better to do what was asked of her until her legs felt stable enough to make a bid for freedom and sanity, Millie turned her gaze to the fireplace.

Lifting both arms above her head, Edna took a second deep breath, and stepping towards the open hearth, began speaking, her voice controlled and slow. "From the depths of chaos, bring yourself to be known! From the bowels of the damned, show yourself to those who would judge you! Show yourself, beast! Show yourself, hellion of death! Bring forth your evil and let it be looked upon!"

Henry jumped to his feet, waving his arms. "Edna, No!"

An inky cold blackness descended over the fireplace, and as Edna dropped her arms to her sides, a tearing sound vibrated through the room, and the darkness bulged, pushing toward Millie as a widening gash appeared in the blackness, a red glow visible beyond.

"No!" yelled Henry.

Millie screamed. She screamed with all the nervous energy that had built up inside her during the time she'd been inside Spellbinder Hall. She screamed at the darkness, and she screamed at the wretched face which was forcing itself through the ever-expanding gash, the eyes a vicious yellow, and ragged strips of rotting flesh hanging from visible bone and sinew.

"Stop it, Edna!" yelled Henry. "I meant a trick such as producing some flowers, or making a book levitate. Not summoning a creature from The Chaos!"

"Oh. My bad!" said Edna.

The blackness faded, and so did the face, and as Henry approached her with concern on his face, Millie found strength in her legs. Pushing the seat from behind herself, she leapt to her feet, barged her way past Edna, and made for the open door.

"No! Let her go!" she heard Henry shout as the sound of footsteps followed her. "Let the poor girl go!"

Millie ran. She ran fast. She retraced the route along the corridor and down the stairs, and flung the main entrance door open, gasping as cool night air filled her lungs.

She stumbled down the steps and ran into the darkness, through the car-park and along the driveway, her breath leaving her in grunts and gasps.

She ran until her lungs burnt and her legs ached, and she wasn't sure how much further she would have run if the twin beams of bright oncoming headlights hadn't almost blinded her. She stopped running and looked around. She'd left Spellbinder Hall a long way behind, its lights visible high on the cliff above her, and had found her way onto a narrow country lane.

She shielded her eyes as the car headlights illuminated the lane, and with a sigh of relief as the headlights dipped, she sank to her knees. It was a police car, the bright stripes and lights on the roof a welcome sight.

"There you are!" said a voice as the car door opened.

She'd only heard the voice once before, earlier that same day, but it was as welcome and familiar as a mug of hot chocolate on a cold winter night. "Sergeant Spencer," she said, her face warm from exertion.

"Are you okay?" said the sergeant, placing a hand on Millie's back. "I've been looking for you."

"You've been looking for me?" said Millie.

A strong hand helped Millie to her feet, tucked beneath her arm. "Erm... yes," said Sergeant Spencer. "Because of what happened earlier today. I needed to ask you some questions about what Albert may have spoken to you about, and I knew you were going to Spellbinder Hall. I guessed you might still be there. I was wrong it seems — you're about a mile away, and you look like you've run a marathon. Is everything okay? What's wrong?"

Millie allowed herself to be led towards the waiting car. "You wouldn't believe me if I told you."

Opening the passenger door, Sergeant Spencer helped Millie into the car. "Try me, Miss Thorn. You may be surprised."

Chapter 9

*W*hen Sergeant Spencer had turned the car around, and was driving downhill towards the bright welcoming lights of the town, Millie began to partially relax.

"So?" said Sergeant Spencer. "Why did you look like you were running for your life when I found you?"

She hadn't taken much notice of the policeman when she'd been standing outside the lighthouse earlier that day. She'd been in shock, she suspected, but looking at him now, Millie decided he was a kind man. At least he looked like he should be.

With his hat removed, his salt and pepper hair, illuminated by the dashboard lights, gave him away as being at least in his late forties, and the creases below his eyes and around his mouth seemed formed by excess laughing. The twinkle in his eyes further backed up her assumption that he was a pleasant man. "You won't believe me, seriously," said Millie. "I'm beginning to doubt myself."

Sergeant Spencer slowed the car down as the lane

narrowed. "Did they… tell you things?" he said. "Things that scared you?"

Millie froze. "Why would you ask me that?"

Sergeant Spencer sighed. "I get the sense that you trust me, Millie. So I'm going to be honest with you. There's no point in pretending — it's dishonest, and you're worth more than that."

"What are you saying?" said Millie, already certain she knew.

The sergeant glanced to his left, and smiled. "Okay. I didn't come looking for you because of what happened at the lighthouse — although I do need to speak to you about that. I came looking for you because Henry phoned me, Millie. When you ran away. He was concerned for your safety. They all were, but they didn't want to follow you. It would have frightened you even more. Nobody wants to scare you, Millie. That's the last thing on anybody's mind."

"Are you telling me you're part of… whatever is happening in this town? This cult or whatever it is," said Millie, her legs tense.

Sergeant Spencer gave a polite laugh. "There's no cult, Millie. Or if there is, it's not the sort of cult you're thinking of. Think of it as belonging to a group — a very special group."

"A paranormal group?" said Millie, her mind struggling to process the events of the day.

"Yes," said Sergeant Spencer. "And you must believe that by now, Millie? You *must* know that's the truth? Henry told me everything that's happened to you since he visited you in London, and if by now, you don't believe what you've been told is true, then you must be either having a very realistic dream, or refusing to see what is in front of your eyes. I don't think you're asleep, Millie, so it must be the latter… right?"

Millie stared at the road ahead. The narrow lanes had given way to built-up streets, and the lights of the harbour twinkled on her left. Her breath caught in her throat. *Of course it was true.* It was the only logical explanation. She was a witch, and her whole world belief had been abruptly and terrifyingly turned on its head. Seemingly incapable of dealing with events, she asked the only rational question she could think of. "Can you take me to the train station, please?" she said. "I want to leave this town, I want to go back to…" Where did she want to go? She had nowhere to go. "I want to go somewhere else, anywhere else."

"I can't do that, Millie," said Sergeant Spencer. "Not that I don't want to. If you hadn't seen what happened to Albert Salmon today, then of course I'd help you leave town, but until we get to the bottom of what happened at the lighthouse, I can't let you leave. I've got questions to ask you and George, and anyway — you won't get a train at this time of night. This is Spellbinder Bay. We don't enjoy the pleasures of a regular train service."

"Am I in danger?" Millie spat the words out, and she was ashamed to hear her voice trembling.

Sergeant Spencer drew the car to a halt outside a pub, and turned in his seat. He smiled. "No, Millie," he said. "No. I promise you that. In fact, you're probably safer than you've ever been in your life. You're surrounded by people, both paranormal and non-paranormal, who are some of the kindest people you're ever likely to meet."

A group of men and women left the pub, laughing

as they crossed the road towards a fast food restaurant. To all intents and purposes, the group of revellers seemed normal. "So those people," said Millie, indicating the group with a nod of her head. "Are they paranormal?"

Sergeant Spencer studied the group. "Two are. I'm not sure about the other four. I have my suspicions about the big guy at the back. I think he's a wolf, but it's not polite to ask, and our paths have never crossed in a situation in which he's been charged with a crime. He'd be obliged to tell me in that instance."

Millie swallowed. "A wolf?" she shook her head, pushing the images from her mind. "No, never mind. Don't answer that. I don't think my brain could take it," she said. "And you? Are you… paranormal?"

"No!" said Sergeant Spencer with a smile. "I'm the only normie, as the paranormal kids call us, who isn't affected by the concealment magic."

"Concealment magic?" said Millie.

Sergeant Spencer put the car into gear. "That's for other people to explain to you, Millie. People who can relate to you, people who have been where you are now — scared and confused, that is." He paused. "How about I introduce you to one? Tonight? She's around your age, and she'd be happy to stay with you in your new cottage tonight and help you begin to understand what's happening. She likes wine, too, and you look like you could use a glass. Or two."

Millie gave in. She gave in to the fear. She gave in to the undeniable truth of her situation, and she gave in to the obvious sincerity of the big policeman who smiled kindly at her. "Okay," she said. "If you promise me I'm safe, I believe you. I'll put my trust in you."

What else could she do?

"Right!" said Sergeant Spencer, with a grin. "We'll go to my house, pick Judith and some wine up, and I'll take you both to Windy-dune Cottage."

"Your house?" said Millie.

"Yes," said Sergeant Spencer. "Judith lives with me. She's my daughter… my adopted daughter. She's a witch, just like you. She'll help you understand that Spellbinder Bay is just like any other town. Almost."

As Millie formed her next question, the voices of shouting men drew her attention. Sergeant Spencer took the car out of gear, grabbed his hat, and opened his door. "Wait here, Millie. Let me deal with this."

Two men stumbled from the pub doorway, grappling with each other as they screamed obscenities. The larger of the two men, clearly stronger than the thin man he was manhandling, pulled his arm back, ready to throw a punch.

"Don't you dare, Frank!" shouted Sergeant Spencer, reaching the fighting men. "If that punch connects, you'll be spending the night in a cell!"

"He started it!" said the big man. "He's been bumping into people all night. Annoying them! The last straw was when he spilt the round I'd just bought. Thirty quid it cost me, and Billy just laughed!"

"I told you!" slurred the thin man, slumping against a wall as Frank released him from his grip. "I've lost my glasses. I can't see properly."

"Drank too many glasses of whisky, more like," snarled Frank. "If you can't handle your booze, you shouldn't be drinking. You've only been in this town for a few months, and you've already managed to get banned from two pubs!"

"Calm down, fellas," ordered Sergeant Spencer, stepping between them. He looked at the thin man, who was in the process of slowly sliding down the wall. "Look at the state of you, Billy Mckenna. You can't stand up, and you stink of whisky. Vile stuff that it is."

Frank looked down at his clothing. "And look what you've done to my shirt, Billy. I'm covered with hair!"

"My dog," mumbled Billy.

"It needs a bath," said Frank, brushing hair from his clothes. "It stinks! Like you!"

"It's your fault," said Billy. "You grabbed me. I didn't rub myself on you!"

"That's enough," said Sergeant Spencer. "I've got more important things to be doing than stopping grown men fighting. Frank, get back inside the pub. Billy, go home. You've had too much to drink."

Frank rubbed at his jeans, sniffed his hands, and pushed the pub door open. "And make sure you give your dog a bath. It stinks!" he shouted, as he ventured back inside the building.

Sergeant Spencer stared down at Billy. "Come on, on your feet. Time to go home."

"I've lost my glasses. I told you," said Billy. "I can't see."

"Right. In the car," said Sergeant Spencer. "I'll take you."

"I've had a stressful day," slurred Billy, pushing himself to his feet. "I drank too much. I'm sorry if I spilt Frank's drinks."

"I'm sure you can reimburse him," said Sergeant Spencer. "When you've sobered up."

Billy wobbled behind Sergeant Spencer, and swayed

on the pavement as the policeman opened the car's back door.

"Get in," said the policeman. He winked at Millie. "Not a word about what we've been talking about, and you'd better hold your nose. Frank was right. He stinks of dirty dogs."

The journey to Billy's home was short, and Millie was thankful for that small blessing. The stench of alcohol breath mixed with wet dog emanating from the back seat of the car, was not something she could have stomached for much longer.

"See," said Sergeant Spencer, as he climbed back into the car after helping Billy to his front door. "It's a normal small town — men falling off lighthouses, drunkards, and fighting."

Millie wound her window down and sucked in a breath of nostril cleansing air. "Well if this is normal, I've had enough of normal for today. You mentioned something about wine?"

Chapter 10

*M*illie had liked Judith as soon as she'd met her. Her face hid no secrets that Millie could discern, and her smile was infectious. Before they'd even arrived at Windy-dune Cottage, Millie's spirits had lifted as Judith's easy manner and warm personality forced her to feel at ease for the first time that day. Her sparkling blue eyes and golden blonde hair matched her fun sense of humour, and despite the day's events, Millie found herself looking forward to spending some time with her.

"Enjoy your night, girls," said Sergeant Spencer, as he stopped the car outside the cottage, and Millie and Judith climbed out. "And, Millie. I *will* need to speak to you tomorrow — about what happened at the lighthouse."

"Okay, Dad," said Judith, nudging Millie with an elbow, and winking. "But give it until the afternoon, huh? We've got three bottles of wine to finish off. I suspect we'll be having a lie-in."

As the police car disappeared into the night, Millie

turned to face the cottage. *Her cottage*. Apparently. If it *was* her cottage, why did she feel so much like a trespasser?

"Are you going to invite me in, then?" said Judith. "I'm dying to find out how much it's changed since Esmeralda died."

Millie shrugged. "Of course. Let's go."

As Millie opened the door and stepped inside, she immediately relaxed. The sensation of safeness which enveloped her when she flicked the light on and stared at her surroundings, made her smile. She *felt* at home.

"It's gorgeous!" said Judith, brushing past Millie and investigating the decor. "The kitchen looks amazing! I bet the bedrooms are beautiful?"

Millie glanced at the doorway next to the fireplace. "I haven't even seen a bedroom," she said. "I didn't get much time here earlier before George arrived and whisked me away to the lighthouse."

"We'll explore properly in a minute," said Judith, opening and closing kitchen cupboards. "I need a corkscrew and two glasses. Where do you keep them?"

"I don't even know if there are any here," said Millie, gazing at Reuben. Was the little bird ignoring her? Was it even possible for a bird to ignore a person? "Hello, Reuben," she said. "I'm sorry I left you on your own all day."

The cockatiel sat facing the wall, his back to Millie, and one eye peering over his shoulder. He made a sound like a snort and forcefully span his head to his front. "Whatever," he said.

"Come on, Reuben," said Judith, over the sound of a cork popping. "Have some manners and show some respect. Millie is your witch now, treat her as such."

"I don't like her!" said Reuben. "I've been locked in this cage all day and she hasn't fed me!"

"She's been busy," said Judith, pouring wine. She offered Millie a glass. "He'll be okay when he gets used to you."

Millie took the glass and swallowed half of it quickly, wiping her mouth with the back of her hand. "Is the bird talking?" she said, her mouth already dry again. She swallowed more wine. "Is that bird *talking*?"

"Oh!" said Judith. "You two haven't been properly introduced?"

"I asked her to feed me, and she left me here while she ran off with that bloodsucker!" said Reuben, peering over his shoulder, an accusatory eye on Millie. "She left me on my own! Behind bars! Esmeralda never locked me in my cage! I don't like you, Millie Thorn. You're not my real witch!"

"Don't you dare say that!" snapped Judith. "That's very rude. She is your real witch!"

"He's talking," mumbled Millie, snatching Judith's glass from her hand and chugging half of the contents. "He is, isn't he? He's speaking. *Really* speaking."

"Nobody told me you hadn't met your familiar," said Judith, filling Millie's empty wine glass and claiming it for her own. "I'd have made a point of introducing you properly if I'd known." She walked to the cage, bent down, and opened the door. "Millie, this is Reuben. He's what we call your familiar. Just think of him as a companion and an advisor. Of sorts. Don't take *too* much of his advice to heart, though."

"Erm… hello, Reuben," said Millie. "I'm sorry I left you on your own for the day… things have been a little… weird for me."

"I'm not speaking to her," said Rueben, closing his eyes and pressing his chin into his plumage. "Tell her I've been lonely and hungry, and that I have feelings too. Tell her my life is important to me! Tell her, Judith! Tell her right this second!"

"Grow up, Reuben," said Judith. "Tell her yourself."

"I heard what you said, Reuben," said Millie, the alcohol helping the situation seem less insane than it had a minute before. "And I'm sorry. Would you like something to eat? Can I get you some fresh seeds? You haven't touched the ones in your bowl."

"Tell her I explained to her this morning that I don't like seeds!" said Reuben, swivelling on his perch to face Millie. He fixed an eye on her. "*Tell her* that since Esmeralda… left, and George has been *looking after me* — that he's been making me eat seeds. He thinks it's funny. I think he's a bloodsucking bastard! Tell her, Judith! Tell her that a vampire has been toying with my emotions!"

Millie sighed. "I didn't know you could *really* talk, this morning," she said. "I just thought you were very well trained. I'm sorry. I don't know what you like to eat. What would you like, Reuben?"

"Tell her I like Pizza, Judith," said Reuben, lifting his chin. "Tell her I like thin crust pizza. Tell her I specifically like to eat thin crust mighty-meaty pizza from Pepino's pizza and kebab parlour in town, whose food is both tasty and affordable, *plus* they will deliver for free within a three-mile radius. Tell her this cottage is within that radius, Judith. Tell her I'm more affable on a full stomach. I think it's a blood sugar thing. You don't need to tell her that last part, though — it was simply an observation on my behalf."

Millie sipped her wine, and smiled. "Judith, would

you please tell Reuben that I'm very fond of pizza, too. I haven't eaten all day, and I'm starving. Perhaps I'll order some. If it's safe for birds to eat pizza, of course."

"Oh, it's safe for *this* bird to eat pizza," said Judith. "He's magical. A little junk food won't hurt him."

"Pizza it is then," said Millie.

"I'll phone it in," said Judith, taking her phone from her pocket. "And while we wait, how about we have a good look around the cottage while Reuben gathers his thoughts, *and* finds some manners?"

———

The two bedrooms couldn't have been more perfect if Millie had decorated them herself, and the roof window theme in the living room continued throughout the cottage, with one in each bedroom, and another above the large jacuzzi style bath in the modern bathroom. Millie had imagined herself laying in hot water, surrounded by bubbles while gazing at the stars, and had shuddered in pleasure. "I don't understand," she said, studying the colourful canvas which hung above the headboard of the huge oak bed in the main bedroom. "Why do I feel so calm about all this? Why do I feel so... safe? After everything that's happened today, I'd have thought I'd be feeling a little more frightened, not imaging bubble baths beneath a view of the moon, and appreciating modern art."

"Come on," said Judith. "Let's go back to the living room, pour some more wine, and I'll begin trying to help you understand a few things. There's far too much about Spellbinder Bay for me to explain in one night, but I can make a start."

Millie nodded. "That sounds like what I need."

Reuben had left his cage, and had perched on a coffee table, pecking at the TV remote control when Judith and Millie entered the living room. "I can't get it to turn on!" he complained. "Esmeralda's TV was far simpler to operate! In fact, I liked the whole place a lot more when Esmeralda lived here. The cottage feels empty now. It's bare."

"I think the term is minimalistic," said Judith. She looked at Millie. "Esmeralda was a hoarder. You could barely move in here without knocking over a cauldron."

"It felt lived in," said Reuben, glaring at Judith as she slid the remote away from him. "Esmeralda made the cottage feel cosy. I'm not a fan of the way you've done things around here, Millie. Really, I'm not."

Millie poured another wine and slumped into the sofa. "I didn't do anything," she said. "I only arrived here this morning. You can't blame me. My suitcase is still next to the door, for heaven's sake. I do have to admit that I like the cottage, though."

"Of course you do," said Reuben. "Why wouldn't you? It designed itself around your energy. It could have been worse, I suppose."

"What do you mean?" said Millie. "It designed itself around my energy?"

Judith sat down next to Millie. "Reuben, would you let me explain things to Millie, please?"

Reuben sighed. "If you must. I know my place. I'll just be over here, pretending you think my input is of any value whatsoever."

"You'll have plenty of time to speak your mind, Reuben," said Judith, "if Millie chooses to stay in Spellbinder Bay."

"What did he mean?" said Millie. "About the cottage?"

Judith sipped her wine. "I'm going to give you the short version, okay? Spellbinder Bay in a nutshell."

"Any version will do," said Millie. "I'm finding everything very surreal — particularly the fact that after everything I've seen today, I'm sitting here with a speaking bird, and not whimpering in a corner somewhere — in a state of catatonic shock."

Judith smiled. "It's because of the energy surrounding you, Millie," she said. "It's helping you adjust. Without it, you probably *would* have gone into shock today. Your whole world has been turned upside down, and I'm guessing you still don't *quite* believe what you've seen and been told today, although somehow you *know* it's all true, right?"

"Right," confirmed Millie. She couldn't have explained how she was feeling any better herself.

"Well," said Judith. "You're surrounded by the energy of people who came before you. Witches who belonged to the same coven you belong to. Witches who died, but whose energy remains in the very essence of this cottage. That energy grounds you. It makes you calm, and it's what shaped the cottage to match your personality before you arrived."

"It's why I'm not more upset about Esmeralda's death," said Reuben. "Her energy is here. I can still feel her in the cottage."

"Okay," said Millie.

"And it's the energy which is making you accept things like we've just told you, at face value, without questioning them too much. It's helping you accept the truth."

Millie looked around her. "So you're saying that this cottage moulded itself into a place I would like? A place based on my personal likes and dislikes, which it gleaned from an energy I emit?"

"She said it better than you did, Judith," laughed Reuben, flapping his wings.

Judith laughed, too. "She did, Reuben. Yes, Millie, that's about it. You see, this cottage and Spellbinder Hall are both built on pieces of land beneath which many ley-lines intersect. Windy-dune Cottage has less magic than Spellbinder Hall, but it's powerful enough to make you feel safe and at home."

"What is Spellbinder Hall?" said Millie. "That place terrified me. The *thing* that Edna made appear in the fireplace terrified me."

"You'd have been a lot more frightened if you hadn't been under the influence of magic," said Judith. "I was with dad when Henry phoned him. Henry told him what Edna had done. It was unforgivable, but Edna is an old-fashioned witch. She believes in throwing people in at the deep end and seeing if they can swim."

"That thing though," said Millie, recalling the face which Edna had summoned. *Was summoned the correct word*? It seemed like it should be. "That… face. What was that?"

"Spellbinder Hall is a school," said Judith. "For people like us. Paranormal people. It's not just a school, though. It's also a precaution. It's a locked gate which prevents things like you saw making their way into the world. It's a barrier between chaos and order, between good and evil."

"That face was real?" said Millie.

"Yes," said Judith. "It couldn't have harmed you,

though. I promise. Edna used a spell to open a one-way window into The Chaos. The face couldn't see you, and it wasn't *really* in the room with you — it just appeared that way. Henry told dad that Edna had used some unnecessarily scary language when she cast the spell. It was uncalled for. Henry is very angry with her."

"I don't know what to think," said Millie. "I have so many questions."

Reuben strutted along the table-top, pausing in front of Millie. "Do you want the Reuben version?" he asked. "I'm supposed to be your familiar, so let me attempt to help you understand."

Judith sighed. "Go on then, Reuben. Let's hear what you have to say."

The little bird cleared his throat. "Spellbinder Hall guards the entrance to an underworld known as The Chaos. It has done for centuries. It's also a school, and it also emits a powerful energy, a spell if you will, which conceals the reality of the town from non-paranormal people."

"Concealment magic," said Millie, recalling what Sergeant Spencer had said.

"Yes," said Reuben. "It prevents people from seeing what is really going on here. People *see* things with their eyes, but the magic prevents them from *really* seeing it. It fails to work on some humans — Judith's father being a prime example, but generally, most human's will never know that Spellbinder Bay is any different to a normal town, and if they do think something is different, nobody else will believe them.

"Now, onto you, Millie. You're a witch, whether you believe it or not. Judith is a witch. There are many witches in this town, along with vampires, ghosts and werewolves. We're a diverse community in Spellbinder Bay, and you'll fit in perfectly well. You simply need to accept your new situation. Answers to all your questions will come in time." He became quiet and looked at the door, his head on his shoulder. "Enough of that for now. I hear a car outside! It's pizza time."

Judith stood up, placing her wine glass on the table. "I'll get it."

"What if I want to leave, Reuben?" said Millie. "What if I don't want to be any part of this place?"

"Then you can leave," said Reuben. "But you'll always know what you left behind, you'll always know there was a better life here for you, and you'll always be curious about how it may have been. You'll never know what it's like to be a witch. To have such power. To be something that many humans dream of being. If you leave, you'll live to regret it, Millie. I'm sure of that."

The door slammed shut, and a cold breeze followed Judith as she placed two large pizza boxes on the table. "How's about we forget about the politics and magic of Spellbinder Bay for the rest of the night, and concentrate on pizza and wine?"

"Sounds great to me," said Reuben.

Millie slumped deeper into the sofa, the friendly and familiar aroma of baked dough making her mouth water. "Sounds good to me, too," she said. "Let's eat."

Chapter 11

"*M*illie! Wake up! Dad's here. Albert's body has washed up, and it seems you were right. There are marks on his body to suggest he was in a struggle. Somebody else *was* in the lighthouse. Dad's treating his death as murder. He needs to speak to you."

Her head hurt. Wine and pizza tended to do that to her. Especially the amount of wine and pizza she'd consumed. Millie opened her eyes, squinting at the light pouring in through the roof window. "What time is it?"

Judith stood next to the bed, smiling down at her. "Just gone nine. I've been up since seven, but I didn't want to wake you. You had a stressful day yesterday."

Millie yawned and rubbed her eyes. "I've got a hangover and I'm being woken with the news that I witnessed a murder. It doesn't feel like today is going to be any less stressful."

Judith raised an eyebrow. "I asked Dad to bring some groceries with him, so there are bacon sandwiches. Maybe that will help with the hangover part?"

"Maybe," said Millie. "A little."

"He brought coffee, too," said Judith.

"Now we're talking," said Millie, swinging her legs off the bed. She stared at the doorway. "Can I hear shouting?"

"It's Reuben and Dad," said Judith, rolling her eyes. "Don't ask." She put a hand on Millie's shoulder. "I'm sorry the first morning in your new home is so hectic, but Dad had to come as soon as he heard about Albert."

"Of course!" said Millie, the term 'new home' sounding alien to her ears. "I want to help. I only met Albert briefly, but he seemed nice. Give me a few minutes to get ready and I'll be through."

After a quick shower, and with little choice about what to wear, Millie slipped into jeans and a loose sweater. Her small suitcase remained unpacked, placed at the foot of the bed. The clothes she wore were creased from their time in the case, but that didn't matter. What did matter was that the glass in the framed photograph of her mother, which she'd carefully wrapped in two t-shirts before stuffing into the case, was cracked. Her wrapping hadn't been careful enough it seemed, and Millie shed a tear as she ran a finger along the splintered crack which dissected her mother's smiling face. "Sorry, Mum," she said, placing the photo on the little bedside table. She planted a kiss on her fingertip, and applied it to her mother's rosy cheek. "I'll get it fixed. I promise."

She smiled at the photograph. She'd often wondered what it would be like to have a picture of both parents together, but none existed as far as Millie was aware. Millie had been conceived during a brief fling, and her mother had explained that the man who fathered her could not be tracked down. He had gone through life oblivious to the fact that he had fathered Millie.

Closing the bedroom door behind her, Millie heard raised voices again. Reuben sounded angry. "She might not be Esmeralda, but I have a duty to her nonetheless. You tell me right now if you're treating her as a suspect! She's a fragile girl. She'll break if you're not careful."

"Everyone involved is a suspect until their innocence is proved," came the frustrated voice of Sergeant Spencer. "That includes Millie, George, and anybody else who was at that lighthouse yesterday. I *know* Millie didn't do it, or George for that matter, but I have to look as if I'm following *some* sort of procedure, Reuben. And as for Millie being fragile — don't be so quick to judge. She went through a lot yesterday, but she didn't run away, did she?"

"She's still processing everything," snapped Reuben. "You just be gentle with her, okay. Oh, and would you be so kind as to scoop a little scrambled egg onto my plate please."

Millie took the moment to clear her throat and breeze into the kitchen. "Good morning," she said. "So, I'm a suspect, Sergeant Spencer?"

The policeman stood up, wiping greasy hands on his uniform jacket. "If you heard our conversation, you must have heard me say I know you didn't do it, Millie? It's just procedure, and we'll have your innocence proved within the hour."

Millie ignored the red-faced Sergeant, her attention drawn to the scene which was unfolding at the stove. Like a scene from a Disney cartoon, Judith stood at the hob, a frying pan on the gas flame, and four rashers of raw bacon levitating above it. The bacon fell into the pan with a loud sizzle, and an egg rose from the counter next to Judith, floating into position above the pan and cracking open in mid-air, to deposit its contents alongside the frying meat.

"What the —" said Millie. "Judith, how did you—"

Judith looked over her shoulder. "I hate touching raw meat. The egg was just laziness on my behalf, admittedly."

"But—" said Millie.

"Come on, Millie!" said Reuben, the yellow feathers of his face smeared in what Millie assumed was ketchup. "You know Judith is a witch. We told you. Close your mouth, you'll catch a fly!"

"Do you want to try?" said Judith, with a wink. "Levitating objects is easy. You must be feeling some magic within you by now? You've been in Spellbinder Bay for almost a full day."

Millie blinked twice and gazed around the kitchen. Sergeant Spencer stood next to the table, greasy finger marks on his bright police jacket. A colourful cockatiel pecked at a plate of scrambled eggs, his face as messy as a one-year-old child's who was learning to use cutlery properly. A smiling witch stood at the stove, seemingly unaware — or unconcerned, that what she had just done had denied physics — and they all acted as if everything was normal.

Taking the seat which Sergeant Spencer pulled out from under the table for her, Millie sat down. She took a deep breath, and did the first thing that came to mind. She laughed. She laughed so hard her body shook and her stomach ached. She laughed until Sergeant Spencer's expression changed from amusement to concern, and Reuben stopped gulping down eggs and stared at her.

"Are you okay, Millie?" said the sergeant. "Do you want some water?"

Judith sat alongside Millie, and took her hand. "She's fine," she said. "I think she's been in delayed shock. She's finally accepted her new reality, and I think…" She looked into Millie's eyes, a smile on her lips. "She's okay with it?"

Was she okay with it? Millie wasn't sure. What she was sure of was the fact that she was no longer scared. No longer afraid. She nodded. "I think I am. I think I'm okay with it all."

"I hate to be a stick in the mud during this little revelation of yours, Millie," said Sergeant Spencer. "But we have to be going."

"Where?" said Millie. "The police station? The lighthouse?"

"No," said Sergeant Spencer. "Spellbinder Hall."

Millie's stomach flipped. "Really?"

"It'll be fine," said Sergeant Spencer. "I promise. It's a lot less spooky during daylight hours, and Edna will never scare you like that again. Okay?"

"Okay."

Millie placed three bacon rashers between two slices of buttered bread. She smiled as Sergeant Spencer offered her the bottle of brown sauce next to his empty plate. "Surely you'll want brown sauce with bacon?" he said.

"I've said it before, Dad," said Judith, plopping a bottle of ketchup in front of Millie. "Most people like ketchup. You're in a minority."

Millie reached for the brown sauce and applied a

generous squirt to her sandwich, wondering what the day had in store for her.

JUDITH SAT IN THE FRONT OF THE CAR WITH HER FATHER, and Millie sat behind her, nervous of the place she was being taken. "Why Spellbinder Hall?" she said. "Shouldn't we be going to a police station? I thought you wanted to ask me some questions."

"This town isn't policed like any other town you've lived in," said Sergeant Spencer. "We do things a little differently around here."

Judith laughed. She turned in her seat and peered at Millie through a gap in the headrest. "A lot differently!" she said. "The concealment magic prevents other police taking an interest in the town. Dad still gets paid, and he has full access to all the police systems and experts, but he's on his own. He's got the cushiest job of any policeman in the world!"

"I wouldn't say it's cushy," laughed Sergeant Spencer. "I have to deal with humans *and* paranormal people. There's nothing cushy about that. It's stressful sometimes, although I will admit it's better than when I worked in the city."

"And easier," smiled Judith.

"Alright. I admit it. I've got a pretty cushy job here," said the sergeant. "Happy?"

Judith winked at Millie and faced the front again. "Happy," she confirmed.

"Why doesn't the concealment magic affect you, Sergeant?" said Millie. "What's special about you?"

Judith answered for him. "We think it's because of me," she said. "When I was adopted by Dad."

"Why?" said Millie.

"That's a conversation for you two to have another day," said Sergeant Spencer. "When I'm not about. It makes me sad to talk about it. Anyway. We're here."

Judith leaned across her seat and gave her father a kiss on his cheek. He blushed, and brought the car to a halt. "Okay, we'll do what we need to do here, and then we'll go to the lighthouse and have a proper look around. Remember, Millie — I've only brought you here to prove your innocence to anybody who might doubt it. I don't doubt you one tiny bit."

"That's okay," said Millie. "I don't mind answering a few questions."

Sergeant Spencer looked away. "Well… erm, that's good then. Just a few questions. Come on then, let's get it over with."

Sergeant Spencer had been right. Spellbinder Hall was a *lot* less spooky during the day. Gone were the long creeping shadows, replaced with vivid green grass and bright flowers in neatly kept beds. Even the gargoyles and stone dragons seemed less sinister beneath sunlight.

The policeman parked the police car alongside four other vehicles. "Okay, Millie," he said, leading the way towards the door. "You're only here to prove you didn't do anything, okay? It's just a formality — everybody knows you're innocent."

"But why a school?" said Millie, gazing up at the old building.

"It's not just a school, Millie," said Sergeant Spencer. "It's the nucleus of the paranormal community. If you were human, I'd be taking you to the little police station in town to ask you some questions. This is where we bring paranormal people. Henry can get to the truth a lot quicker than I can."

"Who is Henry?" said Millie, following the sergeant up the steps. "Or what is he, I mean. Is he a vampire? A witch? A wizard?"

"Henry is just Henry," interjected Judith. "He's nothing, and everything. It's complicated. You'd be better off hearing it from Henry himself. He'll explain it to you when he's ready."

The door swung open and a group of laughing children swarmed through it, almost knocking Millie over.

"No running on the steps!" snapped Judith. "You know the rules!"

"Sorry, Miss Spencer," said a young girl with a mass of curly red hair. "We're on a break."

"You'll break your leg if you're not careful," said Judith. "Now go on. I'll see you next time I'm teaching."

"You're a teacher here?" said Millie, smiling at a small freckled boy in an oversized blazer.

Judith laughed. "Only for a few hours each week. I'm what you might call a temp. I teach the witches among the kids a little magic. It's fun."

Stepping into the school, Millie realised just how much less frightening it was in the light of day. It smelt old, and the wall hangings and furnishings were ancient, but it was nice — in an old country manor sort of way. The suits of armour, which peered at her from dark corners, were the only thing that suggested any sort of spookiness. Until she looked at the stairs.

Millie froze. She'd already seen one. The day before. Florence had been a ghost, but the ghost descending the stairway was different. Florence had been almost humanlike, in form anyway, and her face had seemed outwardly friendly. The ghost on the stairway was very dissimilar to Florence — in shape, and in the way it carried itself.

Judith must have heard Millie's breath catch in her throat, because she came to her side and took her hand, squeezing it gently. "Don't be scared," she said. "There are a lot of ghosts here. Some communicate, and some, like him, don't."

"Is he a monk?" said Millie, hoping the figure wouldn't lift the hood which shrouded its head and face.

"Probably," said Judith. "Of some description. Florence says he's from the medieval period, but that's all we know. He doesn't make himself visible often — it's possible he sensed your energy and didn't recognise it. Maybe he's just curious about who you are."

Millie jumped and gave a low shriek as warm breath tickled the back of her neck, and a voice spoke into her ear. "Or maybe he wishes to suck your soul from your body and take it back to hell with him, where it will remain trapped for eternity."

"Enough of that, Timothy!" said Judith, spinning to face the person behind Millie. "She had a hard day yesterday, she doesn't need you teasing her today!"

Millie wasn't sure whether she should keep her eyes on the shrouded figure floating down the stairs, or turn to face the person who'd violated her personal space. As the ghostly apparition began to fade — its robes becoming so transparent Millie could barely see them, she chose the latter. She swivelled quickly, the small hairs on the back of her neck still upright. "You scared me!" she said.

The man looking at Millie was shorter than she was,

and appeared to be trapped between puberty and adulthood. His fluffy brown beard covered a portion of his chin, and acne scars cratered his cheeks. "I'm sorry," he said. "Henry saw the police car arrive and sent me down to greet you all." He extended a hand towards Millie, and licked his lips before smiling. "I'm Timothy, but *you* may call me Tim. It's a fine pleasure to meet you, Miss Thorn. As you've probably worked out by now, I'm the practical joker around these parts!"

"The clown more like it," said Judith. "And not a very funny one. You scared her, Timothy!"

"That was not my intention," said Timothy. "Please accept my apologies, Miss Thorn."

Millie took his hand. "That's okay," she said. "No harm done. The ghost did most of the scaring, not you."

"Where is Henry?" said Sergeant Spencer.

"Upstairs," said Timothy. "Edna has just been tested, and has been proved innocent. George told us she had argued with Albert on the morning of his unfortunate demise."

Millie bristled.

"It's okay," said Timothy, sensing Millie's unease. "Edna has left Henry's office. Don't worry, Miss Thorn — she won't be summoning any faces from the fireplace today!"

"You know about that?" said Judith. "Is nothing private around here?"

"Florence is quite the gossip," said Timothy. "Ladies of her era were prim and proper, and *never* showed an ankle or a bosom, but good grief — they enjoyed talking!"

"Shall we go up then, Timothy?" said Sergeant Spencer. "I *do* have a murder to solve."

"Of course," said Timothy. "The interrogator awaits Miss Thorn."

"Interrogator?" said Millie. "That sounds… vicious. You're joking again, right?"

Timothy smiled. "You'll be perfectly fine, Miss Thorn. It's just some questions." He gestured at the staircase. "This way, please."

The ghost had vanished, and the staircase appeared void of anything paranormal. Millie wished her head was as clear. So much had happened in so little time, and she wasn't sure she was acting in her own best interests as she followed Sergeant Spencer, Judith and Timothy up the creaky stairs.

Chapter 12

"The owls," said Millie, glancing at the empty glass cases on the wall. "Where are they? There were owls in those cases when I was here last night."

"They've gone for the day," said Timothy. "They required some fresh air."

"They come to life?" said Millie. "Seriously?"

Timothy stopped at the same doorway Millie had escaped through the night before, and smiled. "I don't know what world you live in, Miss Thorn," he said, a bewildered expression on his face. "But in this world, dead owls *don't* come to life."

"What did you mean, then?" said Millie, annoyed at the patronising tone of Timothy's voice.

"They needed some fresh air, as I said," explained Timothy. "They were stuffed a long time ago, Miss Thorn. When taxidermy methods weren't quite as advanced as they are these days. They were beginning to smell. Quite badly. The owls are currently in the basement, with the new taxidermist in town, who is airing and filling their body cavities with a more modern material." He smiled, and shook his head. "Owls coming to life! I've heard it all now!"

"It wouldn't be the strangest thing that's happened to me in the last two days," said Millie, narrowing her eyes. "Don't be so sarcastic. It's not a nice quality to have. It's rude."

"My apologies. *Again*," said Timothy. "You really are a sensitive soul, Miss Thorn."

The door opened before Millie had time to reply, and Henry Pinkerton stepped into the corridor, peering over his spectacles. "How are you, Millie?" he said, genuine concern in his eyes. "I was worried about you last night. So worried! Edna should never have scared you like that. It was unforgivable!"

"No harm done," said Millie. "And to be honest with you, what Edna did was just the last straw. I was already pretty scared before she even came into the room."

"Yes," said Henry, fiddling with his cufflinks. "I can imagine. Myself and Mister Dickinson behaved well, in my estimation, but I can understand perfectly well why Florence and Fredrick may have made you nervous."

"It was a lot to take in," said Millie. "But thanks to Judith, and Reuben, I understand a little more than I did yesterday."

"And you'll understand more and more as time goes by," said Henry. "Thank you for coming here today, Millie. It was brave of you. I hoped to give you time and space to yourself before inviting you back, but the murder of poor Albert Salmon must be solved, and you are Sergeant Spencer's most important witness, Millie."

Millie sighed. "And his most important suspect? You may as well just come out and say it."

Henry's expression softened. "No, no, no, Millie. Please don't get the wrong end of the proverbial stick. Nobody thinks you did it, but as you were present at the murder scene, we need to eliminate you from any enquiries. The same applied to George and Edna, who have both been found innocent."

"Albert mentioned other people were there yesterday, too," said Millie.

"Yes, yes," said Henry. "George has told us what he remembers Albert saying. Something about him having an argument with Jim Grayson, and a blonde-haired woman seen skulking around his property. I'm only interested in finding out if a paranormal person killed Albert, Millie. Sergeant Spencer will deal with investigating any humans who may be involved."

"I'll be happy to answer your questions," said Millie. "Albert seemed like a nice man. I'll do what I can to help find out who killed him."

Henry smiled. "Thank you, Millie, although I won't need to ask you any questions. Sergeant Spencer will deal with that aspect of things. All I need to do is prove your innocence with a little help from a magical artefact."

"The interrogator," said Timothy, scratching his chin.

"I wish you would stop calling it by that name, Timothy!" snapped Henry. "It will never stick! Nobody likes it — it sounds cruel." He smiled at Millie. "I like to call it the jewel of integrity, and it's nothing to be feared. It's a simple test which will take mere seconds to conduct. Would you mind?"

Millie looked at Judith, who nodded. "It's nothing to worry about," she said. "It's like a lie-detector, but with fewer wires and a much higher success rate. A flawless success rate."

"Alright," said Millie. "I'll do it. I've got nothing to hide."

"Then please step into the office, Millie," said Henry. "But remember to bear in mind that we don't think you have anything to hide. This test is simply our procedure when a paranormal person's innocence, or guilt, has to be proved." Henry blocked the doorway with an arm as Timothy tried to follow. "Do you mind if the others come in with you, Millie?"

"No of course not," said Millie. "After what happened in this room last night, I'll feel safer with more people here."

Millie studied the fireplace with suspicion as she entered the room, but it contained no evil faces, only the ashes of a fire and a set of pokers and bellows which appeared to be antiques.

"If you would be so kind as to take a seat," said Henry. "This won't take long, and then Sergeant Spencer can get on with the important task of discovering who *is* guilty of Albert Salmon's murder."

Millie did as Henry asked, sitting in the same seat she'd sat in the night before. This time she felt far safer, and it was hard to believe that it was less than twenty-four hours ago that she'd seen the horrific face in the fireplace.

Henry walked behind the long desk, and unlocked a cupboard built into the wall behind it. He removed a small leather pouch and opened it, tipping a blue golf ball sized crystal into the palm of his hand. "Would you open your hand please, Millie?" he said, walking around the desk. "There's nothing to worry about."

Millie glanced at Judith, who smiled her encouragement. She opened her hand.

Henry placed the stone in the centre of Millie's palm, and smiled. "Can you feel anything?" he asked.

"Yes," said Millie, staring into the depths of the stone. "A throbbing sensation. Almost like a heartbeat."

Henry approached Millie, and stood before her. He bent at the waist and stared into Millie's eyes. "That's tremendous news," he said. "That proves Fredrick wrong!"

"Proves Fredrick wrong?" said Millie, the stone sending pleasant vibrations along her wrist and arm. "Wrong about what?"

"He had his doubts about you. The fear you displayed in this room last night, and the lack of magical ability you've shown since arriving in Spellbinder Bay, gave him cause for concern. He was of the opinion that your magical bloodline was weak, maybe too weak to justify you taking over Esmeralda's cottage, after all — only a true coven witch should inhabit that cottage. Not one with overly diluted blood. I never doubted you, of course, but the fact that the stone responds to you shows you have true blood in your veins. Fredrick must accept that truth and welcome you back to Spellbinder Bay."

"Back?" said Millie, the stone becoming heavier in her hand. "I've never been here before."

"A figure of speech," said Henry, looking away for a brief moment. "Would you focus on the stone, and look into my eyes, please?"

The stone throbbed in her palm, and Millie focussed on Henry's eyes — his pupils magnified by his spectacles.

"Millie," said Henry. "It pains me to have to ask you,

as I'm already certain of the answer — but did you have anything to do with the death of Albert Salmon, or do you have any idea who the perpetrator, if not you, may be?"

"No to the first question," said Millie, the stone warming in her hand. "And no to the second question, too. I didn't, and I don't."

The stone seemed to gain more weight in her hand, and Millie stared into the depths of the crystal as it began to glow, a soft peaceful blue glow which appeared to beat in time with her heart. "It's beautiful," she said.

"And it shows you have integrity, Millie," said Henry. "It shows you speak the truth from a good heart, as I was certain you did." He closed his hand over the stone and lifted it from Millie's palm. "There we are. The stone has proven the innocence of George, Edna — and now Millie. Sergeant Spencer, it's down to you to find a human murderer, or to bring another paranormal before me to be tested by the stone."

"Let us hope the murderer is a human," said Timothy, with a frown.

"Indeed," said Henry, placing the jewel in its pouch.

"Why?" said Millie, standing up.

"It's not what you're probably thinking, Millie," said Sergeant Spencer. "It's not a favouritism thing between humans and paranormals."

"Heavens no!" said Henry. "I wouldn't stand for that sort of nonsense!"

"Then why do you hope the murderer is a human?" said Millie.

Henry sighed, and placed the leather pouch inside the cupboard. He locked the door and turned to face the room. "Because the punishment handed out for murder by the human courts in this country, is far less cruel and unusual than the punishment I would be forced to hand out if one of the paranormal community had committed such a heinous crime. That is why we hope the murderer is human, Millie. The consequences leave a less foul taste in the mouth. Having said that — I hope the perpetrator is brought to justice quickly — whoever, or whatever, it may be."

"Okay," said Sergeant Spencer. "There's no time to waste. I want to head to the lighthouse and have a look around. Millie, Judith, are you two going to join me?"

"Is that allowed?" said Millie. "It's a police investigation."

"It's *my* investigation," said the sergeant. "And as we've told you. We do things differently in Spellbinder Bay. Judith helps me on a regular basis, and I'm not adverse to accepting help wherever I can find it."

"Should you require any help from me, just let me know, Sergeant," said Henry. "I hear there were marks found on Albert's body. Maybe a clue can be found there?"

"Doubtful," said Sergeant Spencer. "The pathologist is taking a good look at the body, but from what was pointed out to me, there was just a little bruising on his wrists, consistent with being held in a tight grip. With the multitude of injuries he sustained when he hit the rocks, it's hard to be sure what was caused by the fall and what wasn't."

"Where was his body found?" said Timothy.

"Not where the coastguard expected," said the sergeant. "He expected it to end up a few miles to the east, but instead it washed up just a couple of hundred metres from the lighthouse. He thinks a freak wave must

117

have pushed him ashore because the wind was blowing away from the beach, and the tide usually drags objects east."

"Who found the unfortunate soul?" said Henry.

"Who always finds these things?" said Sergeant Spencer. "A dog walker of course. Without dog walkers, there would be a lot more dead bodies awaiting discovery."

Henry nodded. "Well," he said, "should Albert's ghost make an appearance, I shall let you know. Perhaps he'll remember precisely who killed him."

"Or perhaps he'll never come back," said Timothy.

"His ghost?" said Millie.

Henry smiled. "Yes, Millie. His ghost. Don't look so shocked. You've already met Florence."

"And the shrouded monk," added Timothy. "On the stairs."

"It's hard to believe, that's all," said Millie. "Two days ago, I was wondering how I was going to pay my rent. Now I'm finding out that I'm a witch and that there is some sort of afterlife — it's all a little hard to take in."

"You'll get used to it," said Timothy. He dropped his gaze to the floor. "I could help you if you like? Maybe we could meet up for a meal, or a drink? I'll answer any questions you have. I'm pretty knowledgeable about all things paranormal, and I'm said to be good company by people who know me. Everybody says I'm super fun to be around!"

Millie looked left, but Judith simply smiled and looked at her feet.

She looked to the right, and Sergeant Spencer came to her rescue. "On that note, I think we should get going. Come on, Millie. Let's get you back to the light-house and see if we can trigger any memories which might help in solving Albert's murder." He cast a warning glance in Timothy's direction. "Other things can wait."

"Maybe another time, Timothy," said Millie, her cheeks warming. "Duty calls, it seems."

"Perhaps you'll come to the beach party tonight?" said Timothy, clasping his hands together. "It's all been arranged. Everyone would love to meet you. I'm sure."

"Timothy!" snapped Henry. "That's unfair of you! I heard George explaining to you that he was arranging a surprise party for Millie. George wanted to be the one to surprise her, Timothy. It wasn't down to you." He smiled at Millie. "I trust you'll pretend you had no prior knowl-edge of the get together when George makes you aware of it, Miss Thorn? He was rather looking forward to the surprise."

"Oh," said Millie. She'd liked George — a lot, if she was honest, but with the knowledge that he was a vampire, Millie wasn't sure how to think about him. She guessed it was unfair of her, but the thought of George being able to suck blood from a human sent a chill along her spine. "I'm not sure I'm in the mood for a party."

Judith slapped Timothy on the shoulder. "Trust you, big mouth!" She took Millie's hand. "You've got to come," she said.

"You knew?" said Millie.

Judith laughed. "Of course I knew! George is really excited about it! We're all going to be there. All the paranormal people, that is."

Henry cleared his throat. "Of a certain age, may I add. It seems that George is only inviting the younger generations. He's made an exception for vampires and ghosts of course — the concept of age merely offends most of them."

"It is offensive," came a voice from nowhere.

Millie stared around the room, convinced she was about to see another disembodied head in the fireplace, but relaxed fractionally when the transparent form of Florence floated through a bookcase and into the room.

"It's *highly* offensive," continued Florence, shimmering as she floated towards Henry, her dark hair in a high bun on top of her head. "I was under forty years of age at the time of my death, yet my gravestone indicates I'm one-hundred-and-sixty-eight-years-old. How am I to be treated? As a relic, too old to enjoy oneself, or as a vibrant young woman — capable of appreciating an evening time gathering of people on a moonlit beach?"

"George did invite you, Florence," said Timothy. "You told him you had better things to do than mingle with commoners and drunken scoundrels."

"Indeed. I do have better things to do," said Florence. "I was merely explaining why the concept of age is offensive to a sizeable and important portion of the paranormal community."

Henry gave Millie a gentle smile. "Go to the party, Miss Thorn. I think it would be good for your soul to let your hair down. So to speak."

"Yes! Come! But remember to act surprised when George tells you," said Judith, scowling fiercely at Timothy.

Millie shrugged. It was apparent that she had no choice in the matter. "It seems I'm going to a party arranged by a vampire tonight," she acknowledged.

Chapter 13

*M*illie was surprised to realise she was relieved — relieved that she'd passed the magical stone of truth test. Of course, she'd known she was innocent, but it was nice that everyone else now knew it, too. Guilt was a strange thing, she decided — even a person completely confident of their innocence could still find guilt worming its way through some dark recess of their mind, making them feel uneasy.

Sergeant Spencer drove slowly through town, in no apparent rush to get to the lighthouse in order to begin his investigation, and as they passed the harbour, he stopped the car next to the seawall. "You and George said Albert mentioned Jim Grayson, Millie?" he asked.

"Yes," said Millie. "He said Jim had accused him of stealing lobsters from his pots. Albert said he was at the lighthouse yesterday."

"Jim reported it to me, too," said Sergeant Spencer. "A couple of weeks ago. He reckons his pots are getting cleaned out every time he drops them."

"I don't know what he expects you to do, Dad," said Judith. "It's just some lobsters."

"It's his livelihood," said Sergeant Spencer. "I can understand his frustration. He's a bit of a hothead, but I very much doubt he'd go as far as to push Albert off the lighthouse because of a few shellfish."

"Stranger things have happened," said Millie. "I heard of a man who killed his neighbour because he stole some apples from his tree."

"You're right, Millie," said Sergeant Spencer. "Murder is often committed over the most trivial of things. Come on, we're here now and I can see Jim's boat in the harbour, which means he'll be around too. Let's talk to him before we go to the lighthouse."

It was good to feel the sun on her face, and the crowds of tourists admiring the boats in the harbour and staring out to sea, lifted Millie's spirits. She'd always enjoyed trips to the seaside when she'd been little, and the smell of salt air and seaweed reminded her that Spellbinder Bay was not all murder and monsters — it was a quintessential English seaside town, too. A characterful one at that. "What are they looking at?" she asked, as they passed a group of people shielding their eyes from the sun as they gazed towards the horizon.

"Dolphins," said Judith. "We have a resident population. People come from all over to watch them playing in the surf."

Using a hand to shield her eyes from the bright sun, Millie stared out to sea. "I see them!" she said, pointing. "Look! A long way out, near that red boat — I saw one jump!"

Judith laughed. "Forgive me for not sharing in your enthusiasm," she said, "but we're pretty used to seeing dolphins in the bay. They're exciting for the first fifty times, but then it gets a little… samey."

Sergeant Spencer stepped out of the path of a woman pushing a pram. "Is it the first time you've seen dolphins in the wild, Millie?" he said.

"I think so," said Millie, walking alongside Judith. "But I'm not sure. The more I watch them, the more I think I've been here before."

"Been here?" said Sergeant Spencer. "Spellbinder Bay?"

"It's just déjà vu," said Millie, shaking her head. "I get it sometimes. I've never been *here* before, maybe my mother took me somewhere like it when I was little. Somewhere similar."

"It's a pretty standard seaside town," said Judith. "They all look a little similar, especially the harbours."

That was true, but as Millie looked up at Spellbinder Hall, perched high on the cliff to her left, she couldn't shake the feeling that she'd seen that view before. A long time ago.

She stepped to the right, avoiding a collision with an elderly couple sharing a cone of chips, and shook her head. Of course she'd never been there before. Déjà vu could be very convincing, but ultimately it was a simple misunderstanding in the brain — a mix up of memories, probably brought on by smells, sights, and sounds.

"There's Jim," said Sergeant Spencer, interrupting Millie's chain of thought. "And you don't need to be a skilled policeman to come to the conclusion that he hasn't got to the bottom of his missing lobster problems yet."

Jim was still kicking lobster pots when they arrived at his boat. The tall man swore once or twice, and placed his hat back on his head when he saw them. "Finally," he said, his eyes on Sergeant Spencer. "You've come to investigate what I reported a fortnight ago!" He looked at Millie and Judith, and his expression softened. "And you've brought back up, I see. Hello, Judith."

Judith replied with a smile. "Hi, Jim."

He turned to Millie, his weathered skin and sun-kissed complexion suggesting he'd been working outdoors for most of his life, and judging by the wrinkles beneath his eyes, and the slight stoop in his posture, Millie guessed it had been a long time. "We haven't had the pleasure," he said.

"This is Millie," said Sergeant Spencer. "She's new in town."

"Welcome to Spellbinder Bay, Millie," said Jim, with a friendly wink. "Are you part of Sergeant Spencer's unorthodox investigative team?"

"I'm not sure what you mean," said Millie. "But thanks for the welcome. It's a lovely town." *This part of it, anyway*, she thought. The part that wasn't the creepy Spellbinder Hall.

Jim kicked another lobster pot, the empty cage rattling across the stone quayside. "I mean, not many towns have a police sergeant who more than occasion-ally takes his daughter to work with him. Are you a new member of the little family police team?"

"No, she's not, Jim," said Sergeant Spencer. "Not that it matters."

"It doesn't matter at all," said Jim. "Quite the opposite. The townspeople like having such a small and friendly police force." He crossed his arms and nodded towards the scattered lobster pots. "*When* they do their job properly. I hope you've come to tell me you've caught the bugger who's been stealing my catch."

Sergeant Spencer shook his head. "Not quite, Jim. I'm here concerning the death of Albert Salmon."

Jim frowned. "We never saw eye to eye, Albert and I — ever since he came to this town — but I wouldn't wish death on my worse enemy. Especially from a fall like that. He didn't stand a chance. Lost his balance did he? That old wooden leg of his finally give up?"

Sergeant Spencer took a step closer to Jim. "Not quite. We believe he was pushed. We have a witness who says she saw somebody on the balcony with Albert, and we found finger marks on his wrists — as if he'd been in a struggle. He was murdered, Jim."

"What? Murdered! And what's that got to do with why you're here?" He took a slow step backwards, realisation evident in his thin smile. "Oh, I see! You think it might be me! Some busybody told you I was up at the lighthouse arguing with him, did they? You think I murdered Albert!"

"I have to ask questions of anybody who was at the lighthouse, Jim," said Sergeant Spencer. "You can understand that?"

Jim dropped his arms to his side. "Aye. Of course I can. I'll do anything I can to help. I'm not proud that the last words I spoke to him were accusing him of something he never did. He died yesterday, and my pots were raided again last night. It wasn't him, and I shouldn't have gone accusing him without any proof."

"Why did you think it was Albert?" asked Judith. "He could hardly get out of that lighthouse as he got older. People even had to take him supplies — why did you think he was capable of it?"

Jim shook his head. "I don't know. I was irrational. My most productive pots have always been the ones I've dropped near the lighthouse. I began dropping all my pots in that area a year ago. The lobsters like the rocks, you see? They can hide away. All Albert needed to do was hop in that beat up old rowing boat of his and he'd have been on my pots in minutes. I didn't think it through, but anger does that to a man, you know? It clouds his judgement. If I could apologise to him, I would."

"Why was there bad blood between you and Albert?" asked Millie, uncertain whether she was over-stepping the mark by asking a question.

Nobody seemed to mind, and Sergeant Spencer kept his eyes on Jim as he answered. "He was just one of those people, you know? He and Betty moved here about fifteen years ago. They bought the lighthouse for cheap just after it was decommissioned. I went up to see them a few times during the first year they lived there. They kept themselves to themselves, you see, and with Albert's wooden leg, and Betty and her spine and balance problems, it seemed a daft place to live with all those stairs. They didn't want my help, though. They didn't want anyone's help back then. Albert would come into town on his boat when they needed anything, and Betty hardly left the place. Rapunzel, we called her — trapped in that tower like she was."

"That was the extent of your argument with him?" said Judith. "The fact that he didn't want any help?"

Jim looked at the floor. "Not really," he said. "There was more to it than that. I interfered where I wasn't needed. My wife worked for the county council before she died. She worked in housing — helping people with disabilities and suchlike to get adequate housing. I asked her if she could help, and she did. She found them a lovely bungalow, with a sea view and everything. A lovely garden — the works. They didn't want it, though. Well, Albert didn't."

"What happened?" Asked Millie.

"Betty was over the moon!" said Jim. "She wanted to move, but Albert was having none of it. He pushed me up against a wall and told me to keep my nose out of their business, said they liked the safety of the light-house, said they didn't want people nosing around. I would have punched him if it wasn't for poor Betty. She stood next to Albert, trying to pull him off me, telling him they'd stay in the lighthouse. Telling him she'd do what he wanted. That poor woman never liked it there, I'm sure."

"I had no idea," said Sergeant Spencer. "Poor Betty."

"Not many people did know what was going on, Sergeant," said Jim. "They kept themselves private since then, until Betty died and Albert's health deteriorated. Only then did Albert start asking for help every now and again. He even put the lighthouse up for sale for a brief period, but decided against selling it when he got an offer. He went downhill after that."

"How sad," said Millie.

"Sad indeed," said Jim, staring out to sea. He ran a large finger beneath his eye, and glanced at the wedding ring on his finger. "Life can be very sad indeed."

Millie stumbled, and Sergeant Spencer prevented her from falling with a hand on her back.

"Watch yourself, young Millie," said Jim. "This is a harbour — plenty of trip hazards here."

"Yes. Yes… I tripped on something," said Millie, her eyes hot with tears. "Silly me."

Sergeant Spencer took his notebook from his pocket. "I'm sorry to have to ask this, Jim, but where were you yesterday, after you visited Albert?"

"Right here," said Jim. "My boat engine needed a service. The young fella from the boatyard brought me out some filters and plugs and helped me fit them. We were here all afternoon, you can ask him."

Millie heard Sergeant Spencer snap his notebook shut, but she'd turned away, staring out to sea — a warm tear running down her cheek. She took a deep breath. *What had just happened?* When Jim had looked at his ring, Millie had been overcome with emotion. Emotion so intense it had caused her to stumble. Emotion so awfully sad that it had brought pain to her heart.

It hadn't been *her* emotions, though. It had been Jim's emotions. *Jim's thought.*

It was true what she'd been told in Spellbinder Hall the night before. She *could* read people's thoughts. She closed her eyes. *The magic in Spellbinder Bay was real.*

The last slivers of doubt left Millie. She did possess some sort of power. *She had magic.* She spoke quietly, allowing her whisper to blow out to sea on the wind. "I am a witch," she said.

Chapter 14

Sergeant Spencer unlocked the door. "And you're certain you locked this door before you left?" he said, pocketing the key Millie had given him when she'd first reported Albert's fall to the police.

Millie nodded. "When Albert gave me the key he was insistent that I locked the door behind me. Nobody could have got into the building after I'd left. Not without a key."

Judith took a step backwards and gazed up at the tall building. "So, we've got a locked lighthouse mystery! It's like being in one of those cheesy television detective shows," she said. "And you're sure there was nobody in the lighthouse apart from you, Albert, and George?"

"As sure as I can be," said Millie. "George and I only went up as far as the second floor, but I'm sure Albert would have known if somebody had sneaked in. Anyway — he seemed serious about his security. Jim Grayson confirmed that much."

Sergeant Spencer pushed the heavy steel door open. "Okay," he said. "I had a cursory look around when

Millie reported seeing Albert falling, but not a proper look. To be honest, I thought Jim had just gone out somewhere, and Millie had imagined the whole thing." He reached into his pocket and withdrew a small packet of plastic gloves. He handed a pair each to Millie and Judith, and proceeded to put one on himself. "We'll do this properly. I'll start at the top — where he was pushed from, and work my way down. You two begin down here. If you find anything, try not to touch it, and let me know."

"What are we looking for?" said Millie, struggling to coax her fingers into the tight latex.

"Nothing and everything," said Sergeant Spencer. "The best clues are always the most innocuous. If something seems out of place, then treat it as suspicious."

The three of them stepped into the building, and Judith wrinkled her nose. "It's a bit smelly in here," she said. "I wouldn't like to live in a building with that sort of smell greeting me every time I came home."

"It's an old building," said Sergeant Spencer, looking around. "Built right next to the sea. I'd be more surprised if it didn't smell a bit damp." He withdrew his notebook from his breast pocket and flicked it open. "Before we start searching, let's just refresh our memories." He looked at the page. "You and George came here to deliver Albert his supplies, Millie. You stayed for a few minutes. And then George left before you, on his motorbike. Is that right?"

"That's right," confirmed Millie.

"While you were here," Sergeant Spencer continued, "Albert told you he'd argued with Edna Brockett and Jim Grayson, *and* he'd thrown out a tradesman that morning for being too noisy?"

"Yes," said Millie. "I thought it was cute that he used the word *tradesman*. He didn't elaborate on what sort of tradesman it was."

"He was from a different generation," said Sergeant Spencer. "What else did he tell you?"

"He mentioned a blonde woman," said Millie. "He'd seen her skulking — his word, not mine — around the lighthouse."

Sergeant Spencer nodded, turning the page. "I was getting to that," he said. "It says here that Albert told you he didn't recognise her, so we can assume it's nobody he knows well, if at all."

"That's what he said," said Millie. "As far as I can remember. I'd just arrived in town, though, for reasons I didn't understand. I wasn't thinking straight. Maybe I didn't listen to everything Albert said. George might remember more than I do."

"I've already spoken to George," said Sergeant Spencer, closing his notebook and placing it back in his pocket. "He says the same as you, although he says he heard Albert call your name as you were leaving? He says Albert told you something, but George didn't want to eavesdrop on your conversation."

"He told me not to go on George's motorbike," said Millie. "That was all. Albert lost his leg in a motorbike accident, he was just trying to warn me of the dangers. I thought it was nice of him."

"He told you that?" said Sergeant Spencer. "You should feel honoured. As far as I know nobody knows how he lost his leg. There's been a lot of speculation and guesses, but nobody was certain of the real reason. Nobody I know of, anyway. Most people think it was down to a health problem — I heard rumours that he was a recovering alcoholic when he arrived in Spell-binder Bay."

"That makes sense," said Millie. "I promised him I'd bake for him. He was adamant I didn't add any alcohol to any of the cake mixes."

"Such a shame," said Judith, opening a cardboard box placed on a rickety table. "He was worried enough about his health to not want alcohol in his cakes, and he ends up being pushed off the top of his own lighthouse. It seems… unfair."

Sergeant Spencer took his hat off and hung it on a brass hook next to the door. "It is a shame," he said. "And very unfair. So, let's see what we can do to get him some justice. I'll head up to the light-room. You girls get started down here."

As Sergeant Spencer headed up the spiral staircase, his heavy boots clanking on metal, Millie helped Judith search the cluttered ground floor. Nothing seemed out of the ordinary, although ordinary by Albert Salmon's standards, may not have seemed ordinary to most people.

The first box Millie searched contained a carefully wrapped collection of glass paperweights, and an equally well protected collection of vintage cigarette lighters — one in the shape of a handgun, and another in the shape of an aeroplane.

Judith prised open an old tin biscuit container, to reveal a collection of postcards which would have been considered risqué when Albert was a young man. Millie laughed as Judith held up a card portraying a young brunette woman standing outside a greengrocer's shop, holding two large pieces of fruit against her chest.

A short balding elderly man gazed on, his eyes wide

open, commenting on the size of the young lady's melons, as his wife prepared to hit him over his head with her rolled up umbrella.

It seemed that either Albert, Betty, or both, had been hoarders, and Millie quickly concluded that there was no point in searching through every box and pot in the room. Using the questionable skills she'd learnt from television detective shows, she scoured the floor — checking for giveaway footprints or discarded cigarette butts which, on television, always led to the villain.

Having found nothing of interest on the ground floor, Judith and Millie ascended the spiral staircase and began searching the cosy living room.

"He enjoyed reading," noted Judith, running a finger over the book spines which lined the bookcase beneath the stairway.

"And art," said Millie, impressed by some of the framed watercolours which hung on the wall, depicting what Millie guessed were Scottish mountains and lochs.

It took a skilled artist to use watercolour well, and the pictures were unsigned, leading Millie to wonder whether perhaps they were the work of either Albert or Betty.

Judith sighed. "It's horrible, isn't it? To think that all these belongings were owned by an old man who was pushed to his death."

Millie opened a drawer in a small oak sideboard. "Too horrible to think about," she said, flicking through a stack of business cards, the uppermost card crisp and new, and the rest of the pile dog-eared.

She placed the cards on top of the sideboard, and withdrew a well stuffed tatty old envelope which had been pushed towards the rear of the draw. Withdrawing the contents, she took a seat in a comfy armchair. "Look at these," she said, flicking through the sheets of paper. "Letters. And lots of them." She unfolded the bottommost letter in the stack. "This one's from nineteen-fifty-four. It's from Betty."

"A love letter?" said Judith, with a smile. "They'd been together for that long?"

Millie scanned the first few lines of the letter and folded it closed. "Yes," she said. "It's a love letter, but I'm not going to read it. It's private and it won't help us with what we're looking for."

Judith sat down next to Millie. "Let's look through them all at least. Maybe we'll find a clue. There doesn't seem to be anything else of interest in this room."

"A quick look won't do any harm," said Millie. She kept the top half of the stack to herself, and handed the rest of the letters to Judith. "This feels very intrusive," she said. "We'll read the first few lines of each letter, and if they're *too* personal, we'll stop."

"Agreed," said Judith, unfolding a sheet of yellowed paper.

The majority of the letters were from Betty, the dates showing they spanned almost a decade. Millie soon became accustomed to Betty's neat handwriting, and moved directly to the end of the letter when she didn't recognise the hand it was written in. The letters not penned by Betty included letters signed off by Albert's mother, and a couple from his grandparents.

As Millie neared the top of the pile, the paper became more modern, and she noticed that the address the letters had been mailed to had changed from a street in Edinburgh, to a road in Glasgow. With only two letters left to read, Millie had already decided that there would be no helpful information hidden in the stack of personal correspondence.

She unfolded the final letter, a plain unlined sheet of white paper tucked into a faded brown envelope, and read it slowly, her blood running cold as the words made sense. She tapped Judith's leg. "Read this," she urged, handing Judith the letter.

Judith read it slowly, and gasped. "That's a death threat if ever I've seen one," she said.

"Look at the date on the franking mark," said Millie, handing Judith the envelope.

"Two-thousand-and-three," said Judith. She looked at Millie. "I don't understand why that's relevant?"

"Remember what Jim Grayson said?" asked Millie. "He said that Albert and Betty had moved here about fifteen years ago. And the content of that letter makes me think I know why they came here."

Judith nodded. "Of course!" she said. "And didn't Jim say that Albert was very concerned about his security! It makes total sense. They moved here to hide!"

"Where better to hide than in a concrete tower next to the sea?" said Millie. "But who were they hiding from? The letter is just signed with initials."

Judith stood up. "Come on. We need to show this to my dad."

Millie followed Judith up the stairs, and as they reached the next floor and began climbing the final flight of steps, they heard a shout from above them. "Stop right there! You! Stop!"

Judith clambered up the last of the stairs quickly, and Millie followed close behind. They emerged into the light-room to see Sergeant Spencer on the balcony, waving his arms. "Stop!" he yelled.

"What's happening?" said Judith, stepping onto the balcony alongside her father.

Sergeant Spencer pointed at an outcrop of rocks below them. "Look," he said. "Our mystery blonde haired woman."

Millie looked at the section of rocks at which Sergeant Spencer was pointing, cold wind whistling in her ears. There she was — staring up at the lighthouse, using a hand to shade her eyes. She wore a flowing white dress, and her long golden hair blew parallel to the ocean in the onshore breeze.

As Sergeant Spencer shouted again, the woman turned her back, and with surprising agility began hopping from rock to rock, quickly putting distance between herself and the lighthouse.

"We'll never catch her," said Sergeant Spencer.

"Can't you call for a helicopter?" asked Millie.

"Police helicopters might be a common sight where you've come from, Millie," said Sergeant Spencer. "But the nearest one is based almost thirty miles away from here. She'll be long gone before it's even in the air."

"We might not be able to get a helicopter," said Judith. She looked at Millie, and smiled. "But I know somebody who can provide us with aerial surveillance."

"Me?" said Millie, gazing at the long drop below the lighthouse balcony. "Even if witches *can* fly, I haven't got a broomstick, and the first trick I try is certainly not going to be launching myself from the top of a light-house! You're a witch too, Judith — you do it!"

"Not you!" said Judith. She pointed at Windy-dune Cottage. "I mean Reuben! Summon him!"

Millie gazed at her cottage. A few hundred metres separated the lighthouse and her home, but the wind was blowing in the right direction to carry her voice. Reuben had insisted that Millie left a window open for him before she'd left that morning, so there was a high possibility that he would hear her shouting. She'd give it a try. What did she have to lose?

She made a funnel around her mouth with her hands, and shouted. "Reuben!" she yelled. "Reuben! We need your help! Come here!"

Judith laughed. "No," she said. "He won't hear you shouting. He made you leave the TV on for him. I mean *summon* him, as in use magic to call your familiar to your side."

"I can do that?" said Millie.

"We'll find out whether or not you *can* do it," said Judith. "The fact is, you *should* be able to do it. You're a coven witch. Reuben is your familiar. It's how things work."

"If you're going to do it," said Sergeant Spencer. "Do it soon. She's heading around the corner of the peninsula. It's about three-quarters of a mile until she crosses the open ground and sand dunes, but if she reaches the forest even Reuben won't be able to see her. Not without a thermal imaging camera anyway."

Millie looked at Judith and Sergeant Spencer in turn. What did they expect of her? She'd only known she was a witch for two days, and she was expected to know how to summon a magical cockatiel to her side? "How?" she said. "How do I summon him?"

"I don't know," said Judith. "I don't have a familiar, but the knowledge should be within you. You should just *feel* what you have to do — that's how magic works. There are no special ingredients and no chant that needs to be incanted. Just reach within yourself. You must be able to feel something different since you came to Spellbinder Bay? Find that thing, focus on it, and you'll know what to do."

Millie closed her eyes. *Pressure*. She never worked well under pressure. "I'll try," she promised.

Bewildered, and even a little amused at the fact that in the space of two days she'd managed to move from London to Spellbinder Bay, discover she was a witch, and somehow find herself at the top of a lighthouse preparing to summon a magical cockatiel through the use of her magic — she closed her eyes. That seemed the most appropriate method to attempt first. Maybe she should try wiggling her nose, too? No. That would just make her look stupid, and bring attention to the fact that she had been born with a nose which was a little askew.

Doing as Judith suggested, Millie allowed herself to look inwardly, placing all her focus on the warm spot deep within her chest, the spot which seemed to have blossomed since she first stepped off the train at Spellbinder Bay station. The same spot which made her feel calm and safe when she was in the cottage.

She wasn't sure what the spot was, but it felt like it *should* be there. Like it should have always been there. Like a part of her body had been unknown to her until she arrived in the strange town she found herself in.

A hand fell on her shoulder, startling her. "Are you okay?" said Judith. "You're wobbling a little bit, and you're quite close to the railing. We don't want somebody else falling off."

Millie kept her eyes closed, and nodded. "Yes," she said. "I'm fine. Give me a moment."

She focused on her chest again, using the techniques

she'd learned during the spiritual month she'd taken up meditation and yoga. She allowed everything around her to become superfluous. The sound of the wind, the annoying scraping sound Sergeant Spencer's boots made as he shuffled impatiently on the metal balcony grid, the calling of the gulls, and the sweet aroma of salt air mixed with the pungent stench of rotting seaweed.

She ignored everything around her, and focused only on what was within her.

Then she found it. It was that simple. Like switching on a light. The feeling in her chest was no longer merely a feeling. It was a *thing*, and she felt like she could touch it. Closing her eyes tighter, and conjuring an image of Reuben in her mind, she allowed the ball in her chest to do what it wanted — almost as if it had free will, knowing that it would respond to the request she made of it.

She opened her eyes, her chest heaving. "I've done it," she murmured. "I think I've done it."

Chapter 15

Sergeant Spencer saw him first. "Look," he said. "I see him. At the back of the cottage."

Millie narrowed her eyes. Sure enough, there he was — a tiny speck in the air above the cottage, but rising higher, and heading in their direction.

Within seconds the little black speck took on colour, and soon enough it was possible to make out the bright red dabs of colour on his yellow cheeks. For such a little bird, he could move fast.

"Reuben! You heard me!" said Millie, as the little bird landed on the balcony rail next to her hand.

Reuben gave Millie an intense scowl. "You summoned me! I haven't been summoned for years! How dare you! You've hardly paid me any attention since you arrived in Spellbinder Bay, and now suddenly you think it's okay to summon me? And not only did you summon me — you waited until I was in the middle of a Jeremy Kyle episode I haven't seen before! I was waiting for the DNA results. Trevor denies he fathered Chantelle's baby, but the red hair speaks for itself! This had better be good, or we are going to have some serious issues."

"I'm sorry I interrupted your viewing, Reuben," said Millie, a little startled at the bird's vitriol. "But this is important. We need you to fly in that direction," she said, pointing. "And follow the blonde-haired woman you'll see running away. She can't have got far. At the speed you can fly, you'll soon catch up with her."

"Hurry!" said Sergeant Spencer. "Don't lose track of her. I'll head around the coast in the car with Judith and Millie, and cut her off. You just follow her to wherever she goes if she does manage to evade us. Have you got that, Reuben?"

"And why, may I ask, am I following a woman? Could that not be construed as weird, Sergeant Spencer? I may be a bird, but I still have morals," said Reuben.

"We think she might be involved in Albert's death," said Millie. "Just get going. Aren't you supposed to do what I tell you? I am your witch, aren't I?"

Reuben flapped his wings. "Okay, I get it. Ignore your familiar for a couple of days, and then when you want something, summon him. I see how it is. I'll do what you ask, but only because I have to, and because I happened to have liked Albert."

The little bird swooped low as he took off, and gained height as he neared the crashing waves and sea spray. Millie watched him until the bright sunlight hid him, and turned to follow Judith and her father down the stairs.

"Quick," said Sergeant Spencer. "It will take us ten minutes to get to the road which will cut her off. There's no way she can run that fast."

"We found a letter, too, Dad!" shouted Judith, as the three of them hurried towards the ground floor. "We think we know why Albert and Betty came here in the first place. To hide!"

"Tell me about it when we catch up with *this* suspect," said Sergeant Spencer. "One thing at a time."

Millie pulled the door shut behind them as they left the lighthouse, and Sergeant Spencer made sure to lock the door. He rushed to the waiting police car, and as he opened the door, looked skyward as a voice drifted down on the wind.

"There's nobody there!" squawked Reuben. "She's gone."

"What do you mean, gone?" said the sergeant. "That's not possible. Even an Olympic athlete couldn't have crossed that much ground in so little time!"

Reuben landed on Millie's shoulder, which she took as a mediocre compliment. "I mean, gone," said the cockatiel. "I'm not speaking in riddles. She's gone. G-O-N-E. I even found her footsteps, but they just stop in the sand. Like she vanished into mid-air."

"A paranormal?" said Sergeant Spencer. "Is she a ghost?"

"Not one I'm familiar with," said Judith. "But if she is a paranormal, she must be a ghost — no other para-normal person can simply vanish like that."

"Can a ghost push somebody?" said Millie.

"Yes," said Judith. "A ghost *could* find the strength to push somebody. It would need to be a well-established spirit though. A ghost must be dead for well over fifty years before they find that sort of power.

"They can pull duvets off people's beds and move teacups around kitchens pretty much straight away after dying, but people pushing? That takes time. Even being able to leave footsteps in sand requires some serious energy. If she is a ghost, she's been around for a long time."

"You're sure she's gone, Reuben?" said Sergeant Spencer. "She couldn't have just been hiding somewhere?"

Reuben sighed. "There *is* nowhere to hide around the corner. It's beach and sand dunes. Nothing else. I'm telling you — she vanished!" He pecked at Millie's ear. "If you're going to insist on being the sort of witch who summons her familiar, then please also be the sort of witch who insists that her colleagues respect the information I give them!"

"Okay, Reuben," said Sergeant Spencer. "I trust you. She vanished. We should get this information to Henry. If a ghost is involved in Albert's death, Henry will need to deal with it."

"You'll want to see the letter Millie and I found, too, Dad," said Judith. "It's a clue."

Sergeant Spencer climbed into the car. "Come on, get in," he said. "Show me the letter when we get to Spellbinder Hall. If a ghost is involved in a crime, we need to inform Henry quickly. The letter can wait a little longer."

***

"Absolutely not!" said Florence, the contents of a bookshelf visible through her midriff. "I'd know about it if there were a new spirit in the bay. We ghosts can sense one another. We operate on a different spiritual level than the rest of you. There is absolutely no possibility that a ghost pushed Albert Salmon from the lighthouse."

"Then how do you explain the vanishing footprints on the beach?" said Millie, warming to her new role as an unofficial policewoman, and realising that her fear of the paranormal had diminished exponentially over the last twenty-four hours.

She still experienced a healthy dose of chills running along her spine when she reminded herself she was speaking to a ghost, but the cold hard fear which had gripped her heart was now just a light pressure. An almost insignificant pressure.

Florence scowled. "I don't know, Miss Thorn. Perhaps she's a *witch*. Perhaps she made herself vanish — I've heard stories about people such as you being able to perform such feats."

"And that's what they are," said Henry, sitting at the table. "Stories. Yes, it's possible for *some* witches to make themselves temporarily invisible, but not like the woman on the beach. It takes a lot of skill, and a surprising amount of time to perform. It's not the sort of spell which can be cast instantaneously in the conditions the mystery woman found herself in."

"Then who or what was she?" said Sergeant Spencer. He looked at the cockatiel on Millie's shoulder. "I trust Reuben. I believe him when he says she vanished."

"How kind of you," muttered Reuben. "I'm honoured."

"I think it's fair to say that the woman in question should be found," said Henry, ignoring the bird's sarcasm. "But in the meantime, I suggest you focus your investigation on the contents of the short letter which

Judith and Millie found." He smiled at Judith. "Read it once again, would you?"

Judith unfolded the letter, and paced in front of the fireplace as she read. "I'm coming for you, Albert. You can't hide. You need to pay for what you did to her. When I get out of prison I'm coming for you. You ruined her life. My new year's resolution for two-thousand-and-four is to get revenge. I'll be seeing you soon, Albert." She looked up. "It's signed — W.M"

Sergeant Spencer frowned. "The lack of anything identifying in the letter leads me to believe it was smuggled out of prison. No letter which contained threats would have gone through the normal channels. They get vetted, and that letter wouldn't have passed. Whoever sent it probably paid an unethical guard to post it for them," he said.

"The postmark says Glasgow," said Judith, studying the envelope. "That helps, doesn't it? The prison must have been in Glasgow."

"Maybe, but there's more than one prison in Glasgow," said Sergeant Spencer, "plus, we don't know if it was a man or a woman who wrote it. The handwriting doesn't give it away. I can ask somebody to check for male and female prisoners in Scotland with the initials W.M, who were incarcerated during that period, but I don't hold out much hope."

"And who does the letter refer to?" said Millie. "Whose life did Albert allegedly ruin? His wife, Betty? Jim Grayson said he kept her locked away — maybe Albert's treatment of her made him an enemy."

Sergeant Spencer shook his head. "I don't know," he said, "it all sounds very unrealistic. A threatening letter smuggled out of prison fifteen years ago… if somebody harboured enough hate to kill Albert, they'd have killed him long before now. They've had plenty of time."

"Unless Albert and Betty were in hiding," said Millie. "Jim said they arrived here about fifteen years ago, and kept themselves to themselves. Maybe they were *very* good at hiding."

"I'll ask some questions," said Sergeant Spencer. "But my money is on the mystery blonde woman being the killer. If somebody runs away when a policeman tells them to stop, they usually have something to hide."

Henry stood up. "What about the tradesman Albert mentioned?" he asked, tidying a stack of papers on the table. "The one he asked to leave for being too noisy. Have you had any luck finding out who that may have been?"

"No," said the sergeant. "I've been in touch with Albert's telephone company, and I'm still waiting for information about any calls he made. I found no evidence of any unfinished work having been done around the lighthouse, so we're in the dark as to what sort of tradesman came to his home."

Henry straightened his dicky bow. "Well," he said. "I'll leave it in your capable hands, Sergeant. I'm afraid I need to be downstairs in five minutes. I always give a speech to the teachers and children on the last day of term. They'll be waiting for me in the main hall."

"It's the last day of term?" said Judith. "I hadn't realised."

Henry gave her an apologetic smile. "I'm sorry you didn't do much teaching this term, Miss Spencer. There just weren't enough pupils. Next term will be busier, I promise. There are over thirty paranormal children reaching school age in the coming year, and the ones we already have will still require your very important input." He turned his gaze to Millie, and smiled. "Maybe we'll have enough pupils to warrant taking on another teacher. One with experience of life outside the paranormal community."

"Me?" said Millie. "I'm not a teacher."

Henry peered over his spectacles, a twinkle in his eyes. "Everybody's a teacher deep down. We all have valuable knowledge to pass on," he said. "Think it over, Miss Thorn. If you decide to stay in the bay permanently you'll need something to do with your time. Money will no longer be an issue for you, and you'll discover that having no need to earn a living leads to an unfulfilled existence." He gave a small bow. "Now, if you'd all excuse me. I have a speech to give. Be sure to enjoy your beach party tonight, Miss Thorn. I think you'll find it… both interesting and enlightening."

Chapter 16

"*A*re you sure you won't come in?" said Millie, aware that she'd hardly spent any time alone in the cottage, and not certain that she really wanted to.

Judith smiled from the passenger seat of the police car. "I can't," she said. "I have to wash my hair before a certain beach party that's happening tonight." She waved her phone out of the window. "And George has been texting me all day. He wants you to be here alone so he can come and get you. He's going to pretend he wants to take you on a bike ride to the beach to watch the sunset. He's really excited about surprising you."

Millie licked her lips. "I'm not sure I want to go on his bike. Albert's warning rattled me a little. I've never been a fan of motorbikes — two wheels travelling at speed have never seemed safe to me."

"Albert didn't know George was a vampire," smiled Judith. "It's highly unlikely that a vampire would crash a motorcycle — they have reactions that would put a striking snake to shame. Just go along with it, there'll be plenty of booze to steady your nerves when you get to the beach!"

"The silver lining," smiled Millie.

Judith opened her mouth to speak, but her father silenced her with a hand on her arm. "That's the pathologist," he said, reaching for his phone, which vibrated on the dashboard. "I need to answer it."

Millie and Judith remained silent as Sergeant Spencer spoke on the phone, his raised eyebrows indicating that the news he was receiving was welcome. "Thank you," he said, before he finished the call. "I think I know exactly who those hairs belong to. I'll let you know."

"What is it, Dad?" said Judith, when the call was over.

Sergeant Spencer smiled. "You can forget all about that threatening letter you found. The pathologist has found several long blonde hairs snagged on Albert's clothing. No prizes for guessing whose head they came from — that woman was running from something, and I'll bet my house on it that when we catch her, we'll have a match for the DNA the pathologist will extract from the hairs."

"How will we find her?" said Millie.

"Shall we start looking now?" asked Judith.

"*We'll* do nothing for the moment," said Sergeant Spencer. "You girls are going to enjoy your beach party. I'm going to go and ask some questions in town. If I need your help again, it can wait until your hangovers have passed tomorrow."

After a quick shower, Millie threw the meagre contents of her suitcase onto the bed, and picked out a warm sweater and a pair of jeans. She took the time to hang the remainder of her clothes in the wardrobe, and slid the suitcase underneath the bed.

As she dried her hair, she glanced at the photo of her mother she'd placed on the bedside table that morning. *That wasn't right.* She looked again. Sure enough — the crack that had run the length of the glass had vanished. Picking the photograph up, she ran a finger over the unblemished glass.

No evidence of damage could be felt beneath her fingertip, and she frowned as she gazed at her mother's smiling face. "Reuben!" she yelled, making her voice heard over the TV which the cockatiel had insisted was switched on. "Reuben!"

"What?" came Reuben's squawking voice. "Are you summoning me again?"

"Would you just come here?" shouted Millie. "Please?"

She turned the photo over in her hand. It didn't look as if anyone had tampered with the back, which would have needed to be done if the glass had been renewed.

A fluttering of wings heralded Reuben's arrival, and he landed on the bed beside Millie, a rogue piece of pepperoni hanging from the tip of his beak. The bird had been adamant that he wanted leftover pizza instead of seeds or fruit, and Millie had finally succumbed to his begging, reluctantly cutting him a few small pieces from the two slices which remained uneaten.

"Has anybody been here today?" said Millie, as the bird used a toe to guide the scrap of meat into his mouth.

"No," said the cockatiel. "Not while I was here, but who knows what could have happened when you summoned me. That's the danger of asking me to leave the cottage — there's nobody here to guard the place. Just a thought for the future when you next decide to drag me away from my TV shows."

"If nobody's been here," said Millie, "then how do you explain the fact that the glass in this photograph was broken when I left this morning, and now it's not?"

Reuben gazed at the picture. "Who is it?" he said.

"It's my mother," said Millie. "It's the nicest picture I have of her."

Reuben hopped closer to the picture and studied it for a few moments. "She seems familiar," he said. "I feel like I've seen her before."

"People say we look alike," said Millie, running a finger over the glass. "It's such a shame that she never lived long enough to see me grow up."

"What happened when you broke the glass?" asked Reuben, his attention still on the picture.

"It was broken when I opened my suitcase," said Millie. "I hadn't packed it well enough."

"What did you do when you found it?" said Reuben. "Did you touch the broken glass? Were you sad that it was broken?"

"Yes," said Millie. "I was sad. I touched it like I am now, and put it on the bedside table. It was definitely broken. I didn't imagine it."

Sharp claws dug into her leg as Reuben hopped onto Millie's thigh. "Then it was your magic which fixed it," said the bird. "Most people experience powerful emotions when they see photographs of people they love, especially those that are no longer with them.

When you saw that your favourite photograph of your mother was broken, you released emotions, and with those emotions came magic. You mended it, Millie. You used your powers."

Millie placed the picture back on the bedside table, and closed her eyes. The idea that she had the power within her to mend broken glass, both scared and thrilled her.

"The photograph looks *so* familiar," said Reuben. "Her face. I know I've seen it before."

Millie opened her eyes. "That's impossible," she said. "You can't have seen her before. She died fourteen years ago, when I was ten. You're probably just noticing the similarities between us."

"Probably," murmured Reuben. He looked at Millie, studying her face. "You've both got that bent nose thing going on. Maybe it's that."

"Bent nose?" said Millie. "That's not a very nice way of putting it. Anyway, a lot of people think it's cute."

"A lot of people think wearing sunglasses indoors is cute," said Reuben. "But that doesn't make it a fact." He flew to Millie's shoulder. "Your nose does have a certain cuteness to it, though," he relented. "It gives you character, it takes the focus away from the fact that your eyes are a little too close together."

"I suppose I should take that as a compliment," said Millie, "because the only other option is to take offence, and that might make me mad."

Reuben took off and flew to the top of the wardrobe, where he perched, scanning the room. "Are you ever going to make this into your place?" he said. "It would be worth your while."

"What do you mean?" asked Millie. She looked around. *Was it her place, though?*

"I mean it's as if you're living in a hotel," said Reuben. "It's as if you don't believe this cottage is yours. It's like you're just waiting to leave — as if you're not going to stay." He fixed a sparkling eye on Millie. "You are going to stay, aren't you?"

Millie sighed. She lay back on the bed, her feet still on the floor. "I don't know what I'm going to do, Reuben," she said. "I feel like I'm in a dream. I feel like I belong in this cottage, but I also feel as if I'm trespassing. There's also a part of me that still believes that this whole *thing*, this whole place, is just a dream. A dream which I know I need to wake up from."

"This is all real," said Reuben. "And you know it."

She did know it, but that only made things seem even stranger. She wondered how most young women of her age would react if they were told that they were witches, and decided that she'd reacted well under the circumstances. "It's a lot to take in," she said, "that's all."

"I expect it is," said Reuben. "But you *should* make this cottage your own. The cottage transformed based on your energy, but even magic can't see into your soul. You should add some personal touches to the place. It would be worth your while. I promise."

Millie raised an eyebrow. "Why?"

The bird fluffed up his chest feathers. "I can't say too much," he said. "It's not my place to do so. It's down to you to work things out for yourself. All I will say, is that when the energy within the cottage knows you're going to make this place your home, it will reveal things to you."

"What things?" said Millie.

"I've said too much," said Reuben. "I shouldn't have said anything, I just get the feeling you're going to leave, and I don't want that."

"Why do you sound so sad?" said Millie, sitting up again. "You hardly know me. You can't tell me you'll miss me if I leave?"

"I *might* miss you," said Reuben, rubbing his beak along the top of the open wardrobe door. "But it's more than that. It's a lot more than that. It's a matter of—"

Millie jumped as a voice called her name. "Millie? Are you here? The door was unlocked, I hope you don't mind that I let myself in?"

"Bloodsucker!" squawked Reuben, swooping from the wardrobe and fluttering towards the door.

"Don't you dare tell him I know about the surprise party," hissed Millie.

Reuben circled the room, his wingtips skimming the walls. "Are you asking nicely, or demanding as my witch?"

"Urm, demanding?" said Millie. "As your witch."

Reuben nodded. "Your demand will be met," he said. "May I go and greet our guest?"

"Sure," said Millie.

Reuben flew through the door at speed. "What do you want?" he screeched as he left the bedroom. "Come to try and force feed me seeds again, have you? Well, it won't work, bucko. My witch summoned me today. She claimed me as her familiar — I've got Millie Thorn watching my back now, and I'd like to see a bloodsucker try and take on my witch! She'd wreck you, vampire boy!"

"Calm down, you feathery fool," came George's

voice. "I was asked to look after you when Esmeralda passed — until another witch arrived. That's what I did. Your demands were outrageous, Reuben. I'm not some sort of soft witch who's going to order in pizza when you demand it. You should be glad I fed you at all. I only looked after you because Fredrick asked me to."

"Oooh," cawed Reuben. "Got to do what your maker tells you! I'm freer than you, and I lived in that cage for a whole week, until Millie came and freed me."

"I am free, Reuben," said George. "Fredrick turned me into what I am today. I owe him, so I do what he asks of me. Within reason. He doesn't force me to do anything. Anyway, where is Millie? Is she here?"

"I'm coming," said Millie, slipping her sweater on. "What do you want?" *As if she didn't know.*

"I want to take you for a ride on my bike. Nothing exciting — just a trip to the beach. I thought you might like to see the sunset?" lied George. "After what happened to you when I left you alone at the lighthouse, I wanted to show you something nice."

Millie smiled.

There was a vampire in her living room. A vampire with a motorcycle parked outside. A vampire who had arranged a surprise party to welcome her to town.

What else could she do but smile?

"I didn't hear your bike," said Millie, as she entered the living room.

"Because I rode it slowly," said George. "And the walls of this cottage must be at least two feet thick. With the windows closed you'd be hard-pressed to hear a bomb going off outside."

"Or did you fly here? As a bat?" said Reuben.

"You can do that, George?" said Millie. "Really?"

155

George laughed. "He's joking. No — vampires can't turn into bats, but we can tell when we're in the presence of courage, and you have courage, Millie. I can sense you're not afraid of me, even though you've learned the truth about me since we last met."

"I try to judge people… and vampires, on first impressions," said Millie. "And you gave a good first impression. What do I have to fear?"

"The fact that he might try and suck the blood from you, leaving you as a broken husk?" suggested Reuben. "A mere vessel of bone and sinew for your darkened soul."

"That's not true either," said George. "Ignore him. He's a bird-brain. I couldn't suck the blood from you even if I wanted to. You're a witch — your blood would cause me *severe* pain. And even if you *were* fully human, I wouldn't suck your blood.

"Vampires don't do that anymore — not vampires who don't want to hide away in the shadows for the rest of their very long existence, anyway. Those days are long behind the majority of the vampire community, and I'm so relieved that I was turned in an era in which I never had to feed on human blood."

Millie focused on George's eyes as he spoke. The depth of emotion they conveyed gave her no reason to doubt him. George was telling the truth, and the fact that his eyes sucked Millie into their mysterious depths was a bonus.

He really was an attractive man. Or was that vampire? She wasn't sure. She reached for one of the helmets George held. "I'm glad to hear you won't be sucking my blood — I don't think I'd have liked that. Shall we get going then? I'd like to see the sunset."

If George guessed that Millie already knew about his surprise, he didn't show it. He gave a huge smile which made Millie chuckle, and zipped his jacket closed. "It will be a sunset to remember," he said. "I promise."

GEORGE TOOK HIS TIME AS HE NAVIGATED THE NARROW winding lanes, the motorbike's headlight picking out the occasional rabbit in the gathering dusk, and the sound of the engine startling birds preparing to roost in the hedgerows.

Millie gripped a hunk of leather jacket in each gloved hand, and held on tight, leaning in the same direction as the bike on each corner they rounded.

The road George followed skirted the base of the cliff which Spellbinder Hall perched on, and the harbour lights twinkled to the right, visible through gaps in the hedge as they zoomed along the lane.

Soon they were at their destination, and George brought the motorcycle to a halt in a small car park which already contained more than a dozen vehicles.

"Here we are," said George, removing his helmet.

Millie climbed off the bike, and removed her helmet, too. She took a deep breath of clean air, enjoying the warm sea breeze on her face. Soft crimson light painted George's face, and the dimming orange sun had dipped low on the horizon, almost completely swallowed by the ocean. "It looks like we've almost missed the sunset," she said, genuinely disappointed.

George smiled. He took Millie's helmet from her and placed it alongside his in one of the panniers. "I didn't really bring you here to watch the sunset," he said. "I've got a surprise for you, Millie Thorn!"

Millie grinned. The fact that she already knew that George had arranged a surprise for her didn't matter. George's eyes twinkled with excitement, and his body language screamed the message that he couldn't contain his secret for much longer. His glee was infectious, and Millie found herself caught up in it.

Realising she was genuinely happy that George had gone to the trouble of arranging a surprise for her, she gave her best impression of a woman in shock. "What do you mean — a surprise?" she gasped, her eyes wide and a hand on her chest. "For me?"

George pocketed the motorbike keys, and turned to face the beach, stifling a giggle. He pointed. "Can you see that?" he said. "At the base of the cliff."

Millie looked. Reflected on the white tips of gently breaking waves, was an orange glow, brighter than the one given off by the dropping sun, and amber fingers of light climbed the cliff wall, dancing higher as the wind irritated their source. "A fire!" she said.

George nodded. "Come on, let me show you."

The path through the sand dunes was hard work on Millie's calves. The soft sand made each step twice as hard as it should have been, and it was with relief that she stepped onto the firmer sand of the beach. She removed her shoes and socks and carried them in one hand as she walked alongside George, the sand cool between her toes. "It's a big fire," she said, as they neared the cliff.

"It's a big crowd of people to keep warm," said George. "Look at them!"

The bright flames made it hard to see beyond the

fire, but by squinting her eyes, Millie could make out the silhouettes of people against the orange glow. "Who are all those people?" she said, genuinely surprised. When Timothy had accidentally let slip that George had arranged the party for her, Millie had not imagined that so many people would be present. She counted the shadows as best she could, estimating there to be at least thirty people mingling in groups around the fire.

"Those are the guests!" grinned George. "To your party!" He took Millie's hand and gave her a sincere smile. "Welcome to Spellbinder Bay, Millie. I arranged this party to make you feel welcome! I hope you have a fantastic night. You deserve it."

Finally, she could let the pretence slip. "Wow!" she said. "All these people have come to welcome me?"

George tugged at Millie's hand, urging her to follow him as he quickened his pace. "Yes. They're all here for you, and they've brought plenty of alcohol and food with them. It's going to be fun!"

Millie jogged alongside him, her hand warm in his, and the heat of the fire on her face before they were within twenty metres of the flames. "It's hot!" she laughed.

"It's not your run-of-the-mill fire," said George. "It was started by one of the witches! It won't go out until she wants it to!"

As Millie and George neared the throng of people, a cheer went up from the crowd. "Welcome to Spellbinder Bay, Millie Thorn!" came Judith's voice.

Other voices joined Judith's, and an open can of beer was shoved into her hand by a heavyset dark-haired man, who Millie guessed was around the same age as her. "Welcome," he said, making no effort to hide the fact that his eyes had wandered the full length of Millie's body. "It's great to meet you, Millie. I'm Sam."

"Millie doesn't need you ogling her, Sam," said the small red-haired girl standing next to the large man. She pointed at Millie's face. "That's where you look when you meet a lady."

"Sorry," grumbled Sam. "I wasn't trying to be offensive."

Millie nodded. "None taken." She wasn't lying. It wasn't every day that a man as handsome as Sam gave her that sort of attention.

The redheaded girl thumped Sam playfully on his arm. "Go and put some music on. We can start having some fun now Millie's arrived."

Even beneath the glow of the fire, it was apparent that Sam's cheeks had turned a shade of crimson. "Music it is," he said, beginning to push his way through the crowd, head and shoulders above most of the other people.

"Sorry about him," said the girl. "Men like him get a bit fired up this close to a full moon. They lose a few of their inhibitions. I'm Eve, by the way."

Millie took the girl's hand as she extended her arm in a friendly greeting. "It's no problem. Honestly. But what do you mean, men like him?" she said, already guessing that the mention of a full moon had a lot to do with it.

"Men like him," Eve said. "Werewolves. It's okay for the males to get a bit frisky before a full moon, but it's frowned upon for us women to do the same. Tell me how that's fair!"

"Enough of that, Eve," said George. "You'll scare

her. She hasn't been here long. She doesn't know much about any of this stuff. Let's do things slowly."

"We're still having the wolf and vampire fight?" said Eve. "We have to have that! You promised party games, George."

"Yes, yes," said George, "we'll have the fight."

Judith grabbed Millie's wrist and guided the open beer can towards her mouth. "Drink up," she ordered. "If the look on your face is any indication of how you're going to react when you see or hear something strange happening tonight, then you're going to need a few more beers inside you."

Millie swallowed. The beer tasted strong and it cooled her throat. She took another gulp, and only stopped drinking when the can was half empty. Dance music began playing from somewhere behind her, and the smell of barbecuing meat mingled with the smoke from the bonfire.

"You look shocked," said George. "Are you okay?"

"Do you know what?" Millie said, licking beer from her lips. "I don't think anything could shock me anymore."

George put his hand on her shoulder. "Never say never, Millie," he said. "Never say never."

Chapter 17

*M*illie and Judith sat a short distance from the rest of the crowd, watching as people danced, ate and laughed. After drinking three cans of beer, the malty taste had become too much for her, and Millie had progressed onto vodka and cola, a fresh plastic cup of which she clutched in her hand.

The alcohol had done its job, and Millie felt more relaxed than she'd done since she'd arrived in Spellbinder Bay. She took another sip of her drink, and laughed as a tall man attempted to lift his dancing partner above his head, in what he obviously considered was going to be a perfectly executed dirty dancing move, but quickly turned into a tangled mess of arms and legs in the sand. "And all these people are paranormal?" said Millie. "It's hard to believe."

"Every single one of them," said Judith. "A non-paranormal person couldn't get near this spot. Apart from my dad of course, but he's a one-off. The concealment magic would just make them turn around before they got within a hundred metres of the cliff. They

162

wouldn't even question their decision — they'd just turn around and walk away."

Millie swivelled her head and looked at the cliff. "What's so special about this cliff?" she asked. "I know Spellbinder Hall is built on top of it, but why can't non-paranormal people be down here? It's just sand and rock."

Judith pointed into the shadows. "Can you see that crack in the cliff?" she said. "The one that looks wide enough for a person to walk through?"

The cliff displayed a spider web of cracks, visible in the glow from the fire, but it was apparent which crack Judith was speaking about. Bigger than the others, it was wide at the bottom, and tapered into a point high above the sand. "Yes, I see it," confirmed Millie.

"There's something very special in there," said Judith. "Something that no normie can ever be allowed to see."

"What is it?" said Millie, tilting her head to get a better view of the fissure.

Judith took a long sip of her drink. "You'll find out by the end of the night," she said.

Millie laughed. *That was vague.* "Come off it! You can't tell me there's something very special inside a crack in a cliff, and then tell me I can't see it straight away. That's not fair! I want to see!"

Judith spilt her drink as she laughed. "Have patience, young lady. The night is young."

Sudden silence washed over the beach as the music abruptly stopped. A man's voice rang out, echoing off the cliff. "Okay, folks! It's fight time. Vampires and werewolves… have you chosen your warriors?"

Judith stood up, wiping sand from her shorts. "The secret in the cliff will have to wait. It's games time!"

"The man said fight time," said Millie. "He definitely said fight time. Not games time."

"It's both," smiled Judith. "There's going to be a fight, but it's just a game. A bit like a boxing match, but without gloves and walk on girls."

A tickling sensation ran the length of Millie's forearms as the small hairs stood on end. She swallowed the last of her drink. "Does this mean I'm going to see a vampire and a werewolf?" she said. "I mean — am I really going to see them? In their... *other* forms?"

"Better than that," said Judith, grabbing Millie's hand and pulling her to her feet. "George told me he's been chosen as the vampire's warrior. You're going to see *him* in his *true* form!"

The crowd had formed a tight circle around a patch of sand bathed in the heat and glow from the fire, and a young man stood in the centre, addressing the crowd. His bare chest glistened, and his long black hair flowed over his broad shoulders. "Where is the guest of honour?" he shouted, looking around the circle of people. "Where's the new arrival in the bay?"

Judith grabbed Millie's wrist and pushed her hand into the air. "Here she is, Daniel!" she yelled. "Millie Thorn. The New witch in Windy-dune Cottage!"

A loud cheer rose from the crowd, and friendly hands slapped Millie's back. "Welcome to Spellbinder Bay!" somebody shouted. "Where anything goes!" laughed another.

Millie gave a wide smile. "Thank you," she said, her voice almost lost among the excited chatter. "It's an honour to be here among you all." She put her mouth close to Judith's ear. "Was that okay?" She whispered. "An *honour*?"

"Of course," said Judith. "It sort of is an honour to be a part of this community. I feel blessed to count myself as a paranormal person in Spellbinder Bay."

"Bring Millie to the front!" shouted Daniel, flicking hair from his eyes with a toss of his head. "The guest of honour should have a good view of the fight!" He paused, and smiled at Millie, his eyes narrowed. "Unless she's afraid of monsters, of course?"

Judith guided Millie through the warm bodies of the revellers. "They're testing you," she said over her shoulder. "They know you haven't seen a vampire or were-wolf yet. They want to know if you're going to fit in around here before they fully trust you."

Somebody replaced the empty cup in Millie's hand with a full one, and as Judith guided her to the inner edge of the circle of bodies, Millie took a long swallow, the liquid burning her throat. *Whiskey.* One of her least favourite things in the world. She grimaced as she took another sip, not wanting to show any weakness. "I'm not scared!" she shouted, alcohol partly fuelling her courage, but her innate determination providing most of the fuel. "Show me the monsters!"

A cheer went up from the crowd, and Millie grinned. She gasped as Judith elbowed her in the ribs. "Ow!"

"That's the way!" said Judith. "You'll fit right in with that attitude!"

The crowd quietened as the ringmaster raised an arm above his head. "Vampires!" he yelled. "Have you chosen your warrior?"

"Yes!" said a young woman, the bronzed skin of her

SAM SHORT

arms intricately patterned in black tattoos. "We choose George Brown!"

"That's his surname?" said Millie. "He doesn't look like a Brown. He looks more like a Pitt, or a Clooney!"

Judith laughed. "Don't tell him that. It will go to his head!"

The crowd parted to form an aisle, and Millie put a hand to her mouth as George entered the ring to cheers from one portion of the crowd, and jeers from another. "What happened to him?" she said. "His chest... what happened?"

The ragged scar ran from his bulging left pectoral muscle, in a raised welt which continued almost all the way down his torso, stopping an inch shy of his navel. As George pumped both fists above his head, in a show of fighting spirit, the wound stretched with his skin, daubed in the dancing glow of flames.

"It happened a long time ago," said Judith. "It almost killed him. He was a British soldier during World War One. He was disembowelled by a German bayonet, which also cut into his heart. He'd have died if Fredrick hadn't been on the battlefield."

Millie smiled at George as he gave her a wink. "That's when Fredrick turned him?" she said.

Judith nodded. "Yes. Fredrick was a German soldier — an officer. He'd been a vampire for centuries before the war, though. He had vowed to neither take, or save a life on the battlefield. He wanted to be neutral, but he'd wanted to do *something* for the country he called home at the time — so he enlisted as a medic, with the intention of helping people who could be saved by natural methods, not paranormal methods."

"Then why did he turn George into a vampire?"

said Millie. "He was an enemy. If Fredrick was going to break his vow of not saving anyone's life, why would he chose an enemy to save?"

The crowd roared a cheer as George pumped his fists again, and Judith smiled. "He said that George reminded him of the son he'd once had. His son had refused to be turned, and had died of old age. Fredrick didn't want to let a reminder of his son die, so he turned George into a vampire.

"George had just enough life left in him to give his permission, and when he'd been changed they both left Europe until the war was over. They found their way here in the nineteen-fifties, I believe." She sipped her drink. "That's all I know about it. George told us all one night — at a beach party like this. He doesn't mention it much, and we *don't* speak to him about it unless he brings it up."

Millie nodded, understanding the veiled advice. "I won't mention it to him. I promise."

Another raucous cheer from the crowd prevented Judith from answering, so she chinked cups with Millie, and smiled.

"Werewolves!" shouted Daniel. "Have *you* chosen your warrior?"

"Yes!" came the call from the group of people opposite George's supporters.

Millie kept her eye on Sam, who stood next to Eve. Having learned they were both werewolves, she was certain that Sam would be chosen to fight.

He stood head and shoulders above everybody else, and his broad chest was twice as wide as the average man's. If he was that large as a man, Millie wondered with trepidation and concern how George had even the smallest of chances against him when he became a wolf.

"We've chosen Timothy!" came a shout.

"Timothy?" said Millie, nudging Judith. "The Timothy I met? The short man-child in Spellbinder Hall?"

"The very same," said Judith.

Millie frowned. "He's a werewolf?"

"One of the strongest," said Judith.

The crowd parted, and Millie stared in astonishment as Timothy sauntered into the ring, his bare belly wobbling a little, and his attempt at a beard as unkempt as it had been when she'd last met him. He pummelled his naked chest with both fists and gave the crowd a wave.

"But he's so small," said Millie. "Why didn't they choose Sam? He's a man mountain."

"The size of the wolf is not based on the size of the person's body," explained Judith. "It's based on the courage contained in the heart. Sam might be a big man, but his wolf is tiny and, well… a little bedraggled, if I'm honest. Timothy's wolf, on the other hand, is huge. Just wait and see!"

With the sun completely set, moonlight vied with the glow from the fire to illuminate the two adversaries in the ring as they turned to face each other.

Daniel looked at each of them in turn. "Are you ready to fight?" he asked.

"I am," said George, his voice deep and calm.

"Me too," Timothy half squeaked and half groaned.

The ringmaster took a step backwards. "Remember the rules. The winner must transform as soon as the loser does."

George and Timothy nodded their agreement and each extended an arm, shaking hands with one another.

Daniel stepped out of the circle and lifted a fist. "As the old saying goes — let battle commence!"

Wondering if she was ready to witness two apparently human men turn into monsters, Millie held her breath and waited.

Chapter 18

$\mathcal{T}$hings happened quickly, and Millie wasn't certain who'd changed first. She'd seen Timothy suddenly gain at least four foot in height in the same instant his arms had bulged with muscles, and coarse dark hair had coated his body. The shorts he wore disintegrated into shreds, unable to contain the monster within.

George's transformation had been quicker, and less dramatic. More reserved. Millie hadn't noticed his eyes darken, but it was evident they had, and the blackness gave him an eerie appearance.

He crouched into a fighting stance as he approached Timothy, two prominent fangs protruding from his upper jaw, and his muscles even better defined than they already had been.

Millie instinctively took a step backwards, but Judith placed a hand on the small of her back. "Don't worry," she said. "You're perfectly safe. And there won't be any blood — it's just a wrestling match, and it's friendly — it's just a game."

Timothy tilted his chin, his snout toward the moon, and let out a bloodcurdling roar which reverberated in the air and echoed over the beach, amplified by the cliff wall.

"George doesn't have a chance!" said Millie. "Look at the size of Timothy. He's terrifying!"

"They said the same about David when he fought Goliath," shouted Judith, making her voice heard over the roaring of the crowd. "And look what happened there!"

"Yes, but George doesn't have a slingshot," said Millie, her attention stolen by the huge claws which extended from all four of Timothy's dinner-plate sized paws.

"No," said Judith. "But he has got incredible strength while he's in his vampire form. Timothy's strong too, but not as strong as George. He has to rely on his teeth and claws, but as this is strictly a wrestling match, he's not allowed to use them. He'll be forced to use his superior weight."

Millie tried to step backwards again as Timothy gave another roar, but Judith applied more pressure to the base of her back. She took a deep breath, calming herself. "Won't instinct takeover?" she asked. "I've seen it in films! The werewolf can be lovely in his human form, but when he turns into a wolf he goes mad!"

Judith laughed. "I can promise you that no film-maker has ever approached the werewolf community to find an adviser for their films," she said. "If they had, the films would be very different. Both Timothy and George are in full control of themselves. Don't worry — they do this all the time."

Attempting to relax, Millie loosened her shoulders

and took a sip of her drink. As Timothy continued to howl at the moon, George circled him, keeping his body low — resembling a thinner and better toned version of a sumo wrestler. Suddenly, and without his body language giving any warning, George leapt at the wolf, his legs propelling him high in the air — high enough to land with a heavy thud on Timothy's back.

The werewolf howled and spun on the spot, attempting to remove George with swats of his large paws, his howls becoming louder.

George held on tight, scrambling higher on Timothy's back, until the wolf's large head was trapped between his thighs. George twisted his upper body, and as Timothy lost his balance, the vampire utilised the momentum of the stumble to slam his opponent into the sand, his neck still trapped firmly between George's knees.

The crowd roared their approval, and Timothy roared his frustration. Sand flew from beneath his rear paws as he scrambled to his feet again, casting George off his back with a powerful swipe of a large forearm.

The two creatures circled one another, but this time Timothy took the chance to attack first. With all four feet burrowing into the sand, he launched himself at George, like a lion hurling itself at a Gazelle.

The sound of the two muscled bodies slamming into one another was almost as loud as the crowd, and Millie winced as she heard George's breath leave him in a ragged gasp. His abdominal muscles rippling, and his fangs glistening in the moonlight, he struggled to force the wolf from on top of him.

"Change, George!" shouted somebody in the crowd. "You know you want to!"

Judith turned to Millie, a hand still on the base of her back. "If George changes into human form, he loses," she said. "It's the vampire and werewolf fight equivalent of a wrestler tapping out."

"But if he changes back into a human he'll be crushed by the weight of Timothy!" said Millie, wincing once more as Timothy placed a massive paw on one of George's arms, and forced it into the sand.

"No, he won't," said Judith. "The moment that George changes — Timothy will know, and he'll change too. Werewolves and vampires have been playing this game for centuries, and no one's ever been hurt." She paused. "Well, no one's ever been killed, I should say."

"That sounds less reassuring than I think you meant it to sound," said Millie, beginning to enjoy the spectacle unfolding before her. When she factored out the fact that she was witnessing two of the most common creatures which populated children's nightmares, wrestling on a moonlit beach, the fight was intensely exciting to watch.

Timothy slammed George's other arm into the sand and let out an ear-splitting roar as his supporters cheered him on. "You've got this, Timmy boy!" yelled a woman.

"Finish it!" shouted a man.

Timothy hunched over George, the yellows of his eyes piercing in the gloom. George struggled in the sand, a heavy paw on each of his limbs and a drooling werewolf looming over him.

"When will he change?" said Millie. "He's lost! Shouldn't he just give in?"

"Give him a moment," said Judith. "He's just regaining his strength, look how calm his face is."

Judith was right. Although not a picture of serenity,

173

George's face was not the face of a vampire about to be beaten in a wrestling match with a werewolf. His black eyes shone, and Millie was sure he was smirking.

As the crowd's demands for George to change grew louder, the vampire tensed his body, his abdominal muscles tightening, and his hands closing into fists. George seemed to slip deeper into the sand, and the werewolf jolted on top of him as the vampire made an upward thrust, using all four of his limbs to shake Timothy from him.

The werewolf howled again, and George's fists tightened, the veins in his forearms bulging. He looked into the crowd, and when his eyes fell on Millie, he gave her a wink, and this time Millie was certain he was smirking.

With a shout that came from his gut, George pushed himself upwards in a show of power and strength. The werewolf had no chance. Even with soft sand beneath him, the pure brute force he employed propelled George upwards, forcing the werewolf to travel with him.

Timothy attempted to release his grip on George's arms, but George took the initiative and gripped a chunk of hair in each fist, keeping the werewolf close to him.

The two creatures flew through the air together, switching positions as they reached the peak of their arc, leaving Timothy beneath George as they slammed into the sand, this time Timothy expelling his breath in a gasp.

The force of the landing pushed half of the werewolf's body beneath the sand, but George wasn't finished, he put a forearm on the werewolf's neck, and pushed hard — forcing Timothy's head deeper into the beach.

The werewolf relented, and in the blink of an eye, the scene changed from a werewolf and a vampire struggling in the sand, to a vampire straddling a short naked overweight man.

No sooner had Timothy transformed back into his human form, than George joined him, releasing his grip and allowing Timothy to breathe.

George rolled off Timothy, and lay in the sand next to him. "Somebody get the man some new shorts!" he demanded, wiping a hand across his stomach. "His todger touched my belly when he changed!"

Millie laughed. "Todger?" she said. "Who says todger?"

Judith giggled, too. "It was probably a common term during the period George lived as a human," she explained. "He often forgets what era he's living in, and reverts to old slang. You have to admit that todger is better than a lot of words he could have used!"

Timothy did his best to hide his dignity as he struggled into the fresh pair of shorts somebody tossed him, and magnanimous in defeat, he slapped George on the back as the two men stood up. "Good fight!" he said. "I almost had you, though!"

"Almost isn't good enough, Timothy," said George. "But I must admit I thought I was beaten at one point."

Daniel stepped back into the ring, and grabbed George's wrist. He pushed it upward. "We have a winner!" he shouted. "George of the vampires!"

Both Timothy and George's supporters showed their appreciation, clapping and cheering. Somebody thrust a drink into each of their hands, and the crowd began to disperse — some of them heading back to the fire, and others making a beeline for the barbecue.

"Not so fast!" shouted Daniel. "Everybody come back! There's a new witch in town, remember? It's time for her to show us what she can do. It's time for Millie Thorn to entertain us with a magic trick!"

"We don't do tricks, Daniel," said Judith. "We cast spells."

"And I don't know how to cast any," protested Millie. "I can't entertain you with magic. I know a few card tricks which I don't mind performing?"

"Of course you can cast spells!" said Judith. "Have some faith in yourself."

"I've got faith in you," said George, rubbing the sand from his hair, which had collected there during the fight. "I know you can do it."

"But I wouldn't know where to start," said Millie. "All I've done so far is summon a cockatiel, and I think I read the mind of Jim Grayson in the harbour."

"Remember what you did when you summoned Reuben?" said Judith. "Do you remember how you did it?"

Millie nodded. "Yes, I remember."

Judith smiled. "Then just do what you did then, but instead of focusing on summoning Reuben, focus the magic on something else. Whatever you want your magic to do when it's built up within you, it will do."

"What sort of thing do people want me to do?" asked Millie. "Turn somebody into a toad? Send somebody to sleep for a hundred years? I don't know what sort of magic witches can do — the only magic I've seen since have been here was you showing off while you made breakfast. I could try that I suppose. I could try to float some meat over the barbecue?"

"You can do far more than that, Millie," said Judith. "You're standing very close to the source of magic in Spellbinder Bay right now, you should be able to access your magic easily." She passed her empty cup to George. "I know. Let me show you the sort of thing they expect. It doesn't serve any real purpose — it's just showy magic, for these sorts of events. I suppose you *could* call them tricks."

"Told you," said Daniel, with a smirk. "Magic tricks."

Judith rolled her eyes. "It's more than you can do, Daniel," she said. "Walking through walls is hardly the best trick in the world. It gets very boring very quickly."

"Maybe so," replied Daniel. "But how many ghosts do you know that can keep a solid form for as long as I can?" He smiled. "Look at Millie's face! She didn't even guess I was a ghost! Did you, Millie?"

She hadn't. Daniel appeared as real as everybody else on the beach. "No," she said, genuinely amazed at the man standing before her was dead. "I had no idea."

"It's only because you're so close to Spellbinder Hall," said Judith. "Try keeping such a solid form on the other side of town — you'd be as see-through as the rest of the ghosts who wander the streets!"

"Ghosts don't wander," countered Daniel. "We travel with purpose. Anyway, enough about my powers, are you going to show Millie and the rest of us some of yours?"

A single voice in the crowd began chanting, soon joined by others. "Magic! Magic! Magic!" they shouted.

Judith rubbed her hands together. "Okay, a quick trick and then Millie can have a go. She turned to face the sea, and looked at Millie. "All I'm going to do is focus on my magic, and then let it go in any way I want it to. Watch this. It's simple"

She took a deep audible breath, and thrust her hands away from her body. A green orb flashed into existence, hovering a few feet above the sand. It dipped and rose, growing steadily in size and becoming brighter.

As the orb grew, it began changing shape, until Millie recognised what it was. "An egg?" she said.

"It's all I can think of!" said Judith, controlling the orb with her hands. "You reminded me what I did at breakfast time — so an egg appeared in my mind. It's not just any egg, though — watch."

The egg shimmered, and a small crack appeared at the tip. As the crack widened, a red light seeped from the shell, becoming brighter as the crack grew. As the egg split open, the two pieces of shell fell to the beach and disappeared into the sand, leaving a faint glow where they'd landed.

The red light began to take on a form of its own, and Millie laughed when she saw what it was. "A dragon?" she said. "It's amazing!"

The hatchling dragon spread its fiery red wings wide, and looking around as if exploring its new world, it made long sweeping strokes with its wings, powering it quickly across the sand. The dragon quickly gained momentum, tracing the gentle curve of the beach as it followed the coastline.

"Where will it go?" asked Millie, as the dragon rounded the base of the cliff and disappeared, leaving only dim red sparks in its wake.

"It will fizzle out within a mile or two," said Judith, "you might even see a few stories in the newspapers over the next few days, fishermen reporting UFOs — that sort of thing!"

Daniel clapped, raising a spattering of copycat applause from the crowd. "Not bad," he said. He looked at Millie. "Now let's see what you can do."

Millie handed Judith her drink, and stood with her feet shoulder-width apart. "I'll try my best," she said. "But I'm not sure I can do anything quite like Judith just did."

"Just draw on your magic and imagine what you want it to become," said Judith. "It's easy. I promise."

Millie closed her eyes. It seemed easier that way. She concentrated on the space within her chest where she'd last experienced the sensation of magic. A gentle warmth rose within her, and she sucked in another breath of air, concentrating hard and trying to recall what she'd done to summon Reuben.

The air around her seemed to warm, and she heard somebody gasp.

"You're doing it," said Judith, "the air is electric. Open your eyes!"

Millie opened her eyelids slowly, aware that tingles of static surrounded her body. Not only could she feel it, she could see it, too. Small sparks flashed and died as they hovered around her, gaining life above her head, and dying in the sand at her feet as they dropped slowly to the beach.

The electric in the air buoyed Millie's confidence, and with purpose and intent, she explored the ball of heat which burned inside her. It was as if another life-force resided within her. A life-force which demanded release.

The quick beat of her heart was evident in her ears, and delicate spider webs of tingling energy sent tendrils throughout her body. She smiled at Judith. "I think I can do it!"

Chapter 19

"*J*ust let it happen," said Judith.

Her hands trembling, and the muscles in her forearms giving tiny spasms, as if she'd taken hold of an electric fence, Millie gazed at the expectant faces around her. They wanted a show, and it was Millie who was to provide it.

With the fire on her left, and the beach and ocean to her front — shrouded in moonlight filtered by the growing cloud cover, she concentrated on the burgeoning ball of heat within her chest. Running on a newly discovered instinct, Millie tightened her focus, willing the powers which swirled within her to take on a physical form. A form which her spectators would enjoy.

"Look at her hands," said a female to her right. "If this really is her first time casting a spell, then she's going to be really good when she's had some practice!"

Millie looked at her hands, and gave a small gasp of delight. Tendrils of blue light swarmed over the surface of her skin, flickering and sparking with every move-ment she made, and every thought she processed.

She gazed towards the sea again, only the brightest tips of the tallest waves visible in the dark.

"Let it go," said Judith. "The magic you've built up will respond to your thoughts, the way you want it to. It will mould itself to the images in your mind. It will do what you want it to do."

Millie opened and closed her fingers, her imagination running wild. She knew what Judith had said was right — she could feel the magic waiting for instructions. She sensed it raring to go — like a powerful racehorse awaiting a heel from its rider.

The image of a horse was a strong one, and as the white foam from a wave shimmered under moonlight, Millie recalled that sailors often referred to the crests of waves as the white horses of the ocean.

That was it! That's what she'd do with the strengthening build-up of magic! Making two tight fists, she drew her hands close to her chest, and with a push from deep within her, she expelled her magic, thrusting her hands forward in the same moment.

The force with which the magic left her caused her to stumble backwards, and she was only prevented from falling to the floor by a pair of strong arms.

"Are you okay?" said George, his mouth close to Millie's ear, and his hands on her waist.

"Yes," whispered Millie.

Shouts of astonishment rose from the crowd as Millie's spell rushed across the beach, the white ball of light morphing into the majestic form of a galloping stallion, its mane long, and its hooves kicking up sand as it sped towards the ocean. Muscles rippled in its strong thighs and flanks, and it tossed its head from side to side as it ran.

"You did it!" said Judith, a hand on Millie's shoulder. "It's beautiful!"

As the shimmering horse neared the sea's edge, a warning shout rang out from a man in the crowd. "Watch out!" he yelled. "Get out of the way!"

The warning came too late for the woman standing in the surf. Suddenly illuminated by the brightness of Millie's magic, she stood as if mesmerised by the stallion which approached her at speed.

Waist deep in water, her white dress and long golden hair reflecting light from the fast approaching spell, she attempted to step out of the way, but had no chance of avoiding the galloping horse.

As the horse collided with the woman, a sound like a cracking whip filled the air, and a vivid blue light spread across the ocean as the horse lost its form and collapsed in on itself.

With the beach dark again, Millie joined the stampede of people as they rushed to help the woman in the surf. George reached the water's edge first, moving fast, his arms pumping quickly as he ran. He rushed into the sea, and reached the stricken woman who was floating face down, bobbing like a piece of driftwood in the waves.

"What have I done?" said Millie, "what have I done?"

"It's not your fault," said Judith, standing alongside Millie. "She shouldn't have been there. I don't understand how she *could* be there. Non-paranormal people shouldn't be able to get this close — it keeps them safe! From things like that!"

"I've got her!" yelled George, dappled in moonlight as he dragged the unconscious figure towards the beach.

Another man waded waist deep into the heaving surf and held the woman's head above water level, while George dragged her towards the safety of the beach.

A collective gasp went up from the crowd as George laid the woman in the sand, a safe distance from the water's edge. Millie gasped too, staring at the place the woman's feet and calves should have been.

The white dress she wore, water-sodden and clinging tightly to her shapely body, covered half of the appendage, but it was quite apparent what it was which emerged from beneath the hem.

"She's got a fin!" said Eve.

"She had legs when I saw her," said the man who had yelled a warning. "She was standing up in the water!"

Millie knelt in the sand next to the stricken woman, more concerned with the woman's health than the fact that she was encountering yet another paranormal creature. She put two fingers to the woman's throat, and concentrated on what she could feel. "She's got a pulse," she said. "But it's weak! We need to get her to a hospital!"

"Forget the hospital," said Judith. "We need to get her into the moon-pool. She's been hurt by magic, and only magic can cure her."

"Into the what?" said Millie, her finger still on the woman's throat.

"You'll see soon enough," said Judith. "Remember I told you there's something special in the crack in the cliff... well, the moon-pool is that thing."

George stood up. "Everybody else go!" he shouted. "Put the fire out, and leave. Me, Millie and Judith will deal with this."

Nobody questioned the order, and as George hoisted the mermaid onto his shoulders, people began grabbing their belongings and leaving the beach, the fire dying quickly as the witch responsible for it extinguished the flames.

Even with the weight of a woman on his back, George moved with remarkable speed across the sand, making it difficult for Millie and Judith to keep up with him.

As they approached the cliff face, and with the fire now out, Millie noticed a soft green glow emanating from the fissure in the cliff. "What's in there?" she asked, hoping it was something that could reverse the damage her magic had done to the poor woman.

What had she done? Her first spell had led to the serious injury and possible death of a beautiful mermaid. The fact that the mermaid had possibly murdered Albert flashed through her mind, but she put it aside, for later consideration. Helping the mermaid was of far more importance.

"I was looking forward to showing you the moon pool in a less stressful situation," said Judith, following George into the darkness of the crack. "But it seems that wasn't meant to happen."

As Millie entered the cliff face, the air temperature rose, and a soft humming sound reverberated off the damp walls of the narrow tunnel they followed. Millie stayed close to Judith, the soft green glow growing brighter, and the sand beneath her feet warm.

As she followed Judith around a slight bend in the path, ducking her head to avoid a painful collision with a low hanging slab of rock, she stared in fascination at the beautiful sight before her.

She stood in a large cavern, the walls shimmering with the same green glow she'd witnessed emanating from the crack. Crystal encrusted stalactites hung from the ceiling, and equally beautiful stalagmites rose from the sand. Flecks of minerals embedded in the ancient rock shimmered in the ambient light, but what lay in the centre of the cavern was the most beautiful thing Millie had ever seen.

Almost perfectly circular in shape, the large pool shimmered with light. A kaleidoscope of greens and blues, the water seemed to have a life of its own. Like a shoal of fish, submerged lights zoomed in erratic shapes just below the surface, and tiny sparkling lights rose like steam from the mirror perfect surface.

"What is it?" said Millie, "it's amazing."

"The source of all the magic in Spellbinder Bay," said Judith, "and the only hope this poor mermaid has of surviving."

"We need to get her in the pool quickly," said George, laying the mermaid on the soft sand next to the water's edge, and kneeling beside her.

Millie dropped to the sand next to the mermaid's head, and Judith knelt near the fin. Taking the weight between the three of them, they lowered the mermaid over the short rim of the pool and into the water, being sure to keep her face above the surface.

As the water enveloped the mermaid's body, the kaleidoscope of blues and greens merged seamlessly into other colours, seeming to switch between every colour in the spectrum.

"Millie," said Judith, her eyes reflecting the beauty of the water. "It was your spell which did this to her.

The pool will do most of the work, but you need to add some of your magic."

"How?" said Millie. "What do I do?"

"Just do what you did on the beach, said Judith, "but on a less impressive scale. Keep both hands in the water and allow a little magic to trickle into the pool."

"Quick," said George. "Time is of the essence."

As her hands cradled the mermaid's head, her long golden hair silky against her fingers, Millie drew on the strength in her chest. Heat built behind her ribs, and the muscles in her arms warmed gently as her hands became imbibed with magic.

She closed her eyes momentarily, and concentrated on allowing her magic to leach into the pool. She opened her eyes as a soft feminine groan emanated from the pool.

"It's working," said Judith. "She's moving!"

Sure enough, the mermaid's head twisted in Millie's hands, and shimmering droplets of water splashed Judith's face as the mermaid's tail gave a small flick.

The mermaid groaned again, and slowly opened her eyelids, her bright emerald eyes focusing on Millie's face. She licked her lips, and closed her eyes again, groaning softly.

"Will she be all right?" asked Millie. "I've never hurt anybody my life, it was an accident! I didn't know my magic could hurt people!"

"Don't worry about that for the moment," said George. "Let's lift her out of the pool. She's had enough magic to heal her, she should be okay within a few hours."

The three of them hoisted the mermaid from the

pool, her eyes fluttering open and closed, and her fin making feeble attempts to propel her to safety.

Laying her head in the sand, Millie brushed wet hair from the mermaid's face. "She's beautiful," she said. "Absolutely beautiful."

"And a rarity," said Judith. "I don't know anybody who has seen a mermaid in real life. Some people say they are just a figment of human's imagination."

"I've never seen one either," said George, slumping into the sand. "I wonder how long she's been in Spellbinder Bay."

"Long enough to murder Albert Salmon," said Judith. She tentatively lifted the hem of the mermaid's dress, revealing the iridescent scales of her tail. "And she must have some sort of magic which enables her to walk on land. She had legs when we saw her running away from the lighthouse. Everything Reuben said makes sense now. The spot in the sand where he saw the footprints vanish must be where she escaped into the sea."

"Tell me she'll be okay," said Millie. "I couldn't live with myself if I've caused her any damage. Even if she *is* a murderer."

George put a hand on Millie's shoulder, squeezing her gently. "She'll be fine. This pool will cure any paranormal person… if they're brought here in time."

Millie gazed into the pool, unable to shake a growing memory. No, it wasn't a memory. It couldn't be a memory — it was just another episode of déjà vu. The same déjà vu she'd seemed to be experiencing a lot of since arriving in the town. "What is it? Why is it called the moon-pool?" she said, shaking the sensation from her head. *She hadn't been there before – it wasn't possible.*

Judith dipped her hand into the pool, and moved it

slowly left and right, making gentle ripples across the surface. "It's the source of all the power in Spellbinder Bay," she said. "It's directly beneath Spellbinder Hall, and the magic flows up through the cracks and fissures in the cliff. Spellbinder Hall acts as a sort of transmitting beacon, protecting Spellbinder Bay beneath a dome of concealment magic. It's the reason that your horse spell was so powerful, Millie. You were so close to the source of all your powers."

"It's called the moon-pool because it's powered by the moon," explained George. "The cliff face collects moonlight and filters it into the pool where it's transformed into magic."

"How?" said Millie.

"Do I look like a scientist?" said George, with a twinkle in his eye. "I don't know. It just does what it says on the tin — it's a pool, and it's something to do with the moon."

"There are things like this all over the world," said Judith. "Not necessarily pools. The pool is just the way the magic in Spellbinder Bay manifests itself. It could just as easily have been an old monument — like Stonehenge."

"Or an old tree," said George. "One paranormal town I went to in America draws its magic from an ancient redwood tree. The tree is huge, and it transmits its magic for miles around — it doesn't need a beacon like Spellbinder Hall — it acts as its own beacon."

Judith withdrew her hand from the pool, her skin shimmering green for a few seconds. She gazed at the mermaid. "It explains how she escaped from the lighthouse before you got inside, Millie," she said. "She probably pushed Albert, and when she saw you — jumped from the balcony into the sea. It would have been easy for her. No wonder you found nobody in the lighthouse. She was long gone before you even got through the door."

"But what would a mermaid have against an old man in a lighthouse?" pondered Millie. "She looks so gentle, I can't imagine her wanting to kill somebody."

"Who knows?" said Judith. "Albert lives right next to the sea — he could have done lots of things to offend her."

"We'll find out soon enough," said George. "As soon as she wakes up, we'll take her to Spellbinder Hall. Henry will have questions for her."

The mermaid gave a soft groan, and Millie took one of the woman's soft hands in hers, smiling as the mermaid's eyelids fluttered open. "Are you okay?" she said.

The mermaid licked her lips, and swivelled her eyes as she checked out her surroundings. "Where you bring me?" she said in broken English, her accent a thick mix of what Millie guessed was French and Irish. "The white animal in sea. It hurt me."

Millie squeezed the mermaid's hand tighter. "That was my fault — I'm so sorry. It was an accident."

Judith peered down at the woman. "What you did at the lighthouse was bad!"

Focusing on Judith, the mermaid narrowed her eyes. "What I did at the lighthouse was good!" she snapped. "Was very good! I stopped cruel man! And I will do it again!"

George stood up and shook sand from his hands. "Oh no you won't," he said, his voice low and threatening. "Do you know what happens to paranormal people who commit crimes in Spellbinder Bay?"

The mermaid tried to sit up, but crumpled back into the sand. "I did no crime. I do not care what happens!"

"We'll see about that," said George, bending at the waist and fixing the mermaid with an intense stare. "But I can tell you one thing for certain — you will care what happens to you if you're found to be guilty of murder."

Chapter 20

"*H*er name's Lillieth," said Timothy, leading Millie, Judith and Sergeant Spencer into the bowels of Spellbinder Hall. "She's been in a deep sleep since you brought her here last night. She woke up about an hour ago, but she's still very upset."

"Has she admitted anything?" asked Sergeant Spencer. "Is she the person... or mermaid, who killed Albert Salmon?"

Timothy shook his head as he negotiated the narrow set of stairs carved out of rock. "She's too upset about her legs to answer any questions about Albert," he said.

Millie's stomach flipped. *What had her magic done to the poor mermaid?* "Have I damaged her?" she said, "has my magic permanently hurt her?"

"I don't know," said Timothy. "I'm a werewolf, magic is not my forte. Lillieth seems to think so, though — she says she's lost the ability to transform her fin into legs."

The thought that her magic had hurt another living creature filled Millie with shame. She wasn't sure she could look Lillieth in the eyes, let alone watch her being interrogated by Henry Pinkerton and Sergeant Spencer. "What have I done?" she said. "I shouldn't have attempted magic — I was drunk, and I'd just witnessed a fight between a werewolf and a vampire. I wasn't thinking straight."

Timothy glanced over his shoulder. "Would you say that fight was fair, Millie? I'm not so sure. I really think George must have employed some sort of trick to beat me — I had it in the bag."

"Quiet, Timothy," hissed Judith. She took Millie's hand. "It's okay. If it was your magic which caused the problems, then your magic will be able to undo them. That's how it works… most of the time."

"I'm not sure I ever want to try magic again," said Millie. "In fact, I'm not sure I even want to stay in Spellbinder Bay. Last night scared me — not the vampire and werewolf fight, a person could get used to that sort of thing, but learning that I possess a power which can hurt somebody else, scares me. I'm not sure I can live like that. I'm not sure I can live here."

Reuben shifted on Millie's shoulder. "Don't say that, Millie. I don't want you to leave. I'm beginning to like you."

"Thank you… I think," said Millie, running a finger over the bird's chest. "But I have to make the decision that's right for me."

"There's plenty of time for those sorts of conversations later, Millie," said Timothy, leading the group through a narrow archway at the base of the stairs — the walls and floor of rock indicating they were deep within the cliff itself. "But for now, we've got a murder suspect to interrogate." He stopped outside a wooden door set deep in the rock, the thick timbers reinforced with bars of blackened metal. He knocked twice. "She's in here," he said.

The door opened with a creak. Henry Pinkerton stood on the other side, his glasses high on his nose, and a stern expression on his face. "Thank you all for coming," he said. "I've asked Sergeant Spencer here for obvious reasons, and Millie should be here as it was she who captured the suspect."

"Damn right it was," squawked Reuben, from his position on Millie's shoulder. "My witch doesn't mess about."

"We'd have caught her a lot sooner if you'd mentioned that her footprints had vanished right next to the ocean, Reuben," said Sergeant Spencer. "You made it sound like they'd just vanished in the middle of the beach. We had no idea that she might have jumped into the water."

"In a moment of crisis," lectured Reuben. "The quick passage of information is vital. The footprints had stopped in the sand, and the suspect was nowhere to be seen, would my telling you that they'd disappeared right next to the water's edge have changed anything?"

"Probably," said Judith, "but it doesn't matter now." She looked at Henry. "You've explained why Millie and my dad are here," she said. "I'm feeling a bit left out… why am I here?"

Henry's face opened into a smile. "You know why, my dear. Around these parts, you're considered as Sergeant Spencer's sidekick — his deputy, if you will."

Reuben hopped onto Millie's head. His claws tangling in her hair. "And me?" he said. "*I* feel left out now. Why was I asked to come?"

"I didn't ask that you should be here," said Henry. "In fact, I can't think of any valid reason why a simple cockatiel could help in the investigation of a murder."

Millie swivelled her eyes upwards. "I wanted you here, Reuben," she said. "I don't like thinking of you locked away in a cottage all day on your own."

"As long as you leave the TV on," the little cockatiel said, "I'm as happy as a pig in the proverbial. Don't think you must drag me around with you everywhere you go. I'm a home-bird." He hopped back onto Millie's shoulder. "And I wasn't always a *simple cockatiel* as you so eloquently put it, Henry," he said. "I was a wise old owl once. Not that I'm complaining, I think I prefer being a cockatiel — I was always very tired during the day as an owl, and I was often frustratingly on the lookout for small furry creatures to chase down. It was no way to live."

Millie held out a hand, and Reuben fluttered onto it. "You were an owl?" she asked. "What happened to the owl?"

"I'll tell you what happened to the owl," snapped Reuben, grinding his beak. "Some witch, who became an author in the normal world, thought it would be clever to blow the lid on some of our customs. She decided to include owls in her books about wizards and magic. They became a *thing* in the fictional world of magic, and Esmeralda wasn't one for *things*.

"She liked to be different, so when she heard about the books and their popularity, it didn't take her long to decide she wanted me in the body of another animal." Reuben closed his eyes. "I had a lucky escape, actually. She wanted me in the body of a tortoise, luckily, I was watching a David Attenborough programme on the television, and a segment on cockatiels just happened to be on as Esmeralda was considering the merits of finding a suitable tortoise to house my spirit.

"Panicked, I suggested a cockatiel, and sold the idea to Esmeralda by explaining that I'd be able to speak in public without arousing too much suspicion. She went along with it, and I've never looked at a mouse in a threatening manner since."

A terrible thought crossed Millie's mind. "You weren't in one of those owls in the glass cases in the corridor upstairs, were you? If you were, that's pretty gruesome — to have those poor creatures on display after they were no longer of use."

Reuben shook his head. "Gosh, no. Esmeralda was a kind woman. She released the owl she'd used back into the wild — with a spell on it — allowing it to live a long and healthy life with no memory of ever being possessed by a familiar. Those owls upstairs are a hundred years old. They're nothing to do with Esmeralda."

Henry cleared his throat. "If I may interrupt," he said, "it's very nice to hear you two getting on so well, and it's always good that a familiar and his or her witch find out about each other's histories, but we have a mermaid chained in the corner of the room, awaiting interrogation. Shall we proceed?"

He gave Millie a probing look. "I hear through the grapevine that it was an impressive spell you cast last night on the beach. You shouldn't feel guilty that it damaged the mermaid — it was an accident, Millie. You meant her no malice."

"That doesn't make me feel any better about it," said Millie, following Judith into the room as Henry beckoned them inside. "I feel awful that —" Her words faltered as guilt wrapped its unforgiving fingers around her heart, and squeezed hard. *Poor Lillieth.*

The windowless room resembled the dungeons of castles Millie had visited as a child, and the only light came from the half-used candle balanced on an imperfection in the rock wall. Staring at her from the only piece of furniture in the room — a long slab of wood bolted to the wall to form a bed — was Lillieth, her hair dishevelled, and her accusing eyes focused firmly on Millie's face.

"Why are you keeping her like this?" said Millie. "This is awful. Her wrists are chained to the wall, what could she possibly do to hurt anybody, she can't even walk — she has no legs — thanks to me."

"I understand that it looks bad," said Henry, having the courtesy to drop his eyes to the floor. "But this is how we are forced to treat paranormal prisoners in Spellbinder Bay. They either possess great strength, magic, or sometimes both. The room must be windowless and with little furniture — to prevent escape, and makeshift weapons being manufactured.

"The doorway is protected by a magical force field, and of course the prisoner must be chained. When George brought her here last night, Lillieth was still too dazed to be questioned, otherwise I'd have used the stone of integrity on her right away, and either proved her guilt, or found her innocent."

"And if she was found innocent, we would have released her immediately," said Timothy.

"And if she isn't innocent?" said Millie, taking a step closer to Lillieth. "What happens to her then? George alluded last night to the fact that something terrible would happen to her, and you said the same after you'd used the stone of integrity on me, Henry. What exactly is it that happens to paranormal people who have committed a crime in Spellbinder Bay?"

Henry slipped a hand into his pocket and withdrew the pouch containing the magic stone. "One step at a time, Millie Thorn. Let us first find out if the poor woman in the corner is indeed Albert Salmon's murderer."

Millie gave Lillieth a small smile, but the mermaid looked away. "You took legs from me," she said.

"I'm sorry," said Millie. "Really. I am. It was an accident."

Reuben fluttered from Millie's shoulder and landed on the bed next to Lillieth. "She's beautiful," he said, studying her with a tilted head.

Lillieth's eyes twinkled in the candlelight, and she gave Reuben a kind smile. "Animals always kinder than land people," she whispered. "Thank you, little bird. You beautiful, also."

Henry approached the bed, withdrawing the stone of integrity from the pouch. He gazed down at the mermaid. "Lillieth," he said. "You couldn't say much last night, and you've refused to say much this morning. You're suspected of a terrible crime, and George — the man who carried you here last night, tells me you confessed — he tells me you said the man was evil and you'd do it again."

He offered the stone to Lillieth. "I want you to hold this stone for me, please — it will tell us whether you speak the truth… or falsehoods."

Lillieth pulled her white dress higher over her shoulders, her wrists chains clanking, and gave Henry an accusatory stare. "Mermaids not tell lies," she said.

"Only tell truth. Give me stone — I show you I am good person. I did what I did because I love animals, and yes — I *would* do it again."

"She did it because she loves animals?" said Timothy. "Well, that makes absolutely no sense."

"Crimes often don't make sense," said Sergeant Spencer. "Especially crimes committed in passion. People kill for all sorts of reasons, and maybe that's true for mermaids, too."

Lillieth turned her attention to the policeman. "Kill? I not kill. Life is special — not to be taken. I protect life!"

Reuben leapt out of the way with a squawk as Lillieth slapped her fin in anger, a scattering of iridescent scales falling onto the bed as her beautiful appendage slammed into the hard wood.

The mermaid held out a hand towards Henry. "Give me stone. I give you truth."

Chapter 21

*H*enry placed the stone gently on the mermaid's palm, the jewel beginning to glow the moment it brushed her skin.

Reminding Millie of a sunset, the orb emitted vivid reds and oranges, very different from the way it had responded when she had held it. "It's different," she said. "Why was it a different colour when I used it?"

Because what's in your heart is different," explained Henry. "This stone looks into the very depths of you — your soul, your heart — your integrity. Everybody is different, and the stone translates those personal traits into colour."

Lillieth gazed into the depths of the jewel, her eyes made even more beautiful by the shimmering light. She spoke in a gentle voice. "Please ask the questions. So I can get back to the ocean." She looked at Millie. "I can't be on land anymore. With no legs. I can't grow them — my magic won't work."

Millie looked away from the mermaid. Laid out on the bed like a fish on a chopping board, the mermaid's eyes stoked the fire of guilt which burned hot in her belly. She concentrated on Henry instead, waiting for him to speak.

After clearing his throat, Henry adjusted his cufflinks and stood fully upright. Like a barrister in a court of law, he spoke clearly — with only a hint of an accusatory tone in his voice. "Lillieth," he said, "did you murder Albert Salmon?"

The stone of integrity flickered in Lillieth's hand. "I know not who the person you speak of is," she said, her soft accent complementing the beautiful colours of the orb.

"Did you push a man to his death from the top of the lighthouse?" said Henry.

Lillieth fixed Henry with a fiery gaze. "No," she said, the words leaving her mouth with venom. "I did not push a man to his death. I have never killed. I will never kill."

Before Henry had the chance to give his verdict, Millie already knew Lillieth was innocent of murder. The first time she'd read a thought had been unnerving, but Lillieth's thoughts were far less upsetting than the sad emotions Jim Grayson had broadcast.

The mermaid's thoughts were clear and precise. And the one which Millie's powers focused on, translating it into words and images which Millie could understand, screamed her innocence loud and clear.

The stone glowed blue as Lillieth gave her answer, the surface swirling with colour. Henry nodded. He plucked the orb from Lillieth's hand and slid it into its pouch. "You speak the truth, Lillieth," he said. "I apologise profusely. I hope you can forgive me for treating you in such a manner, but I hope you can also understand that I had no choice." He turned to Timothy. "Unshackle her, please. Lillieth is to be freed at once."

Timothy reached into his waistcoat pocket and retrieved an old-fashioned key. Bending to unlock the mermaid's shackles, he faltered at the last moment. "But she admitted to doing something," he said. "She's done *something* wrong — shouldn't we find out what it is?"

"Unlock her," commanded Henry. "Lillieth has proved she is innocent of the crime she was accused of. Her innocence demands her freedom. Should she be accused of another crime, and brought before me, I will use the stone of integrity again. Until she is accused of any further wrongdoing, she is free to go. We will release her and transport her to the ocean. We have treated her badly. I hope she can forgive us."

Timothy asked no more questions. He used the key, and with a loud rattling, the iron wrist shackles fell to the floor. Lillieth was free.

Sergeant Spencer stepped forward. "Do you mind if I ask you some questions, Lillieth? About why you were near the lighthouse, and why we found your hairs tangled in a murdered man's clothes?" he said, his face open and friendly. "You're not obliged to answer, but your help would be greatly appreciated."

Lillieth rubbed one of her wrists, a red shackle mark marring her perfect alabaster skin. She took a few seconds to answer, staring intently at the policeman. "I sense you are different than the others here. I sense no magic in you."

Sergeant Spencer nodded. "That's right. I'm a human."

"Why should I help you?" said Lillieth. "You are

with these nasty people who hold me captive. You as bad as them. You are horrible man. I give you no help."

"He's not horrible!" snapped Judith, stepping out of the shadows, the anger on her face made less harsh by the soft candlelight. "He's a wonderful man!"

Stretching her fin, Lillieth rolled her eyes. "You jump quickly to his defence. Who are you?"

"I'm his daughter," said Judith. "He's my father."

"Your father?" said Lillieth. "He has no magic. You have magic. I watched you on the beach — making magic red dragon. Every magical being must have magical parent. Your mother is magic?"

Judith's shoulder's slumped. "She *was* magic," she said, her voice faltering. "She's dead. My mother is dead."

The same words Millie had used herself for the past fourteen years, sounded alien coming from another woman so young. She'd known Judith was adopted, but she'd not considered why. Her throat constricting, Millie wiped the building moisture from the corner of her eye.

Another thought crossed her mind. *Every magical being must have a magical parent.* That's what Lillieth had said, and nobody had corrected her. What did that mean? Had Millie's mother been a witch? Or had the father she'd never known been magical?

She swept the thoughts aside. It was Judith's time to speak, and Millie would listen.

Lillieth's expression softened as Judith spoke. "So sad," she said. "A daughter losing a mother and a husband losing a wife. I'm sorry. For you both."

Judith's face crumpled. "My father… my father is —"

Sergeant Spencer placed a protective arm around

Judith's shoulders, drawing her close to him. "You don't have to, Judith. Don't upset yourself."

"It's okay," said Judith. "Everybody in this room knows apart from Millie and Lillieth. Millie would find out soon enough, and I won't listen to Lillieth calling you horrible. I won't have anybody calling you horrible, Dad! The man who saved me, and then gave me a whole new lease of life, is not horrible!"

Lillieth reached for Judith's hand and guided her onto the bench next to her. "Sit, sad girl. Tell me. Tell me what troubles you so much. I sense great despair in you."

Judith kept her hand in Lillieth's. She bowed her head. "My father is dead, too," she sobbed, tears shining on her cheeks. "My real father —" She paused, and looked at Sergeant Spencer, pride in her eyes. "My *first* real father." Her body trembled as she wept. "My mother and father both died. They're both dead, and I killed them. I killed my parents!"

"An accident," said Henry, offering Judith his handkerchief. "It was an accident, Judith. You were a young child. Have some compassion for yourself."

Her eyes conveying a beautiful understanding, Lillieth wiped a tear from Judith's cheek. "You don't need to say more, sweet girl. I will answer your father's questions, and help him. I don't believe he is horrible. I don't believe any of you are horrible. I was angry when I used that word — I understand you all thought I had done a terrible thing. I understand you had to keep me captive."

Wiping her eyes with Henry's handkerchief, Judith composed herself. "No. I want to. I want to tell you how lovely the man who adopted me is. I want to tell you how proud I am to call him Dad."

"Then tell us, sweet Judith," said Lillieth. "Tell us your story."

"It was nineteen-ninety-two. I was two years old," said Judith. "A lot of people don't remember much from that age, but I remember. I remember everything that happened on that day."

As Judith spoke, Millie sensed her thoughts, but couldn't — or wouldn't, focus on them. It seemed discourteous to peer into other people's minds, and Millie was glad that it seemed possible to tune out if she needed to.

"I didn't know I was a witch," Judith continued. "My mother or father never told me. I didn't find out until I came to Spellbinder Bay and met Henry — he told me everything. He told me that my mum had not been a particularly powerful witch, and had preferred to live in the so-called normal world — rather than a town like this one."

"She didn't find out she was a witch until later in life," said Henry. "A little like Millie. She decided she didn't want to give up the life she'd built to live among the paranormal community. There's nothing wrong with that. Nothing wrong with that at all."

Judith stared into the candlelight. "I wish she had decided to live in a town like this. Perhaps being surrounded by magic would have strengthened her own magic, and then maybe she could have saved herself and my father." She turned her gaze to Sergeant Spencer. "You know I love living with you, Dad. You know I love you dearly, but two lives were lost so we could be together. If I could turn back time, I would, but my life would never be the same without you in it."

Sergeant Spencer approached his daughter, and put a big hand on her shoulder. "You don't need to excuse yourself," he said. "I told you before, Judith. I know you love me, and I love you. Of course we treat each other like father and daughter now, but I understand that you wish to some degree we'd never met — because the way we met was unfortunate."

"What I did, accident or no accident," said Judith, "was unfortunate. Meeting you was not unfortunate. I'll never think of it as unfortunate."

"What did happen?" asked Lillieth, Judith's hand still in hers. "What terrible event brought you two together?"

Judith let out a long breath, as if mustering the courage to speak. She looked at the floor. "It was a cold night," she said. "There was ice on the roads, I remember slipping on the pavement before I got into the car. We'd been to pick out a Christmas tree. Mum liked real ones, but Dad didn't like the needles falling on the floor. He wanted a fake tree." She smiled. "Mum always got her way, though."

"It was the coldest winter we'd had for a decade," interjected Sergeant Spencer. "The accident wasn't all your fault, Judith. If there hadn't been ice on the road, your father might have been able to control the skid."

"Perhaps," said Judith, with a shake of her head. "But we'll never know. All I know is that I wanted ice cream, and Mum and Dad wouldn't let me have any. They said I'd had enough treats for the day. That's when I lost my temper. I lost my temper like a spoilt two-year-old. I acted like a brat."

"You lost your temper like a normal two-year-old," said Sergeant Spencer. "You weren't a brat."

"I could see Mum's laughing face in the rear-view mirror," said Judith. "It made me angrier. I struggled to get out of my car seat, but the straps held me in place. That's when it happened."

"What happened?" asked Lillieth.

"The first time I found out I had magic," said Judith. "That's what happened, and with terrible consequences. The more I struggled to get out of my car seat, and the more I shouted, the angrier I became. As I got angrier, I remember a fierce heat in my chest. I didn't know what it was, and it frightened me. When my arms began to tingle, I really got scared, and as the fear grew, my magic was released. It was a simple spell — a two-year-old's spell. It was just a flash of colourful light which filled the car."

"The innocent magic of a child," said Henry.

"The spell might have been innocent, but the consequences weren't," said Judith. "Dad shouted something, and I remember Mum turning in her seat to look at me, and that was the last time I saw her face. The light must've blinded Dad, and he lost control of the car. It happened quickly. We hit a tree and the car crumpled, flipping onto its roof. I shouted for Mum and Dad, but they didn't answer me. Then I saw it… and I smelled it. Smoke and flames."

Judith bowed her head as she sobbed, and Sergeant Spencer wiped a tear from his eye. "Don't upset yourself any more, Judith," he said.

Her body wracked with sobs, Judith relented. "You tell the rest of the story, Dad," she said.

His shoulders slumping, Sergeant Spencer sighed. "I

was a young police constable," he said. "I was on my way home from work. It was a dark night, and I saw the glow from the fire even before I rounded the sharp bend in the road. The car was on its roof, in a ditch, where it had landed after bouncing off the tree. The flames had filled the front of the car, and were spreading quickly. I had to act."

"You were a hero," said Henry.

"Anybody would have done what I did," said Sergeant Spencer, brushing off Henry's compliment. "We had no mobile phones back then, so I couldn't call for help, and even if I could have — there was no time to wait. I saw movement in the back of the car — a small arm banging at the window. The fire was hot, but somehow I managed to get the door open. Then I saw her, hanging upside down in her car seat — surrounded by…" He paused. "Surrounded by what I soon learned was magic, but at the time, thought was a miracle."

"I'll never forget seeing your face when you opened the door, Dad," said Judith.

"And I'll never forget your face," said Sergeant Spencer. "It haunted me for a long time."

Lillieth's fin swayed as she spoke. "And you took her on as your daughter? The little girl you rescued from fire."

"She had no other family," said Sergeant Spencer. "There was nobody else to look after her."

Millie had considered her own story sad, but as Judith's story unfolded, she realised with guilt which she understood was misplaced, that far worse could have happened to her. And her mother.

"Mum's parents were dead," said Judith, "and she was an only child. Dad's family had never cared about him — they certainly didn't care about what happened to me."

"I'd seen what happened to a lot of the children who ended up in the care system," said Sergeant Spencer. "And I didn't want that happening to Judith. It took a while, and a lot of legal arguments, but eventually I was granted permission to adopt her. I never mentioned the… *force field* I'd seen protecting Judith from the fire, to the courts, they would have thought I was mad. I never mentioned it to Judith, either — I didn't want to scare her. Then Henry showed up, and everything changed."

Henry cleared his throat. "If I may?" he asked.

"Of course," said Judith. "It's your story too."

"Please do," said Sergeant Spencer. "It makes me sad to speak about it."

"Thank you," said Henry, his eyes heavy with sadness. "I'm in tune with the magical energies which criss-cross the planet," he began. "It's my job to be aware of magic being used where it shouldn't be. I can't be everywhere, but when I sensed that a young child had cast a spell which had invoked… unfortunate consequences, I had to become involved.

"I watched from afar, at first — wondering if I should intervene. When Sergeant Spencer adopted young Judith, I hoped that Judith's magic would settle down, and she would be able to live her life in the non-paranormal world until she found her own way to us — if she ever did, of course. That wasn't to be, though. Judith had been through a traumatic experience — her magic responded as such."

"Things began happening," explained Sergeant Spencer. "Things I couldn't explain. Windows smashing for no reason, a tree in the garden being ripped out by the roots — things that scared me, and things that I knew deep down Judith was responsible for."

"I couldn't allow Judith to remain in the non-paranormal world," said Henry. "She needed guidance. Her magic was becoming a danger to herself, and other people. So I approached Sergeant Spencer, and gave him a choice."

"What choice do you speak of?" asked Lillieth.

"I explained to him who I was, and who... *what* Judith was — a witch," said Henry. "Sergeant Spencer was remarkably open to such a possibility."

"Of course I was," said Sergeant Spencer. "I'd seen things. What you told me made more sense than anything I could have imagined myself."

"The choice was simple," continued Henry. "And necessary. After explaining everything about the paranormal world, I gave Sergeant Spencer the choice of either accompanying Judith to Spellbinder Bay, where he could continue living as her father, or allowing me to use magic to completely wipe his memory of everything that happened, and his memories of Judith. It may sound harsh, but I couldn't risk allowing any human — even such a fine citizen as Sergeant Spencer, to have knowledge of the magical world if they weren't a part of it."

"I didn't need to think about it," said Sergeant Spencer, smiling at Judith. "We moved here together, almost immediately. When she was three."

"And going against centuries of tradition," said Henry. "I used magic to allow Sergeant Spencer to see through the concealment spell which enveloped our little town. The good sergeant kept his job in the police force — although the police force stays out of his business, thanks to the concealment magic, whilst continuing to pay him a wage."

"The cushiest job in the history of police employment," laughed Judith.

Hearing Judith laugh influenced everybody in the room. If she could be upbeat after telling her tragic story, then so could everybody who'd listened to it. Millie smiled at Judith, and as Judith reciprocated, Millie read a thought which threatened to take her legs from beneath her. Not wishing to alert Judith to the fact that her thought had crossed the short distance between them, she looked away, her mouth dry.

Judith had been right, though. However hurtful her thought was – it was valid.

How dare Millie be so upset about her magic damaging Lillieth. My magic killed my parents! I wish we could swap places! Then she'd know what real regret feels like!

Shaking the hurt from within her, Millie ran a finger over Reuben's plumage as Lillieth stretched out her long fin.

The mermaid tilted her head to look at Sergeant Spencer. "I am ready," she said. "I have heard enough to understand you are good people. I will answer your questions now."

Chapter 22

"Thank you," said Sergeant Spencer, as Lillieth paid him her full attention. "My first question is why were your hairs tangled in the clothes of a murdered man who washed up on the shore?"

Lillieth's face darkened. "That poor man," she said. "I found him a long distance from shore. No life remained within him, and his clothes were sodden, dragging him towards the ocean bed. I pushed him to the shoreline — so that his fellow land people could find him and lay his body to rest in the correct tradition."

"That's why the coastguard was confused," said Sergeant Spencer. "It wasn't a freak wave which pushed him ashore, it was you?"

Lillieth gave a gentle nod. "I hope what I did was right. We are told not to interfere with other traditions, but I thought it was important."

"What you did was perfect," said Sergeant Spencer. "Thank you. I'm sure Albert would be grateful that you saved his body from the sea."

Her eyes still red from crying, Judith asked a question. "What did you mean when you said he was a cruel man and you'd do it again? Were you talking about Albert? The man you pushed ashore?"

"No," said Lillieth. "I speak of the man who captures the long-claws in his baskets. He places cages on the seabed and baits them with morsels of food to attract the long-claws. It is cruel. I release them, and relish his rage when he retrieves his empty prisons."

"You've been releasing Jim Grayson's lobsters?" said Millie.

"Yes," said Lillieth. "And I *would* do it again. I hear the anguished cries of the poor creatures. They are afraid when trapped in the cages. It is cruel."

"I suppose it is," said Millie. "But it's how Jim Grayson makes a living. Without the lobsters he catches, he won't be able to sell them, and *he* won't be able to live."

Lillieth looked away. She closed her eyes, as if in thought. "I do not wish to cause that much harm to the man. I do not wish to prevent him from living. I will make it right. You have my word."

Sergeant Spencer retrieved his notebook from his pocket. "Okay — we've got to the bottom of one mystery — the mystery of the missing lobsters. Now let's try and solve the more pressing mystery." He looked at the page in his book. "Albert said he saw you on the rocks outside his lighthouse, Lillieth," he said. "Have you seen anything suspicious? Did you see anybody at the lighthouse? Two days ago?"

"I watch you land people, sometimes," said Lillieth. "That's why I was near the beach last night. I find you interesting. Yes, I did see people at the lighthouse, two moons ago." She nodded towards Millie. "I saw her, the girl who took my legs. She was with the man who carried me here last night."

"You saw Millie and George?" said Sergeant Spencer. "Did you see anybody else?"

Lillieth shook her head. "No," she said. "I saw nobody else on the day you speak of, but I spend most my time in the ocean, and I don't venture too far away from the water's edge when I *do* walk on land. I long for a home next to the sea, so I may spend more time on the land. The dress I wear gives me legs, but they always feel strange beneath me — I like the safety of water nearby."

"The dress gives you legs?" said Millie. "How?"

"A woman like you gave it to me," said Lillieth. "A witch. From another land, far across the sea. The dress is magic. When I wear it, it gives me legs. I carry it in a purse around my waist while I travel the oceans, and the dress has always worked —" She looked at Millie. "— until now."

"I am sorry, Lillieth" said Millie. "Really. I am. I'll do everything I can to make it right."

Lillieth nodded. "I forgive you. Suffer your guilt no more. I shall speak no more of it. We shall see if it can be made right again. I appreciate your offer of help."

Sergeant Spencer gave a polite cough. "Is there anything else you can think of at all, Lillieth?" he said. "*Anything* that might help us? Did you see anything out of the ordinary at the lighthouse?"

"I am sorry," said Lillieth. "I cannot help. I saw only the people you call Millie and George." She paused, her eyes narrowing.

"What is it?" said Sergeant Spencer, the nib of his

pen hovering over his notebook. "Have you thought of something?"

"I did see something," said Lillieth. "Yes. On the day you speak of. In the early part of the day. I saw one of the things you land people travel around in. With wheels. It was outside the lighthouse, but I saw no people with it. It was already there when I climbed from the sea."

"A vehicle?" said Sergeant Spencer. "You must mean a vehicle. What did it look like, Lillieth?".

"It was painted in your language," said Lillieth. "Decorated with symbols from your alphabet. I do not understand them, though. I cannot tell you what it meant."

Judith stood up, her eyes bright again. "Could you show us?" she asked. "If we show you the letters of our alphabet, do you think you could remember which ones you saw?"

"I am sure I can," said Lillieth. "We mer-people have good memories. I think I can remember."

Henry smiled. "I can help with that," he said. He bowed his head, and took a breath. He pointed at one of the rocky walls of the dungeon, and with an artistic flick of his hand, showered the wall with tiny glowing lights.

The blue lights moved like magnets, attracted to one another, forming shapes as they crawled across the imperfect surface. It wasn't long until the alphabet was illustrated on the wall, written in light.

"Do you recognise any of the symbols, Lillieth?" asked Sergeant Spencer. "It's important you tell us which ones you saw in the order you saw them, from left to right — that is how we write our language."

Lillieth studied the letters, her eyes dancing over them. "That one," she said, pointing. "That was the first one."

"This one?" said Henry, touching the wall.

Lillieth nodded.

"Write these down, Sergeant Spencer," said Henry. "I have a feeling this is important."

As Lillieth pointed out letters from the wall, Sergeant Spencer scribbled in his book. When Lillieth had indicated the fourth letter, Henry held out a hand. "That should be enough," he said. "I think we know what vehicle you saw."

"There were more symbols," said Lillieth. "I remember them."

"It will have been the telephone number," said Henry. "And as there is only one such company which operates in our small town, I don't think we need to trouble you any further, Lillieth. Your fin seems to be drying out. We should get you back into the ocean."

With a gentle nod, Lillieth ran a long finger over her fin, a scattering of scales falling off as her nail dragged across the surface. "You are correct," she said. "I have been out of water for too long."

Henry nodded, the alphabet vanishing from the wall behind him. "Sergeant Spencer," he said. "Timothy and I will transport Lillieth to the sea. You should follow up on our new lead."

Sergeant Spencer slammed his book shut, and tucked it away in his pocket. "Right away," he said.

"IT WAS EITHER DROPPING SOMEBODY OFF, OR PICKING

Albert up," said Millie, the leather of the chair feeling strange beneath her. It was only a chair, but it had been Albert's chair. A murdered man's chair. It felt disrespectful to be sitting in it. She stood up and took a seat next to Judith on the small sofa.

"Perhaps Albert *did* take flowers to Betty's grave," said Judith. "After Edna had come here to accuse him of being heartless. Maybe her words had an effect on him. He couldn't have walked to the cemetery, so he would have needed a cab."

"If he did," said Sergeant Spencer, his head appearing at the top of the spiral staircase. "He didn't use the local company." He slid his phone into his breast pocket. "They have no record of a cab being sent here. Not on the day Albert was murdered. Not on any day, in fact. Albert has never used a taxi from Spellbinder Cabs, and no cab has ever brought anybody here, either."

"Maybe Lillieth was wrong," said Judith. "She'd been through a lot."

"I find that hard to believe," said Millie. "She was sure about the letters she pointed out, and they definitely spell the word *taxi*."

Judith looked at her dad. "What do we do next? Get in touch with all the taxi companies in the county?"

"The owner of Spellbinder Cabs is going to ask around for me," said Sergeant Spencer. "He's friendly with all the other companies. He'll get the information quicker than I can — a lot of the drivers are working illegally, they don't trust the police too much."

"Are you taking the threatening letter any more seriously?" said Millie, addressing the policeman. "Surely that's our best clue now?"

"I did what I said I'd do," said Sergeant Spencer. "I

put out some feelers — I've been in touch with the Scottish Prison Service, and I'm still waiting to hear back from them. Even if they do manage to match a prisoner with the initials WM — the letter was written fifteen years ago. That's a long time to hold a grudge — a lot of water has passed under a lot of bridges since then. I'm sceptical about the author of the letter being our murderer."

"So there's nothing more we can do at the moment?" said Judith. She smiled at Millie. "How do feel about trying out some of your magic again? Lillieth left her magic dress with Henry, hoping you could fix it for her. Do you want to try?"

Millie looked at her new friend. Had she really meant what she'd thought in the dungeon beneath Spellbinder Hall, or was it one of those troublesome intrusive thoughts which haunted most people? The type of thoughts which crossed the mind, but never really stuck. Millie didn't know. What she did know was that Judith had been through a lot. A lot more than she had. She returned Judith's smile. "Okay," she said. "Let's try."

Sergeant Spencer stood up. "I'll take you both to Spellbinder Hall to pick up the dress, and while I wait to hear from the taxi company and the Scottish Prison Service, I'll get on with trying to solve some of the less important cases in town, like finding out which kids have been spraying graffiti on the wall in the park."

As Millie stood up, a flash of colour on the top of the sideboard caught her eye. Looking out of place in the relative neatness of the room, Millie remembered she'd placed the stack of business cards there, while she and Judith had searched the room.

Wanting to keep the room as neat as Albert had, she reached for the pile, with the intention of placing them back in the drawer she'd taken them from.

As her fingers closed around the stack of cards, her stomach flipped. She looked at Sergeant Spencer. "You can phone the taxi company and tell them we don't need their help anymore," she said. She peeled the top card from the stack and passed it to the policeman.

"Well I never," said Sergeant Spencer, studying the card. "The rest of the writing Lillieth saw on the vehicle *wasn't* a phone number. It was the last letters of a word."

Judith peered at the card. "A taxidermy service!" she said. "And the card looks brand-new."

Millie smiled. "And the stuffed bear downstairs looks far from new. I think we've found our tradesman."

"Or our murderer," murmured Sergeant Spencer. He took his car keys from his pocket. "Lillieth's dress can wait. We've got a more important trip to make."

Chapter 23

The address on the business cards led them to an old part of town. Sergeant Spencer had explained that the crumbling quayside had once been a busy dockland, back in the day when Spellbinder Bay had been used as the port from which stone, mined from the surrounding hills, had begun its long journey around the globe.

With no signage on the old stone walls of the building, the little white van parked outside was the only give-away that the premises contained a business. Sergeant Spencer parked the police car behind the van, and switched the engine off. "We assumed that Lillieth had seen a car outside the lighthouse," he said. "It was obviously this van."

"Taxidermy services," Millie said, reading the signage on the side of the van. "By Charles Bannister."

Sergeant Spencer opened his door. "Come on," he said. "Let's speak to Mister Bannister. Be careful, both of you. Stay behind me — we don't know what sort of man we're dealing with."

"One who stuffs dead animals for a living," said Millie. "And one who possibly pushed a man to his death."

"Precisely," said Sergeant Spencer. "Let's be very cautious."

Built long ago, the building had seen better days. Grime on the windows prevented them from peering inside, so Sergeant Spencer tried the door, using a fist to hammer on it when it proved to be locked.

"Who is it?" came a man's voice, muffled by the thick wood of the door.

"It's the police!" shouted Sergeant Spencer. "Open the door please, Mister Bannister. I have some questions for you."

A few seconds passed before the door creaked open a few inches, and a man's face peered out at them from the gloom within. "The police?" he said, his voice as stern as his features. "And what, may I ask, would the police want with me?"

Sergeant Spencer placed his boot against the base of the door. "Let us in, please, Mister Bannister," he said.

With pursed lips and narrowed eyes, Charles Bannister relented, opening the door and stepping aside. "I suppose you'd better come in — all of you — including the two girls who like to pretend they're police, but are in fact witches. I saw you all in Spellbinder Hall, while I was re-stuffing their poor owls."

The muscles in Sergeant Spencer's neck visibly tensed, and he reached for the nightstick hanging from his belt. "You're a member of the paranormal community?" he said.

Charles Bannister smiled, his teeth as white as his complexion. "That... *weapon* wouldn't help you if I did intend you harm," he said. "Your only hope would be the two witches you travel with, and I'm not sure what their magic could do against a vampire of my age and experience."

"You'd be surprised what two witches could do," said Judith.

A chill worked its way up Millie's spine. Maybe Judith was confident in her abilities, but Millie certainly wasn't in hers. She'd seen how strong George had been on the beach — she didn't hold out much hope that she and Judith would be able to take on an angry vampire.

Charles studied Judith for a moment or two. "Luckily for us all, there will be no need for any of us to prove our strength today." He gave a small bow. "Please, why don't you come in. Would any of you like a beverage? A cup of tea?"

Sergeant Spencer stepped inside, with Millie and Judith following him. "That won't be necessary, thank you," he said. "We'd just like you to answer a few questions."

Lit by a single ceiling light, the workshop made Millie uneasy. A single workbench took up space on the left of the room, and a large refrigeration unit hummed in the corner, no doubt containing the furry bodies of Charles Bannister's projects.

"I realise it's quite gloomy in here," said Charles, following Millie's gaze. "I've only recently got back to Spellbinder Bay. I haven't had time to set up properly." He unstacked three stools from a pile behind his workbench, offering them to his visitors.

"Back?" said Sergeant Spencer, wiping dust from his stool, and sitting down. "You've got *back* to Spellbinder Bay?"

"Indeed," said Charles, using his handkerchief to wipe the dust from the stools he'd offered Millie and Judith. "I left over a hundred years ago, I thought it was about time I came back and refreshed my work. Free of charge, of course — I offer a *very* long guarantee on all the creatures I work on, and as with most of us in the paranormal community, money is not something I worry about."

Millie sat down, placing her feet on one of the stool's cross pieces. "You stuffed animals in this town over a hundred years ago?" she said. "That's unbelievable."

Charles Bannister smiled, and began arranging the myriad of tools which scattered the surface of his bench. "In this very building," he said. "Of course, back then this room was full of my projects. As you can see, it's quite empty now — employing taxidermists seems to have fallen out of fashion."

"It was you who originally stuffed the owls in Spellbinder Hall?" said Judith.

"Indeed, it was," said Charles. "And it seems I arrived back in town just in time. The poor creatures had begun to smell quite awful." He dropped his head. "I'm ashamed to say that I wasn't the most talented of taxidermists all those years ago. I was self-taught, and quite shabby at performing the art. I failed to deodorise the carcasses to the extent I should have. I'm righting my wrongs now, though."

"And the bear in the lighthouse?" said Sergeant Spencer. "Was it you who stuffed that?"

"A beautiful animal," smiled Charles, his deep-set eyes twinkling. "The lighthouse keeper all those years ago bought the dead animal from the captain of a ship which docked in the harbour. I was awarded the honour of giving the beast a new lease of life. I was surprised to find it still resided in the lighthouse after all this time. It must've been passed along with the lighthouse every time a new tenant took residence in the building."

"Albert asked you to re-stuff it for him?" said Millie.

"I asked Albert if I could re-stuff it," corrected Charles. "I visited the lighthouse, in the hope that the bear was still there. He wouldn't answer his door, he spoke to me from his window. I lied to him, telling him my grandfather had stuffed the bear, and if it was still there — I would like to re-stuff it for him. The fact that I offered my services for free, and the fact that he admitted the creature was emitting a foul stench, saw him take me up on my offer."

"That's why you were there on the day of his murder," said Judith.

"An unfortunate incident," said Charles. "I overheard Henry Pinkerton speaking of it in Spellbinder Hall. In the short space of time I knew Albert, he came across as being a very rude man, but even a rude man is not deserving of such a violent death."

Millie shifted on her stool. "If I may say so, without sounding rude — I've seen the bear, it looks a little… limp."

"Of course it does," said Charles. "Albert wouldn't allow me to finish my work. He was abrupt with me from the moment I arrived at the lighthouse, claiming he'd forgotten our appointment. He seemed to have other things on his mind."

"It was the anniversary of his wife's death," explained Millie.

"How tragic," said Charles. "But that explains his attitude. I like to whistle while I work, you see? It helps me to focus, but it seems to have been an annoyance to Albert Salmon. That and the fact that I terrified the poor man."

"How did you terrify him? You didn't turn into a vampire in front of him, did you?" said Judith.

"Of course not!" said Charles. "That's against all the rules I hold dear. I scared Albert, because when he heard me whistling, I was crouching inside the bear — completely hidden from view. He wouldn't have admitted it, but I think he was under the impression that it was the bear which was whistling a merry tune. It gave him quite the fright.

"He demanded I leave, in the middle of my work. No wonder the bear appears limp — it is devoid of half of its stuffing. I propped it up with an old broom handle I found amongst the odds and ends which surrounded the poor beast. I still hope to get the job finished, and now that Albert no longer has any need for the animal, perhaps that will become a possibility."

Sergeant Spencer stared directly at Charles. "I have to ask you this," he said. "Did you kill Albert Salmon?"

"Why would I do such a thing?" spat Charles. "How dare you ask me such a question. Of course I didn't kill him!"

"He's telling the truth," said Millie.

"Are you reading his thoughts?" asked Judith.

Millie shook her head. "No," she said. "I don't need to. His van wasn't there when I saw Albert being pushed. Charles wasn't at the lighthouse. He'd been and gone."

"He's a vampire, Millie," said Sergeant Spencer. "Vampires can move quickly, maybe they can even leave their vans somewhere else, and scale lighthouses with thick steel doors — I don't know. A vampire could have easily pushed Albert from the lighthouse, and then leapt off the balcony before you got inside."

Charles's fist came down on the workbench with force. Tools bounced, and small clouds of dust rose from the dirty surface. "How dare you!" he shouted, veins pulsing in his neck. "I will not be accused of murder! Take me to Spellbinder Hall, I will hold the stone of integrity, and you will apologise to me!"

Charles looked at Millie, and her skin crawled with fear. His eyes had blackened, and the sharp tips of fangs protruded from below his thin top lip. An angry vampire was not something she wanted to make more irate.

Calming herself, she focused on the barrage of thoughts that streamed from Charles. She sensed anger, incredulity, frustration, but above all — she sensed his innocence.

She stood up slowly, and approached the workbench. "I know you didn't do it, Charles," she said. "Please calm down, Sergeant Spencer was just doing his job."

With an expression of curiosity, Charles studied Millie. Slowly, his eyes reverted to their human form, and the tips of his fangs slid beneath his lip. "You read my thoughts? Like your friend said you could?" he asked.

"Yes," said Millie. "I'm sorry. I had to. You were becoming angry. It scared me."

"Then you'll know I'm not capable of murder," said Charles. "And even if I was, I wouldn't do it in this town. The punishment which Henry Pinkerton would bestow upon a murderer from the paranormal community, does not bear thinking about."

Millie raised an eyebrow. "I keep hearing about this

awful punishment. What is it? What will happen to a paranormal murderer that is so terrible?"

"You don't know?" said Charles. "Have you been living beneath a rock?"

"She's new in town," said Judith. "She's learning as she goes."

"Then allow me to hasten your learning curve, young lady," said Charles. "If I may?"

Millie nodded.

Charles sat down behind his workbench. "Have you been made aware of chaos and order?"

"Yes," said Millie. "Judith explained that Spellbinder Hall acts as a barrier between the two."

"Do you have any idea what resides in The Chaos?" asked Charles. "What horrors are only a thin dimension away from the reality we inhabit?"

Recalling the face in the fireplace, Millie shuddered. "Yes," she said. "Edna Brockett made me very aware."

"She used magic," explained Judith. "To show her a glimpse of The Chaos — a face. It scared Millie. She doesn't need you scaring her any more."

"I'm quite capable of knowing the truth," said Millie, her frustration getting the better of her. "Thank you for your concern, Judith, but it's not required."

Judith looked away, her cheeks reddening. "Okay," she said.

"If the face which Edna Brockett revealed to you was a source of fear," said Charles, "then imagine being sent to dwell among the creatures who possess such faces. Imagine being banished to a dimension in which hellions rule, and chaos is king."

"It sounds awful," said Millie. "Is that the punishment? Banishment to another dimension?"

"Yes," said Charles. "Permanent banishment to a place of despair and pain."

"Permanent?" said Millie, visions of an eternity in hell swirling through her mind.

"Indeed. Only a few escape The Chaos," said Charles. "And most of the ones who do, escape it to bring chaos to this dimension — hence the importance of Spellbinder Hall as a barrier between the worlds. It is never good when a demon breaks through." He shook his head slowly, and frowned. "Never good at all. For the most part."

"For the most part?" said Millie.

"Not all demons are evil," said Charles. "Some are born into chaos by accident. They are good spirits, trapped in an awful place."

"What happens to them?" said Millie, aware of a tapping sound on glass behind her.

Charles looked over Millie's shoulder. He pointed behind her. "That's what happens to the lucky ones," he said. "They are rescued. I'm assuming that the little bird tapping at my window is the familiar of one of you young witches? Either that, or he's very tame, and some-body's escaped pet."

Millie span on her stool. At the top of the window, where the grime was less thick, hovered Reuben, his beak tapping incessantly on the glass.

"Reuben is a demon?" said Millie, standing up.

"Yes," said Charles. "Rescued from chaos by a person like you — a witch, his spirit homed in an animal's body, so it may have a physical form in this dimension."

"I don't know about him being a demon," said

Sergeant Spencer, "but if somebody doesn't let him in soon, he's going to do himself an injury."

Reuben continued to slam his beak into the window as Millie hurried to the door. She swung it open, and Reuben fluttered inside, shaking his head.

"Are you okay, Reuben?" said Millie, as the bird landed on her shoulder. "How did you find me?"

"When you summoned me," said Reuben, "you accepted me as your familiar. I'll always be able to find you. That's not important, though — what is important, is that two men are using tools to break down the door of Albert's lighthouse. I thought you'd want to know."

Sergeant Spencer hurried to the open door. "Thank you, Reuben. Let's go!" he said.

"May I accompany you?" asked Charles. "I would very much like to retrieve the bear. It will serve no purpose to anybody else in its forlorn state."

Sergeant Spencer nodded his agreement. "Come on," he said. "If the two men are trying to rob from the lighthouse, maybe the strength of a vampire will be useful."

"Thank you," said Charles. "I'll follow along in my van."

Chapter 24

"Technically, there's only one man breaking in, and one man watching him," said Millie.

Reuben pecked at Millie's ear. "Don't be so pedantic," he said. "It doesn't suit you. Anyway, my work here is done. I was in the middle of watching an interesting documentary about volcanoes when I heard the banging on the lighthouse door, would you mind if I got back to it?"

Millie opened the car window just wide enough to allow Reuben through the gap. "You go," she said, wondering how a demon rescued from chaos ever became interested in volcanoes. "Thanks for your help."

Sergeant Spencer drew the car to a halt next to the van and the car which were parked alongside the lighthouse. The two men Reuben had spoken of carried on with the task at hand – one of them, dressed in overalls, working on the door with a hammer and chisel, and the other, dressed in a suit, watching him.

Both men turned to look as Sergeant Spencer

shouted a warning. "Stop that!" he yelled. "What the hell do you think you're doing?"

The man in the suit withdrew a business card from an inside pocket as Sergeant Spencer and the girls approached him. He gave Sergeant Spencer a wide smile. "You must be the local constabulary," he said. "I'm David Rees, from Rees and Wilkinson legal services. I'm in charge of the recently deceased, Albert Salmon's, estate."

"You're breaking in!" said Sergeant Spencer, snatching the business card from the lawyer's hand. "If you're in charge of Mister Salmon's estate, why don't you have a key?"

The lawyer pointed at the thick steel door. "Mister Salmon liked his security," he said. "Some clients without family leave us a key to their property when they use our company to produce their will, but not Mister Salmon."

The man holding the hammer and chisel looked at David Rees. "Should I carry on trying to get in?" he said.

"No, you will not!" said Sergeant Spencer. He glanced at the lawyer's brown leather briefcase. "Do you have any proof that you are who you say you are?" he said.

Mister Rees nodded. "I have all the necessary paperwork with me," he said.

Sergeant Spencer patted his pocket. "And I have a key to the lighthouse," he said. "If the paperwork is in order, I'll let you in."

"You have a key?" said the lawyer. "And how did you come about that?"

"Mister Salmon gave it to this young lady," he said,

indicating Millie with an open hand. "She lives in the cottage you can see over there — Windy-dune Cottage. Albert gave her the keys so she could let herself in with supplies for him."

"Well, this does make things easier," smiled the lawyer. He looked Millie up and down. "You must be Millie Thorn?"

"How could you know that?" said Millie.

"Albert's will names you as the person to receive his inheritance Millie," smiled the lawyer. "He's left the lighthouse, all its contents, and the land it stands on to you."

"That can't be right," said Millie. "I've only just arrived in town. When did Albert make his will?"

David Rees's face darkened momentarily. "If I'm being honest with you," he said. "I find it a little strange, too. I helped Albert write his will a few weeks after his wife had died and all her belongings were made legally his. I know what Albert instructed... or I'm *sure* I remember what he instructed, and I'm positive he demanded the lighthouse be sold after his death and the money made from the sale be handed over to the taxman. I remember thinking it was quite nasty of him, I think I suggested a charity, but he refused. I must be wrong, though. My memory must be muddled. I work long hours, and he made his will years ago."

"Was it changed recently?" asked Sergeant Spencer.

"No," said the lawyer. "There are no records of the sealed envelope being opened, and the matching document on our computer system has not been accessed. Both say the same thing, and according to our systems, both were written years ago. It's as the will says, Miss

Thorn — the land you are standing on belongs to you now."

"I don't understand," said Millie. "It doesn't make any sense. I didn't even know Albert!"

Snapping open the clasp on his briefcase, the lawyer smiled. "It makes no sense to me either, but the law is the law, and the will is quite clear," he said, withdrawing a thin cardboard file from his case. "Albert Salmon's will states quite categorically that his estate should be left in whole to, and I quote — *Millie Thorn. The magical lady who resides in Windy-dune Cottage.*"

"Magical lady," said Millie, "it says that?"

"It seems he held you in high regard," said the lawyer.

"Let's do this inside," said Sergeant Spencer, brandishing the lighthouse key. "I'm sure Millie would like to sit down while she reads Albert's will."

The man with a hammer and chisel stepped aside as Sergeant Spencer slipped the key into the lock. The workman looked at the lawyer. "Do you need anything else?" he asked, slipping his tools into the canvas bag at his feet.

"No," said the lawyer. "Thank you. Send me an invoice for the time you've wasted." He looked inland as the sound of an engine approached.

A grin on his face, he watched as Charles Bannister's van pulled up alongside his car. "A taxidermist?" he said. "I know lawyers have a bad reputation, but there's no need to have me stuffed!"

———

MILLIE PERCHED ON THE SOFA WITH ALBERT SALMON'S

will in her hands. There was no denying what it said — he had left everything to her.

"Are you any closer to finding out who murdered him?" asked David Rees. "I can't arrange his funeral until I get the go-ahead from the police. When I am allowed to go forward with the arrangements, the costs for the funeral will be taken from his estate, and the rest will be passed on to you, Millie."

Sergeant Spencer gave a heavy sigh. "No," he said. "Not yet."

"I'm sure you'll have a breakthrough soon enough," said the lawyer. He smiled at Millie. "What will you do with the lighthouse? It's so close to your cottage — you could rent it out. It'll need a little work, but it's a beautiful old building, and so close to the sea."

It *was* close to the sea, and that gave Millie an idea. "I think I know just the person who would love to live here," she said. "But first I need to right a little wrong I did to her."

David Rees looked at his watch. "Well, I've collected what I need from here," he said, bundling the bank statements he'd found in the sideboard, into his case. "When we've paid off all his outstanding debts — if he has any, the balance of his estate will be forwarded to you, Millie."

As Sergeant Spencer saw the lawyer out of the lighthouse, Judith sat beside Millie. "Are you all right?" she asked. "You've been through a lot in the last few days, and now you find out you're the beneficiary of a murdered man's inheritance. It must be quite a shock."

Judith's eyes held nothing but sincerity, and Millie regretted snapping at her in Charles Bannister's workshop. She'd still been reeling from the thought she'd intercepted from Judith, and she *had* been through a lot in the last few days — she was bound to snap sooner or later.

She smiled at Judith. "I'm okay," she said. "Are you busy tonight? Maybe you could come to my cottage again? We could have wine and pizza. Reuben would like that."

"You said *my*," said Judith, a twinkle in her eyes.

"Pardon?" said Millie, her brow furrowed.

"You said *my* cottage," said Judith. "It's the first time I've heard you refer to it as yours."

"I did, didn't I?" said Millie. "Perhaps I'm finally starting to believe that I belong here. It's a strange town, but it's certainly not without character."

"And you've only scratched the surface," laughed Judith. "Wait until you've been here for a while."

Preceded by footsteps, Charles Bannister appeared at the top of the stairs, his shirt covered in coarse hairs. "I hear from the lawyer gentleman, that you are the new owner of the lighthouse, and all the articles within it, Millie," he said.

"Apparently so," said Millie. "It's come as quite a shock."

Charles raised an eyebrow. "I was wondering if —"

Millie nodded. "— take it. Take the bear — it makes me nervous, and I'm sure Albert would like to think it's going to a place where it will be appreciated."

Charles gave a broad smile. "Thank you, it certainly will be appreciated. I shall load it into my van right away." He held a hand out to Millie. "I found these inside the animal, they must be Albert's, perhaps he was inspecting what little work I'd managed to get done before he threw me out. One of the lenses is missing, I'm afraid."

Millie reached for the spectacles. "I think I must've stood on the other lens," she said. "I remember treading on glass when I rushed into the lighthouse after seeing Albert fall from the balcony."

"Well, they'll be of no use to Albert anymore," said Charles, wiping hairs from his arms. "Whereas his stuffed bear will be of great use to me! Thank you!"

"You've made an old vampire very happy," said Judith, as Charles descended the spiral staircase.

"That's a sentence I never thought anybody would say to me," laughed Millie, reading the sheets of paper attached to Albert's will. She re-scanned the sentence she was reading, something nagging at her memory. "Look at this," she said, "it talks about Betty's belongings being transferred to Albert's estate when she passed away. It has her maiden name written here —"

Her breath catching in her throat, Millie stood up. "I think I know who did it!" she said. "I don't know *why* they did it, but I think I know *who* killed Albert Salmon!"

Chapter 25

*A*s Sergeant Spencer prepared to knock the door of the small house, he turned to face the two girls. "If you're correct, Millie," he said, "we could be dealing with a very dangerous man. Both of you be on your guard."

"I know I'm right," said Millie. "Everything points to him being the murderer."

"We'll soon find out," said Sergeant Spencer, checking his handcuffs were in their pouch. He hammered on the door with a big fist. "Open up, Billy McKenna!" he shouted. "It's me, Sergeant Spencer! I have some very serious questions to ask you."

The door opened within half a minute, and Billy glared at them from the hallway beyond. "To what do I owe the pleasure?" he said. "It's not every day you get a visit from a burly police sergeant and his two beautiful assistants."

Millie peered past Billy, much like Henry Pinkerton had tried to do when he'd visited her flat in London. "No dog?" she said.

The corner of his mouth lifting into a sneer, Billy stared at Millie. "No. Why do you ask?"

"You said you had a dog, Billy," said Millie. "When Sergeant Spencer and I brought you home the other night, when you were fighting outside the pub. You said the hairs on your clothes, and the smell, had come from your dog."

Billy looked harder at Millie. "It was you in the police car with Sergeant Spencer?" he said. "I was very drunk that night, it's hard to remember."

"No dog though?" said Millie.

Billy shook his head. "No, I don't have a dog. I don't know why I said I did."

"And you still haven't found your glasses?" said Millie. "Maybe that's why you don't remember what I looked like."

"No, I still haven't found my glasses," said Billy. "I shall be visiting the optician next week to purchase a new pair." He looked between the three of them. "I'm sure you're not here to ask me if I'm a dog owner, and to check on my eye health. What do you want? Spit it out."

Sergeant Spencer pushed past the thin man, forcing his way into his home. "Billy McKenna," he said, reaching for the suspect's arms. "I'm arresting you on suspicion of murder, you don't have to —"

Billy moved quickly. Stepping backwards along the hallway, he reached for the small of his back. When he lifted his hand again, Sergeant Spencer shouted a warning. "He's got a gun!"

"And I'm not afraid to use it," said Billy, the pistol steady in his hand. "I'm not going back to prison. No way. Not for Albert Salmon!"

As if floating outside of her own body, and with nausea gripping her insides, Millie spoke as confidently as she could manage. "So, it was you?" she said. "You did kill Albert?"

"Of course it was me," confirmed Billy. "And I'm not sorry for it. I could have killed you too, if I'd wanted to. I was right beside you when you came into the lighthouse after I'd pushed Albert off it."

"So you do remember me?" said Millie.

"I do," said Billy, shifting the pistol slightly to the right, the barrel aimed directly at Millie's face. "I may need glasses, but I'm not totally blind. I watched you from the balcony, rushing towards the lighthouse like some sort of wannabe hero"

"Point the gun at me, Billy!" said Sergeant Spencer. "You've already killed one innocent person, you don't want to kill any more."

"Albert wasn't innocent," said Billy. "He ruined my sister's life!"

"Betty was your sister, wasn't she?" said Millie. "Her maiden name was Mckenna — I saw it in a document. Billy is short for William, so your initials are WM — you wrote that threatening letter to Albert all those years ago. When you were in prison."

The gun barrel still trained on Millie, Billy grinned. "I'm happy to know that he kept my correspondence," he said. "It's nice to know that I meant that much to him."

With Millie and Judith still standing on the doorstep, Sergeant Spencer moved slightly to the left, putting himself between Millie and the gun. Billy adjusted his aim, directing the pistol at Sergeant Spencer's wide chest. "Don't move again," he said. "I'm ex-military, and I'm a good shot. I won't miss at this range."

"Why were you in prison, Billy?" said Sergeant Spencer.

"Trying to keep me occupied with conversation are you, Sergeant? So I don't shoot you?" sneered Billy. "Well, I've got nowhere to go. I've got plenty of time to talk."

"Tell me, then," said Sergeant Spencer. "Why were you in prison?"

"I was in prison for making death threats," said Billy. "To Albert Salmon. The police took it seriously when they searched my home and found the Iraqi pistols I'd smuggled back to Britain after operation Desert Storm." He waved the pistol in the air, briefly turning the barrel away from its human target. "They didn't find this one, though."

For such a large man, Sergeant Spencer moved quickly. He ducked low as he threw himself towards Billy, taking his chance while he could, yelling at Millie and Judith to get down.

In the narrow hallway, the gunshot was deafening. Like an angry bee, the round passed close to Millie's ear, buzzing as it screamed a path past her head. Hearing Judith scream, Millie feared the worst. *The bullet must have hit her.*

Billy flew backwards as Sergeant Spencer's shoulder struck his midriff, the big policeman's strength easily overpowering the smaller man.

Judith screamed again as the two men grappled on the floor, Sergeant Spencer attempting to control the arm with which Billy wielded the pistol. *If Judith had been hit by the bullet, at least she was still alive, and well enough to scream.*

No expert on guns, Millie was fully aware that most military pistols were of the semi-automatic variety — the sort that fired one bullet with each squeeze of the trigger — as quickly as the person firing it could pull the trigger.

As the gun barrel found the side of Sergeant Spencer's temple, metal digging into hair and flesh, Billy's finger curled around the trigger, the muscles in his forearm twitching as he applied pressure.

Judith screamed once more, and Millie did the only thing she could think of. Drawing on the bubbling heat behind her breastbone, she focussed on what she wanted to happen, and flung her magic from deep within her, with an anger which startled her.

A flash of flame erupted from the barrel of the pistol, and the explosive bang reverberated in Millie's eardrums as Sergeant Spencer's head jolted sideways, and he gave a drawn-out groan.

"No!" shouted Judith, terror moulding her words. "Dad! No!"

As Millie stared at the pool of blood seeping into the hallway carpet, her mind wandered to the aroma which filled the small space. Surprisingly, the smell of cordite was actually quite pleasant.

Judith's screams broke into her shocked trance, and Millie reached for her phone. The moon-pool wasn't going to be able to help this time — the carnage at her feet was definitely a job for the hospital.

Chapter 26

"*J*'m sorry about your father, Judith," said Billy, one handcuffed to the wooden table, and the other bandaged in thick layers of gauze. "It was an accident. I was scared, I didn't want to go back to jail — I've spent most of my life there since leaving the Army."

Judith shrugged. "Although I wish *nobody* had got hurt, you came off worse, Billy. I hope the three nights you spent in a hospital bed were comfortable, because I've got a feeling the bed you're going to be sleeping in for the foreseeable future won't be so soft."

Billy held up his bandaged hand. "Five fingers are overrated anyway, I'm sure I'll manage with one finger and a thumb. As for the prison bed — I've sort of got used to them over the years."

The door swung open with a heavy thud, and Sergeant Spencer entered the interrogation room, smiling at the prisoner. "Glad to see they patched you up," he said, taking a seat between Millie and Judith. "That will teach you to maintain your weapons in the future, not that I hold out much hope that you'll ever own a gun again."

Billy looked at his hand. "The army taught me how to look after my weapons," he said. "Whatever happened to my pistol wasn't down to a lack of maintenance on my behalf."

Sergeant Spencer turned to Millie and gave her a conspiratorial wink, the stitches above his ear the only sign a bullet had almost penetrated his skull. "Perhaps it was divine intervention, Billy," he said. "Maybe *somebody* was looking after me that day."

Sergeant Spencer had been lucky. *Very lucky*. Millie had cast the spell with a heartbeat to spare. She still wasn't sure exactly *what* spell she'd cast as she'd flung the magic from her fingers — she'd simply envisioned a force field between Sergeant Spencer's head and the barrel of the gun.

Whatever the spell was, it had worked. Meeting an invisible force-field as it had peeped over the rim of the barrel, the bullet had met powerful magical resistance, and the pistol had exploded in Billy's hand.

The wound Sergeant Spencer had suffered was minor compared to the carnage caused to Billy's hand. Even the highly skilled surgeon who'd treated Billy couldn't save his fingers, but at least nobody had died — a positive outcome in Millie's estimation.

It had taken Judith almost a full day to stop shaking after the incident, and then a further day to cease apologising to Millie for not doing more to help while Billy was brandishing a gun.

Millie understood. Of course she did. Judith had already seen two of her parents die — watching her second father almost being killed had pushed her over the edge. All she'd been able to do was scream.

Through gritted teeth, Billy gazed at the tape recorder placed at the end of the table. "I suppose you'll be wanting my confession?" he asked. "I've given plenty of them in my time, but never to a policeman, his daughter, and another girl whose job I can't quite work out."

"They work with me, Billy," said Sergeant Spencer. "That's all you need to know." The recorder clicked into action as he pressed a button. He levelled a stern gaze at his prisoner. "Okay, Billy, would you run through the events of the day on which you murdered Albert Salmon? We'll get to the reasons *why* in due course."

Billy leaned back in his seat, and gave a thin smile. "I'd been planning that day since I'd arrived in Spellbinder Bay a few months ago," he said. "I knew Albert wouldn't discover I was in town, and that I'd finally found him. I'd asked around and found out he was practically a hermit. I knew I could bide my time until the anniversary of my sister's death — what better day to use to get my revenge on the man who ruined her life, and put her in an early grave?"

"How did he put her in an early grave?" said Judith.

"We'll get to that," said Sergeant Spencer. "Just let Billy tell us what happened on the day he killed Albert."

"I went to the lighthouse bright and early," said Billy. "I wanted to get the unsavoury job out of the way so I could spend the rest of the day in the pub. It was the first time I'd visited the lighthouse, and I realised pretty quickly that it wasn't going to be as easy as I'd imagined."

"Why?" asked Millie.

"The door," replied Billy. "I thought I'd be able to break in, but that door is bombproof. There was no way I was going to get through it."

"What did you do?" asked Sergeant Spencer.

"I waited," said Billy. "I hid in the sand dunes. I hoped Albert would venture outside at some point. I didn't wait long before a van arrived — a taxidermist's van of all things. Albert tossed him a key from the window and he let himself in with his tool bag."

"You didn't see anybody else?" said Millie. "Like a woman sitting on the rocks near the lighthouse?"

Billy frowned. "No, why? Was somebody else there?"

"A witness," said Sergeant Spencer. "She saw the taxidermist's van, but evidently she didn't see you."

"The fact that somebody else was there wouldn't surprise me at all," said Billy. "For a man who was a hermit, he certainly had a lot of visitors that day. The taxidermist didn't stay for long, and when he left he had a face like thunder. He was carrying a bigger bag than he went in with, and I heard Albert shouting something as he slammed the door behind them."

"The old stuffing from the bear," said Millie. "That's what he was carrying." She locked her eyes on Billy's. "But you'd know all about that, wouldn't you, Billy?"

Billy smiled. "I'll get to that," he said. "After the taxidermist left, I approached the lighthouse. I had to hide again before I could get close — I heard another vehicle approaching. It was a yellow car, and I recognised the woman driving it — that old battle-axe, Edna Brockett."

"You hid again?" said Sergeant Spencer.

Billy nodded. "Albert wouldn't let her in at first, but eventually he threw her a key. She was only there for a few minutes, and she left with a face like thunder, too. It seems that Albert didn't get on with people very well at all. "

"And that's when you got into the lighthouse, isn't it, Billy?" said Millie. "Albert told us that Edna had left the door open."

"It was just the luck I needed," said Billy. "I used the long grass to cover my approach so Edna wouldn't see me as she drove away, and sneaked in through the door. I could hear Albert complaining, and I could hear footsteps from above, so I looked for somewhere to hide — I didn't want to do anything until I was certain that Edna was a long way away."

"The bear?" said Millie. "That's where you hid?"

"It was the first thing I saw," said Billy. "It was standing right next to the door — it gave me a bit of a fright. I climbed behind it, and then realised I could get inside it. It didn't smell too good, and I thought all the loose fibres inside were going to make me sneeze, but it was the perfect hiding place."

"That's why you smelt so bad when Millie and I took you home," said Sergeant Spencer.

"Yes," said Billy. "Perhaps I should have had a shower when I went home after killing Albert, but I went to the pub instead. I was a little shaken up, and I'd discovered that murder is thirsty work."

"How long did you stay in the bear?" said Judith.

Billy looked down at the table. "I waited for Albert to lock the door. I was tempted to kill him right there and then, as he was standing next to the bear, but I wanted to make sure nobody else was going to arrive. It's lucky I did wait, because within ten minutes somebody else was banging on the door."

"Jim Grayson," said Millie.

Billy nodded. "They had a shouting match," he said. "About lobsters. It was ridiculous. Albert wouldn't let him in, though, and he didn't stay for long."

"Then George and I arrived?" said Millie, "before you had the chance to hurt Albert?"

"It was infuriating!" snapped Billy, wincing as his bandaged hand struck the edge of the table. "When Jim had left, I was about to make my move on Albert. He was muttering about not having coffee, and having to drink herbal tea instead. He must have enjoyed talking to himself, because he wouldn't stop complaining about what time his supplies were going to arrive."

"You knew somebody else would be coming to the lighthouse," noted Sergeant Spencer. "With his supplies."

"Yes," said Billy, "and the smell inside that damn bear wasn't getting any better. I felt sick. Surely stuffed animals shouldn't smell that bad?"

"Let's just say the bear wasn't stuffed properly the first time it was done," said Judith.

"I got used to it," said Billy, "and settled down to wait. I didn't have to wait long as it happens. Not too long after Jim had gone, the supplies arrived."

"We looked right at the bear," said Millie. "George even prodded it."

"Don't I know it," said Billy, with a glare in Millie's direction. "I thought I was going to be rumbled. I had my pistol at the ready."

"You would have killed Millie and George, too?" said Sergeant Spencer.

The only person in the room unaware that George was a vampire, and that he'd have had no chance of killing him, smiled. "Only if I'd been forced to," he said. "And I would have deeply regretted it."

Millie shuddered. "It didn't come to that," she said. "Thankfully."

"I thought about it," said Billy, his eyes on Millie. "Especially when you came rushing back into the lighthouse after I'd dealt with Albert. Luckily for you, I had time to get back inside the bear, and sneak out of the door when you'd gone upstairs."

"Back to the timeline, please, Billy," said Sergeant Spencer. "What happened when Millie and George arrived?"

"I stayed hidden," said Billy. "I listened to their conversation with the grumpy old man. They didn't stay long, and as they were leaving, I heard Albert shouting at Millie — telling her to lock the door because he wasn't letting anybody else in after they'd gone. I waited until I heard the motorbike leave, and made my move."

"Feeling safe that nobody else would interrupt you," said Judith.

"Yes," said Billy. He pointed his bandaged hand at Millie. "I certainly didn't expect *her* to still be around."

"That's because you didn't hear the part of my conversation with Albert that he didn't want George to overhear," said Millie. "If you had, you'd have known I promised Albert I'd walk back to my cottage. He whispered because he didn't want George to know he wasn't a big fan of motorbikes."

"He said that?" said Billy. "About motorbikes? How ironic."

"What's ironic," said Sergeant Spencer, with a scowl, "is that you fired a bullet at my head, and now I'm sitting here alive and well in my police station, interviewing you, and preparing to send you to jail for a long time. Albert wasn't so lucky. Tell us what you did to him, Billy."

Billy's face reddened. "When the motorbike had left, I sneaked out of the bear and went looking for Albert. He was two floors up, in that shoebox kitchen of his, unpacking his groceries. He had quite the shock when he saw me after all those years, I can tell you!"

"What did you do to him?" said Judith.

"He lunged at me," laughed Billy. "I could have shot him right there and then, but he was easy to overpower. I wanted him to suffer for a bit. I wanted to hear him beg, and beg he did — but not for his life."

"What did he beg for?" said Millie, her skin crawling as she looked into Billy's eyes.

"He begged to be taken to the top of the lighthouse," said Billy. "He said it was where Betty had enjoyed spending time. He said if I was going to shoot him, he'd rather me do it up there."

"And you took him up there," said Sergeant Spencer.

"Oh yes," said Billy. "I dragged him up those stairs by his wrist, and when we got to the top, I had a wonderful idea. Why shoot him and risk somebody hearing the bang, when I could push him from the top? And as a bonus, maybe people would think Albert had been the victim of a tragic accident, and slipped. I might never have been caught."

"But I heard him shouting," said Millie.

"So that's why you came back," said Billy. "I had wondered. He did shout a little when he realised I wasn't going to shoot him. I suppose being pushed off a lighthouse onto jagged rocks *is* less appealing than a bullet in the head. It wasn't easy, though. It's quite the struggle to push a panicking man over a balcony rail — let me tell you! He stopped shouting as he went over the edge, though, but that's when I heard a woman's scream." He looked at Millie. "Her scream."

"You knew somebody had seen Albert falling," said Sergeant Spencer.

"Yes," nodded Billy, "but I couldn't see her properly. My glasses had dropped off in the struggle, and one of the lenses had cracked. I grabbed them and got off the balcony quickly."

"And then I rang the doorbell?" said Millie, recalling her actions on the day.

"Not straight away," said Billy. "I had time to get downstairs. I thought I'd be able to sneak out of the door and escape, but then I heard the bell. I'm not ashamed to say I panicked a little. I got inside the bear again, and waited."

"The glass I stood on when I let myself in," said Millie. "That was from your glasses, wasn't it?"

"Yes," said Billy. "I dropped them again when you rang the doorbell. The cracked lens smashed completely, so I left it there before jumping inside the bear."

"And then you left your glasses in the bear," said Millie. "You might never have been caught if you hadn't made that mistake. They were found inside the bear, and straight after that, I discovered your sister's maiden name. I put two and two together after remembering you'd lost your glasses on the night Sergeant Spencer and I took you home, covered in hair and stinking to high heaven."

Billy frowned. "A fair cop," he said. "My glasses were of no use to me with only one lens, so I slipped them inside my pocket. Or thought I did. I must have dropped them. I'd assumed I'd dropped them on the way back into town. If I'd have known they were in the bear, I would have tried to retrieve them."

"When Millie went upstairs, looking for a murderer, you left the building?" said Sergeant Spencer. "That's why it appeared that nobody else had been in the lighthouse."

"Yes," said Billy. "I sneaked down onto the rocks, and followed the coast back into town. I hid my gun at home and went straight to the pub to celebrate. Despite the complications, I thought it was a job well done. I got my revenge on Albert, so I thought I deserved a drink."

Sergeant Spencer shifted in his seat. He narrowed his eyes as he studied Billy's face. "Now you've told us *how* you did it," he said. "Why don't you tell us *why* you did it? Just why did you want revenge on Albert Salmon, Billy? What did he do that deserved such a violent death?"

Billy sneered, but as he looked at Sergeant Spencer, his gaze travelled beyond the policeman. His sneer collapsed into an anxious grimace, and his grimace led to a scream, which chilled Millie's blood.

"I'll answer that," said a voice from behind Millie. "I'll tell you why he killed me, and I'll tell you why I deserved it."

Chapter 27

*C*ompletely drained of colour, Billy's face appeared emotionless, and Millie wondered whether her own face had looked so white when she'd first seen Florence.

Terror rushed through her mind as she picked up on Billy's thoughts, and she took a deep breath to steady herself. The man was scared. Very scared.

Albert Salmon, the panic button on the wall next to the door visible through his torso, stood behind Sergeant Spencer, gazing down at Billy.

"It… it can't be," stuttered Billy, his frightened eyes devoid of anything but terror. "It's impossible."

"Don't be afraid, Billy," said Albert, a gentle softness rounding his words. "I don't want to hurt you — I want to save you from yourself. I want to save you from prison."

"Albert," said Millie, aware that her fear of ghosts had diminished substantially since arriving in the bay. "I'm so sorry about what happened to you."

The smile which Albert gave her banished any pity from Millie's heart. Genuine, and empty of sorrow, the smile conveyed a deep peacefulness. "Don't be sorry, Millie," he said. "Death was the best thing that ever happened to me. It released me from all the things which made my life a living hell — the pain — both physical and emotional, the regret, the shame, the frustration — it's all gone now. I'm free."

"I don't understand," said Billy. "I don't understand what's happening. Is it the painkillers they gave me at the hospital? Am I hallucinating?"

"No, Billy," said Albert. "You're not hallucinating. I'm standing here — a ghost, and I've come to fight your corner. I've come to help you."

As Billy stared at Albert, the corner of his right eye began to twitch, and the fingers on his uninjured hand trembled. He sank in his seat, his face that of somebody whose world had been turned upside down.

He opened his mouth to speak, but the pathetic sound that came out was unintelligible — a wavering moan which tapered off into a deep sigh.

"May I?" said Albert, addressing Sergeant Spencer. "May I speak, and tell you why Billy was led down the path of revenge?"

Sergeant Spencer turned in his seat. "Of course you can, Albert," he said, unfazed by the appearance of a ghost. "But you must understand that this isn't a court of law — what's said here today won't reflect the punishment Billy receives for murdering you."

"I'm hoping it won't go that far," said Albert. "I'm hoping Billy won't go to court for my murder. He's done a lot of things that are wrong, which he rightly deserves punishment for. Pointing a gun at innocent people was unforgivable, and he deserves to face the consequences for that, but as the ghost of the man he murdered, I feel I should have the right to ask that he be forgiven for that particular crime."

"Why didn't you come forward earlier, Albert?" said Judith. "You could have helped us catch Billy sooner."

Albert's ghostly beard seemed to shimmer as he smiled. "It's not easy to make yourself seen when you're dead," he said. "It takes a lot of energy, energy I'm still learning how to harness. I would have made myself visible a lot sooner if I could have, and anyway, I've been focusing the energy I do have on other things. Things I'll explain later."

Sergeant Spencer leaned across the table and turned the tape recorder off. "This tape is useless now," he said, with a glint in his eye. "I'm not sure the courts are ready to hear the disembodied voice of a dead man inter-rupting an interview with his own murderer." He sat back in his seat and smiled at Albert. "Go on," he said. "The floor is yours, tell us what you'd like us to hear."

Albert began pacing, his feet making no sound as he walked. "Sixteen years ago something terrible happened," he said. "Something which ruined Betty's life, and my own. I'd always been a drinker. I used alcohol to mask my inadequacies and my fears. It became my friend, but not a good friend — more like a friend who you know doesn't want the best for you, but is always there when you need him."

"Tell me about it," said Billy, his face regaining a little colour. "It's not been good to me either, but even I knew there were some things you didn't do with alcohol in your belly."

Albert's transparent form flickered for a moment, and his eyes saddened. "If I could turn back the clock, Billy, I would. That's impossible, though. What happened, happened, and there is nothing I can do to change that."

"What did happen, Albert?" said Millie.

Albert stopped walking, and lowered his head. "We lived in Scotland, Betty and I," he said. "The country-side was beautiful, and Betty loved to get out into the mountains. I suggested we get a motorbike so we could explore with more freedom. I'd had one when I was younger, so I had my license. Betty loved the idea — so much so that she wanted to learn to ride herself. She did her test, and within a few months we both had bikes."

Billy shook his head, as if ridding it of bad memories. "She loved that bike," he said.

"She did," said Albert. "And she was a good rider."

"A safe rider," said Billy. "That's why I knew there was something wrong with the story you told the police. Even before Betty came out of the coma."

"Coma?" said Sergeant Spencer. "What happened, Albert? Did she crash her bike?"

"Not quite," said Albert.

Seemingly more at ease with fact that the ghost of his murder victim was in the room, Billy stood up, the handcuff on one wrist preventing him from reaching his full height. "Not quite?" he yelled. "Not at all, more like!"

"Sit down, Billy," barked Sergeant Spencer. "You getting angry won't help things. You murdered this man. Whatever you think he did to deserve it won't take away that fact. You have no moral high ground here whatsoever."

"Please," said Albert. "Allow him his anger. Betty was his big sister – Billy looked up to her."

Billy sat down, his shoulders slumping. "Betty brought me up," he said. "She was like a mother to me rather than a sister. My mother was older than the average mother when she gave birth to me. There was a twenty-six-year age gap between me and Betty. My mother and father liked to drink – it's probably where I inherited my taste for alcohol from. They were no use as parents, so Betty stood in as a mother *and* a sister. She was good to me. Very good."

"That's a big age gap for siblings," said Sergeant Spencer.

"Mum was always late," said Billy. "Late picking me up from school, late remembering to cook my dinner. I'm not surprised she was late having me."

"Betty loved you dearly, Billy," said Albert.

"While she could remember who I was, you mean!" yelled Billy, his face crimson, and veins throbbing in his neck.

"Calm down!" ordered Sergeant Spencer. He looked at Albert. "Tell us what happened. Why is Billy so angry with you?"

Albert vanished momentarily, reappearing a few feet away. "I can't hold my form for much longer," he said. "It takes a lot of energy, which I don't have yet."

"Be quick then," said Millie.

"Betty had gone out with work colleagues for a meal," said Albert. "I'd promised her I'd pick her up when she was ready to come home — in the car. We lived in a small town. There were no taxis at that time of night."

"You had a drink though, didn't you, Albert," said Billy, lowering his gaze to his injured hand. "You couldn't go one night without a drink — even the night you promised to drive your wife home."

"I'm ashamed to say I did," said Albert. "And when it was time to go and collect Betty, I decided I'd use my bike instead of the car. Betty wasn't happy of course… it was a cold night, and she wasn't dressed appropriately for a bike ride."

"Did she know you'd had a drink?" said Millie. "When you collected her?"

"She smelt it on my breath," said Albert. "But I convinced her I was okay to ride. It was only a few miles anyway, and police were very rare in those rural areas. It was unlikely I'd be caught."

"But not unlikely that you'd crash?" said Millie.

Albert nodded. "I misjudged a bend in the road. I skidded and hit a tree. Betty was thrown from the bike, hitting her head and damaging her spine. My leg was mangled and had to be amputated."

"And then the story gets better," said Billy, malice shining in his eyes. "I got a phone call from the hospital. Betty was in a coma, and my brother in law had lost his leg. All thanks to Betty's careless riding."

"Betty's riding?" said Judith.

Albert flickered. "That's what I told the police," he said. "To my shame, that's what I told the police. They told me that Betty was unlikely to ever wake up, and if she did she'd be unlikely to ever be the same again. I lied to cover my shame at what I'd done."

"He didn't want to be prosecuted for riding while drunk and causing the accident," said Billy. "There were no witnesses. Betty's work colleagues had all gone home by the time Albert arrived to collect her. Nobody saw Betty getting on the back of the bike. And when the hospital checked her blood, they found it contained alcohol. Not much — just the glass of wine she'd had with her meal, but enough to make it seem like she was a criminal. A criminal who'd caused terrible injuries to herself and her husband."

"That's awful," said Judith. "Really awful."

"It gets better," said Billy. "Tell them, Albert. Tell them what you did when Betty came out of her coma with spinal injuries and brain damage which Albert was told would get progressively worse and would eventually kill her. Tell them what a good husband you were to a woman with such life-changing injuries."

"She had no memory of the crash," said Albert. "I made her believe it was her who'd been riding the bike. I told her she'd had a drink and insisted she rode the bike."

An uneasy silence fell over the room, broken only by Billy's angry breathing.

"So how did you learn the truth, Billy?" ventured Millie, beginning to understand why the man had been driven to getting his revenge.

"I was visiting my sister in hospital," explained Billy, the knuckles on his cuffed hand white as he formed a tight fist. "When she remembered. Only briefly, but she remembered. She remembered who I was, and she remembered exactly who had been riding the bike.

"I confronted Albert, and he admitted it, but by the time I'd been to the police, Betty's memory had gone again. Albert denied everything."

"So you threatened to kill me," said Albert. "And I knew you had the potential to do it."

"Of course I did," snapped Billy. "I had post-traumatic stress disorder from my time in the army, which made me an angry man."

"And you had the means," said Albert. He looked around the room. "I knew he had guns at home, and I was sure he'd use them."

"So you reported him?" said Sergeant Spencer. "For making death threats?"

"Yes," said Albert. "They found his guns, and he went to prison."

"Most of them," sneered Billy. "And while I was in prison, one-legged Albert decided to go into hiding, taking his poorly wife with him."

"I had to," said Albert. "I was scared. You wrote me letters from prison, and I had no doubt that you'd kill me for what I'd done. I deserved nothing less."

"You came here?" said Millie. "To spellbinder Bay?"

Albert nodded, his shimmering form briefly vanishing again. "The perfect town and the perfect building to hide in. I stopped drinking of course, and tried my best to help Betty, but she was never the same. She remembered me, but she had forgotten everybody else."

"And I never saw my sister alive again," said Billy. "Of course I didn't know she was dead when I finally found out where Albert had taken her. I only found out that little snippet of information when I arrived in Spellbinder Bay, and if I'd had any doubt about killing Albert before, it vanished after I'd visited Betty's grave."

"The brain injury killed her," said Albert. "As the doctors said it would. Her nervous system was affected, you see. Her respiratory system gave out in the end. I was responsible for her injuries, and I hid from the consequences." He looked down at Billy. "Just how did you find me after all that time?"

"You put the lighthouse up for sale," smiled Billy.

"When Betty died," confirmed Albert. "I decided against it, though."

"But you didn't check the photographs the estate agent plastered all over the internet," said Billy. "I was looking for somewhere new to live. I'd been in and out of prison since what happened to Betty — the anger got to me, and I drank too much. When I drank, I got angry, and when I got angry I started fights. Prison was my second home.

"Then my luck came in. I won the lottery. Not millions, but enough to buy myself a house. I decided I would change my ways. And to begin that change I decided to move away from Scotland. I'd always liked the idea of living near the sea, so I began looking for a new home, far away from bad memories."

"And you found me from a photograph?" said Albert.

"Imagine my surprise!" said Billy. "I scoured the internet for homes near the sea, and one day I came across the listing for your lighthouse. It looked very cosy inside, very cosy indeed. I especially liked the paintings on the wall. The same watercolours I knew my sister had painted, back when she could concentrate for long enough to paint."

"That simple?" said Albert.

"That simple," confirmed Billy.

"Well I'm glad you found me," said Albert. "I deserved what I had coming, and I hope Sergeant

Spencer will honour my wishes and not prosecute you for my murder."

Sergeant Spencer frowned. "It's not that simple, Albert," he said. "Billy has confessed, and your body washed up on the beach."

"You said yourself that the tape was no longer admissible as evidence," said Albert. "His confession means nothing. And anyway — Billy didn't kill me. I jumped from the balcony because it was the anniversary of my wife's death. You'll find my suicide note on the table next to my bed. You'll also find my confession about what I did to Betty."

"How?" said Sergeant Spencer. "That's not possible. We searched the lighthouse. There was no such note."

"It is possible," said Albert. "I've not made myself visible before today, because I've been using my energy for other things."

"Writing your suicide note?" said Millie.

Albert smiled. "That, and changing my will. It took a great deal of effort, but I eventually managed it."

Sergeant Spencer leaned across the table and looked Billy in the eyes. "Billy McKenna," he said. "I'm charging you with assaulting a police officer, and possession of an unlawful firearm."

"And when you come out of prison," said Millie. "The lighthouse is yours, Billy. Albert left it to me, but I think you deserve it."

"I don't want it!" spat Billy. "I don't want to be anywhere near the place that my sister suffered in for all those years. I bought that little house in town, and I'm happy in it. I'll take Betty's paintings, but those are all I want."

"I left it to you, Millie, because I knew Billy wouldn't

want it. Why would he?" said Albert. "After my death, I learned all about this town. I learned who Esmeralda *really* was, and I learned that you come from her bloodline, Millie. I didn't thank Esmeralda enough for all the help she gave me while she was alive, so I wanted to forward my gratitude to you instead — the witch who has taken her place. Anyway, after watching your antics from the afterlife, I have a feeling you'll be allowing a certain mermaid to live in it? If she so desires, and if you can mend the magic in her dress."

"Witch?" said Billy, his face losing colour again. "Mermaid? Magic dress?"

"Those *were* some strong painkillers the doctors in the hospital gave you, Billy," said Sergeant Spencer. "I'd advise you forget what you heard in this room after you leave. It may affect your court-case if the judge thinks you're crazy."

"And, Billy," said Albert. "If you do go to prison, you won't be alone. I found somebody who would love to spend some time with you."

Billy stared at Albert. "What are you saying?"

The air shimmered behind Billy, and Millie smiled at the kindly old woman who appeared. "He's saying I'm here with you, Billy," said the apparition. "And I'll visit you in prison whenever you like. I have all the time in the world."

Billy turned slowly in his seat, a tear forming in the corner of his eye. "Betty?" he said.

"I'm here for you, little brother," said the ghost. "I'll always be here for you. Albert found me. You must forgive him for what he did to me, Billy. As I have."

"How can you forgive him?" sobbed Billy, his

bandaged hand passing through his sister as he reached out to touch her.

"Death cleanses a person of all the animosity of life," said Betty, bending at the waist to kiss her brother's head. "You'll find out one day."

Chapter 28

*W*ith Lillieth's dress on the table between them, Henry Pinkerton peered over his glasses at Millie. "Thank you for coming," he said. "I trust Spellbinder Hall no longer holds any fears for you?"

Millie looked around the room. The fireplace failed to make her nervous, and if a ghost *had* walked through the wall, she was sure she would have hardly raised an eyebrow. "None at all," she said, honestly. "After everything that's happened to me since I've been here, I think it would take a lot to frighten me again."

Henry nodded. "It's been an exceptional four weeks," he said. "I'm sorry that your introduction to Spellbinder Bay was so hectic. I had hoped things would have gone a lot smoother for you. You've helped solve a murder, had a gun pointed at you, and inherited a lighthouse from a ghost. I'd say your time here so far has been a little... mad."

"It *has* been a little mad," said Millie, with a shrug. "But I've sort of got used to it."

Henry adjusted his cufflinks, the little squares of gold vivid against the red of his shirt. "But not used to it enough to decide you're going to stay permanently?" he asked.

"How could you know that?" said Millie. "I've only spoken about that to —"

"Reuben," said Henry, finishing Millie's sentence for her. "Yes, I know. He came to me with his concerns."

"Concerns?" said Millie. "What concerns could he possibly have about me staying or going? I'm sure he'd do fine without me being around."

"What exactly do you know about Reuben?" said Henry. "Do you know where he came from? Where all familiars come from?"

"Yes. Charles Bannister told me," said Millie. "He told me that Reuben came from The Chaos, he told me he was a demon."

Henry gazed at the fireplace. "Demon is an unfortunate term — it conjures up images of evil entities, and Reuben couldn't be further from evil if he tried, but not all Demons are bad, some are just born into an unfortunate existence."

"The Chaos?" said Millie.

Henry nodded.

"What exactly is The Chaos?" asked Millie. "I've heard about it, and the face Edna showed me in the fireplace gave me an idea of what sort of things live there, but what is it? I've had so much to learn about since I've been here — I've put it out of my mind."

Henry stood up, and pushed Lillieth's dress across the table towards Millie. "I've tried to fix the magic that this dress is imbibed with," he said. "I can't do it. It's as we thought — only you are capable of giving Lillieth her legs back."

"Not too much pressure then?" said Millie.

"There's no rush," said Henry. "When Timothy and I transported her back to the ocean, Lillieth told us she was going to make sure Jim Grayson would never have to catch lobsters again, and then she was going to travel for a while. There's no need to worry too much about her dress. It can wait for a while."

"It's still pressure," said Millie. "If I can't fix her dress, Lillieth can never walk on land again."

"I'm afraid the pressure is about to go up a notch or two," said Henry. "I didn't just call you here to talk about Lillieth's dress. I called you here to explain some things which I fear should have been explained when you first arrived, but after you witnessed a murder on your first day in the bay, and after Edna had terrified you in this very room, I didn't feel it was right to place further burdens on your shoulders. And the fact that you summoned Reuben, may, I fear, increase the weight of the burdens I speak of."

Millie narrowed her eyes. "What is it, Henry?" she said. "What are you trying to tell me? What's the fact that I summoned Reuben got to do with anything? Judith suggested I do it — she told me *how* to do it."

"Judith doesn't come from a powerful bloodline like you," said Henry. "Witches such as her don't have the ability to keep a familiar. When Judith suggested you summoned Reuben, she had no idea of the importance of such a gesture."

"You're making me nervous," said Millie. "Stop speaking in riddles — just tell me what it is you have to say."

Henry sighed. "Would you like to take a walk? Into the depths of Spellbinder Hall? There's something I'd like to show you."

HENRY LED MILLIE DOWN THE STEPS TOWARDS THE dungeon in which Lillieth had been held captive. Glancing at the door, Millie raised an eyebrow. "Have you got another prisoner in there?" she said. "Is that what you want to show me?"

"No," said Henry. "The room is empty, and thankfully it rarely contains a prisoner." He pointed further along the corridor, into the shadows. "We're going deeper into the depths of the hall."

"What's down there?" said Millie, able to make out an archway in the shadows.

"Chaos," said Henry. "That's what's down there."

Had Millie been told a month ago that the staircase she was descending led to chaos, she would have turned around and ran the other way, but a lot had happened in four weeks. She was braver. More resilient.

She remained close behind Henry as he led her down the dimly lit corridor, deeper into the cliff below the hall. At the bottom of the steps, the corridor curved to the right, lit by flaming torches secured to the rock face by metal brackets.

Henry reached into his pocket as he walked, and retrieved a large set of keys, the jangling sound of metal breaking the eerie silence. He took a few more steps before a door loomed out of the darkness, and he stopped. "We're here," he said.

Set deep in the rock, the metal door clanked as Henry inserted a key into the lock.

"What's in there?" whispered Millie.

Henry pushed the door open, the hinges groaning. Light flooded the corridor, and Henry pointed at the glowing circle of light which seemed to hover in the small room beyond the door. "That's what's in here," he said. "The door to The Chaos."

Henry stepped into the room, and Millie took tentative steps behind him. As she neared the circle of light, it became apparent it wasn't hovering — it was contained by a stone circle, and a small plinth — resembling an altar, was built on the floor before it, carved from stone.

The circle of light flickered and shimmered, and as Millie neared it, she became aware that it was emitting a low sound, reminding her of wind in treetops. "It's beautiful," she said.

"What's beyond it isn't so beautiful," said Henry, standing before the light. "Would you like to see?"

"What will I see?" asked Millie, detecting a soft breeze in the air as the light flickered between bright reds and deep greens.

"I can't tell you," said Henry. "It's always different. When you saw that face in the fireplace, you were looking directly through this door — Edna used a simple spell to show you what we're looking at now, but with the veil removed so you could see into the depths."

Millie nodded. "Show me," she said. "I'd like to see where Reuben came from."

Henry took two steps closer to the glowing circle and lifted a hand. As his outstretched finger made contact with the light, ripples spread across the surface, and the bright colours gave way to a swirling mass of deep blacks and bright silvers.

"I can't see anything," said Millie, stepping closer to the circle and staring into the depths.

Henry put a hand on her shoulder. "Prepare yourself for —"

Wind rushed from the circle in a powerful surge, and Millie screamed. She stumbled backwards, tripping over her feet, and crashing to the floor, the small of her back slamming into hard-rock. "Close it!" she shouted. "Close it!"

The haggard face which glared at Millie appeared to be attempting to force its way through the barrier. Drool hung from the needle-sharp teeth which populated the lipless mouth, and the cavernous hole where a nose should have been, revealed bloody flesh and sinew. The deep-set eyes, filled with anger and hate, stared directly at her as the face pushed against the invisible force field.

Henry touched the barrier again, and the face was gone, the blacks and silvers replaced with vibrant colours once more. "I'm sorry," he said, offering Millie a hand, and helping her to her feet. "I didn't expect that to happen. The creatures are becoming more brazen since Esmeralda died. Are you all right?"

Millie took three steps away from the shimmering circle, and rubbed the painful spot at the base of her back. "What was that, Henry?" she said. "What the hell was that?"

"A creature of chaos," said Henry.

"A demon?" said Millie.

Henry nodded. "Yes," he said. "I'm sorry you had to see it. I was expecting a far less spectacular show."

"What did you mean?" said Millie. "The Creatures are becoming more brazen since Esmeralda died?"

Henry pointed at the stone plinth on the floor. "Do you see that?" he said, indicating a deep circular recess in the stone.

"Yes," said Millie. She looked more closely. A bundle of thin white strands tied together with course string had been laid in the bottom of the hole. "There's something in there. What is that? It looks like hair."

"It is," said Henry. "It's Esmeralda's hair."

"Why?" said Millie.

Henry looked at the floor. "I haven't been completely honest with you, Millie," he said.

Millie took another step away from the circle of light. "Honest with me about what?" she said.

"About why you're here, in Spellbinder Bay," said Henry.

Millie pulled her jeans higher around her waist, the small of her back aching. "Just why am I here?" she said, glaring at Henry. "Tell me, *Mister Pinkerton*."

Henry bent at the waist, and picked up the snippet of Esmeralda's hair, gripping it between two fingers. "This contains magic," he said. "Powerful magic. The same magic which flows through your veins, Millie. The magic needed to form this barrier between good and evil. The barrier between order and chaos. As long as there is a witch from your bloodline living in Spellbinder Bay, the barrier will remain as strong as it has for centuries."

Realisation dawned on Millie. "So you brought me here to use me? To use my magic?" she said. "Was anything you told me true? Did Esmeralda's energy just happen to find me after she died, like you told me it had, or was that a lie, too?"

Henry didn't need to speak, his eyes conveyed everything Millie needed to know. He took a step towards her. "I'm sorry," he said. "I —"

Millie had heard enough. She turned her back on Henry and the terrifying door to another dimension, and ran from the room. She wasn't going to stop running until she'd grabbed her belongings from the cottage, and turned her back on Spellbinder Bay, too.

Chapter 29

*R*euben squawked with fright as Millie barged into the cottage, slamming the door behind her. "What's wrong?" he demanded. "I was trying to have a snooze!"

"I've had enough," said Millie. "That's what's wrong! My life may have been miserable in London, but at least I knew what was happening to me. At least I didn't keep discovering things which made me question who I was, and what I was doing."

Reuben fluffed up his plumage, and fluttered the few feet from the sofa to the table. He looked up at Millie. "Where have you been?" he said. "Tell me what happened, Millie. You look... distraught."

"I've been to see Henry," said Millie. "He began to tell me things, things he'd lied to me about. He showed me the doorway to chaos, too — the awful place that you came from. Everything is getting too much for me, Reuben. I've had enough, I'm leaving, I've come to say goodbye to you and pick up what few belongings I own."

"You've come to say goodbye?" said Reuben. "So

that's it? You're leaving me — just like that? With no concern about what will happen to me?"

Millie scowled. "I'm sure you'll do just fine without me, Reuben," she said. "You've got plenty of other people in Spellbinder Bay to speak to — Henry told me you'd been talking to him behind my back."

"I was scared," said Reuben. "Since all the excitement of solving Albert's murder died down, you've still not committed yourself to staying here — in Spellbinder Bay. *In this cottage.*"

"I made a few remarks," said Millie. "I never once said to you that I definitely wasn't staying. There was no need for you to go airing your ridiculous concerns to Henry. I don't like people talking about me when I'm not there. It's rude."

Reuben looked away. "I don't think my concerns are ridiculous," he said. "When I was retrieved from The Chaos by Esmeralda, she promised I'd never have to go back there. The thought of spending eternity there terrifies me. And as I told you before, when you finally commit yourself to living in this cottage, the cottage will reveal more of itself to you. That's how I know you haven't decided to stay — the cottage hasn't accepted you yet."

Millie gazed down at the cockatiel. "What do you mean, Reuben? she said. "About spending eternity in The Chaos?"

Reuben blinked. "I assumed... I assumed Henry had told you."

"Told me what?" said Millie, lowering herself onto the sofa. She patted the cushion next to her. "Come here," she said. "What's wrong? You look scared."

Reuben swooped from the table and landed next to

Millie. He bowed his head. "I shouldn't have said anything," he said. "I don't want to add to your burdens."

"That's exactly what Henry said," explained Millie. "He told me that by summoning you I may have added to my burdens. What did he mean?"

"He means that knowing what will happen to me if you leave, may affect your decision about leaving, or staying in Spellbinder Bay," he said. "I didn't know whether to tell you or not — it felt selfish to worry about myself when you were having doubts about the path of your own life. I almost told you on the day you called me into your bedroom to show me the photograph of your mother which had been fixed by magic. Thankfully George interrupted us before I could finish telling you."

So much had happened since then, and Millie hadn't had the time to focus much on people around her, and what had or hadn't been said, but as she remembered that day, she recalled the conversation Reuben was referring to. "That's right. You began saying it was a matter of —"

"I'm glad George interrupted us," said Reuben. "I *had* been about to say it was a matter of life and death, but that would have been incorrect — it would be a matter of the wonderful life I'm living now, or a life in chaos."

"I don't understand, Reuben," said Millie. "What is it about Spellbinder Bay? Why won't anybody say what they really want to say, instead of beating around the bush? Look me in the eye, Reuben, and speak to me."

Reuben gave a small sigh, and shook out his feathers. "Okay," he said. "When you summoned me, you formed a link between us — a link that can never be broken. A bond between witch and familiar is a strong one. If you leave Spellbinder Bay the bond will be broken, and my spirit will be ripped from the body of this cockatiel and sent back to The Chaos. Forever."

The cockatiel bowed his head, and Millie placed a finger beneath his chin, gently lifting his eyes to hers. "I could take you with me, Reuben," she said. "If I decide to leave."

Reuben shook his head. "It doesn't work like that," he said. "I need to be within the radius of the magic emitted from Spellbinder Hall. I can never leave this town."

"What about when Esmeralda died?" said Millie. "You didn't go back to The Chaos then. Surely the bond with her was broken?"

"As I told you before," said Reuben. "Esmeralda's energy remains within this cottage. The energy of every witch who has ever lived in this cottage returns here when they die. The energy of generations of witches resides within these walls. Until you summoned me, it was Esmeralda's energy tying me to this dimension — now it's yours, and if you leave Spellbinder Bay, your energy leaves with you, and I go back to The Chaos."

Millie took a deep breath. "Are you telling me I can never leave Spellbinder Bay? And if I do, you'll be sent back to the awful dimension you came from?"

"Not quite," said Reuben. "If the cottage has accepted you, and revealed its secret, then you can leave. As long as you keep returning, some of your energy will remain in these walls wherever you go on the planet, but if you sever all ties with Spellbinder Bay before the cottage has accepted you, then yes, I will be sent back to the awful dimension I came from."

Millie closed her eyes. Was Spellbinder Bay really that bad? Could she envision a life amongst a paranormal community? Amongst people like Sergeant Spencer, Judith and George? Amongst people who seemed to care for her. *Amongst friends.*

When she opened her eyes, Reuben was no longer looking at her — his twinkling coal black eyes were fixed on a point beyond her. "You've decided to stay," said the cockatiel.

"How can you tell?" said Millie. "Am I that transparent?"

Reuben shook his head. "Look behind you Millie," he said. "The cottage has accepted you. It knows you're going to remain in Spellbinder Bay."

Millie turned her head slowly, and stared in disbelief at the new addition to the cottage.

Constructed from thick timber, and with a small circular window set at eye level, the door to the left of the fireplace had definitely not been there before.

"What is it?" said Millie, approaching the doorway and placing a hand on the hard wood, certain the timbers were vibrating beneath her fingertips.

"The real reason for this cottage being here," said Reuben. "I wanted to tell you about it so badly, Millie, but I couldn't — you had to make the decision to stay here before the door was revealed to you."

"What's behind it?" said Millie. "Do you know?"

"Yes, I know," said Reuben. "It was behind that door that Esmeralda rescued me from The Chaos. The door vanished when she died, but Henry assured me it would reappear when another witch took her place."

"*Of course* Henry would know," said Millie. "Is there anything *Henry* doesn't know?"

The door creaked as it opened, and Millie took a nervous step backwards. The familiar face that appeared in the open doorway offered her a wide smile. "There are plenty of things I don't know," said Henry, stepping aside and inviting Millie through the door with a flourish of his arm. "But why don't you come with me and let me explain some of the things I *do* know. Some of the things which may be hard for you to understand."

"What's down there?" said Millie, peering down the steps which Henry stood at the top of. "And how did you get in there?"

"Follow me," said Henry, turning his back and descending the steps. "Welcome to your coven cavern, Millie Thorn."

Chapter 30

Bathed in a soft green light, the large cavern smelt like a spice shop. Rough shelves, crowded with books, colourful glass bottles, and bunches of dried herbs, were hewn out of the rock walls, and the source of the green glow rippled lazily in the centre of the floor, contained in a circle of stones built to waist height.

"Another moon-pool?" said Millie, her eyes adjusting to the gentle light.

"The same magic," said Henry, "but on a smaller scale. Think of it as your cauldron."

"What is this place?" said Millie, picking up a small cork stopped blue bottle. "What is all this stuff?"

"It's centuries of magical knowledge and spells," said Henry. "Every witch who has ever lived here has added to the collection you see before you, and now everything in here is yours to use and add to."

Reuben landed on an old twig broom, propped up against a rickety bookshelf. "I watched Esmeralda doing a lot of magic down here," he said. He dropped his eyes.

"We had some good times in this old cave," he said. "She pulled me from that very cauldron twenty-three years ago."

"From The Chaos," said Millie.

Reuben nodded. "I was lucky. When her magic seeped into The Chaos searching for a suitable familiar, it found me. It was like being reborn when she manipulated my spirit from that green pool and placed me in the body of an owl."

Henry stepped towards the cauldron, and cleared his throat. "This cavern is as old as the planet earth," he said. "The cottage above is a manifestation of the magic contained in the cauldron. The building above us wasn't always a cottage — it has taken on many forms — an iron age round house, a bronze age hut — it has manifested itself in many ways, but it has always been here to hide the cavern from non-magic eyes."

Millie studied Henry with suspicion. She still wasn't sure what secrets he was hiding from her. She began with an easy question. "How did you get in here, Henry?" she said. "Inside this cavern — before the door was even visible to me?"

Henry removed his glasses and wiped one of the lenses on his shirt cuff. "Do you remember when I came to visit you in London — I told you I needed to be in Scotland before the full moon rose — to meet a young man, and you doubted it was possible that I could travel there so quickly?"

"Yes," said Millie. "I remember, and since learning about some of the people who live in this town, I'm assuming the young man in question is a werewolf?"

"Indeed," said Henry, "and he's settled into his new

life in Spellbinder Bay with remarkable ease. As for how I arrived in Scotland with time to spare…"

Henry vanished with a sound like a flat bottle of pop being opened, and Reuben laughed as Millie stared around the cavern.

"Where is he?" said Millie.

"He could be anywhere on the planet," said the cockatiel. "Who knows?"

Another soft fizzing sound came from behind her, and Millie span on the spot to see Henry smiling at her. "I trust I didn't scare you?" he said.

Millie shook her head. "Where were you?" she asked.

"London," said Henry. "I've been paying a certain con-woman a few impromptu and unannounced visits since she stole your savings and your confidence. I told her I was the ghost of the dead father of one of her victims, and if she didn't change her ways, I would haunt her for the rest of her days. It seems I've scared her enough to reset her moral compass. She's given up her criminal ways and is working for a charity helping homeless people."

"You did that?" said Millie. "For me?"

"And her other victims," said Henry. He winked. "But mostly for you."

Millie offered the old man a smile. He had her back covered, it seemed. Maybe any secrets he still held from her weren't so awful. "How did you do it?" she said. "How did you travel to London and back in the space of a few seconds?"

"I'm not like you, Millie," said Henry. "In fact, I'm unlike anybody in this town, either human or paranormal. I'm not made of flesh and blood. Not as you would understand it."

"What are you made of?" said Millie. "You look like flesh and blood from where I'm standing."

"As the building above us is constructed from energy, yet resembles a cottage," said Henry. "The same is true for me. I'm constructed of energy, yet resemble a human. As Windy-dune Cottage is the manifestation of the magic contained in your cauldron, I'm the manifestation of the magic contained in the moon pool beneath Spellbinder Hall. In fact… you could say I *am* Spellbinder Hall. Or a portion of it at least."

"You're Spellbinder Hall?" said Millie. "I don't understand."

Henry gave her a kind smile. "Not many people do understand," he said. "Spellbinder Hall is much like Windy-dune Cottage, and I'm the human face of it. I'm made from energy, and as such, I can travel *through* energy — the invisible lines of energy which criss-cross the planet. I can be anywhere I like in the blink of a human eye."

"Does this place get any stranger?" said Millie. "What else am I going to learn about Spellbinder Bay?"

Henry laughed. "Plenty of things, Millie Thorn, I'm sure, but first let us begin with what I was trying to tell you before you ran from Spellbinder Hall."

"About using my magic to prevent… *things* from coming through the door to The Chaos?" said Millie.

"We can begin there," said Henry, with a nod of his head. "Yes." He gazed into the green glow emitted by the cauldron. "When the moon-pool was created by ancient magic, so was the door to The Chaos — think of it as good and evil, or yin and yang — opposites of one another, yet somehow dependant on each other."

"I understand the concept," said Millie.

"There was a time when the door to The Chaos was completely open," said Henry. "Long before humans roamed the planet. It's where vampires, werewolves and all the other diverse paranormal people came from. Demons crossed between the two dimensions freely, too, and the world we live in wouldn't have been a nice place to inhabit all those years ago."

"Not a nice place at all," said Reuben, with a shudder. "Believe me."

"When humans did arrive," said Henry. "Some of them were able to harness the magic of places like the moon-pool. Gifted people, people like you, Millie."

"Witches?" said Millie.

"They went by many names in many parts of the world," said Henry, "but yes, witches. These witches soon learned about the existence of the door to The Chaos and set about closing it, using powerful magic which has been passed down through a select bloodline."

Millie looked at the cauldron. "My bloodline," she said.

"Indeed," said Henry. "And it is your presence in this cottage which will keep the door closed."

"My hair?" said Millie. "You need my hair — to put in the place of Esmeralda's, on the stone plinth?"

"No," said Henry. "That was only necessary after Esmeralda died. Some of her magic remained in her hair after she cast off her mortal coil. The stone plinth was built with such precautions in mind. We won't need your hair — all you need to do to keep the door as safe as it can be, is to call Windy-dune Cottage your home. Your magical energy will do the rest."

"*As safe as it can be*?" said Millie. "What do you mean?"

"No door, magical or otherwise, is impenetrable," said Henry. "And the door to The Chaos is no exception. Demons pass through it. Not in numbers large enough to cause devastation to this world, but they do pass through."

"Most of them don't survive long," explained Reuben. "They need a host to live in — just like I do. Some demons find a host quickly enough to allow their presence in this world to continue, but most perish before they can take over a human body."

Millie frowned. "And what do these demons do in the bodies they take over?"

"Some of the worst dictators and serial killers in the history of the world have been demons," said Henry. "Others simply become low-level criminals. None are beneficial to this dimension, though. They all mean us harm to some extent."

"You're not making Spellbinder Bay sound the safest of places to live in," said Millie.

"Would you rather live here," said Henry, "with the door to The Chaos nearby — where you can monitor it. Or out there — in the normal world, never knowing what may have passed from one dimension to the other? Never knowing what evil may lurk in the shadows around you."

"Better the devil you know," said Millie.

"Precisely," said Henry.

Millie approached the cauldron and looked into the swirling depths. She lifted her eyes and smiled at

Reuben. "I've made my decision, Henry," she said. "As you know — I've decided to stay in the bay. Now I need to know if there's anything else you're holding back from me. I got the feeling after you'd shown me the door to The Chaos that you'd been selective about what you've told me — about why I'm here. So now's the time to clear the air. Tell me everything I need to know."

Henry nodded. "What I'm about to tell you may come as a shock to you, Millie. Would you like to sit down?"

Millie stood straighter, drawing her brows together. "No. I'm perfectly fine standing here."

"Okay," said Henry. He pointed at a large black metal box, pushed up against the cave wall. "In that box," he said, "is everything you require to begin enjoying the wealth passed down to you by generations of witches. There are bank account details, stocks and shares, bonds — all in your name of course. The cottage would have seen to that when it showed you the door to this cavern. You're a rich woman now, Millie."

"And you own a lighthouse!" added Reuben.

"Is that the shock?" said Millie. "I was expecting worse."

"There are other things in that box," said Henry. "Most importantly, a letter. A letter which you were only supposed to open if this cavern was ever revealed to you. That time has come."

"A letter?" said Millie. "A letter from who?"

Henry crossed the cavern and bent over in front of the box. He lifted the lid and retrieved a thick white book from inside. "It's better I show you," he said.

"The photograph album," said Reuben, fluttering onto Millie's shoulder. "It's all Esmeralda's work! She loved to take pictures. We spent hours looking at her pictures together!"

Henry opened the book, and paused on the first page. "This was the first photograph Esmeralda took when she moved into this cottage," he said. "It's a picture of the witch who lived here for two years before her. The witch who wrote you the letter in the box. The letter which she handed to me fourteen years ago, as she lay on her deathbed."

Millie's chest thumped, and her breathing quickened. A cold chill spread along her arms, and her stomach flipped. "Fourteen years ago?" she said, her voice trembling.

Henry nodded. He passed the album to Millie. "She asked that you should never know that she was a witch unless there came a time in your life when this cavern was revealed to you. That time is here. For better or worse."

Millie held the book in shaking hands, and through a veil of tears, stared at the photograph, already sure she knew who it portrayed. The slight bend in the nose, and the happy eyes of the woman pictured standing outside Windy-dune Cottage confirmed it. "My mother," she whispered. "How can this be?"

***

"THAT'S YOUR MOTHER?" SAID REUBEN, FROM HIS position on Millie's shoulder. "I told you I'd seen her face before! She looked older in the photograph you showed me upstairs, but it's definitely her!"

Millie swallowed, her fingers trembling.

"Yes, she was younger," said Henry. "The picture

was taken twenty-four-years ago, before Esmeralda had rescued you from The Chaos, Reuben." He took a step towards Millie. "See how her hands are closed across her stomach, Millie?" he said.

"She was pregnant," said Millie, her tongue rasping on the dry roof of her mouth.

"Yes," said Henry. "She left Spellbinder Bay when she discovered she was with child."

Millie closed her eyes. She counted to five, willing the rage which was bubbling in her stomach to subside. When she sensed she was ready, she slammed the photograph album shut, startling Reuben, who flew from her shoulder and landed on the rim of the cauldron. "Tell me everything, Henry," she demanded. "Right now. From the beginning. Or I swear I'll explode."

Chapter 31

*H*enry pushed his glasses higher along his
nose and took the photo album from
Millie's outstretched hand. He placed it back in the box,
and closed the lid. "I couldn't tell you before, Millie," he
said, his voice soft. "Your mother made me promise. She
made me promise that you'd only learn the truth if
somehow you found your way to this cottage, and ultimately, this cavern."

"Well, I'm here," snapped Millie. "So get that
tongue wagging, Henry Pinkerton."

With a sigh, Henry lowered himself onto the box,
and removed his glasses. He placed them on the metal
lid beside him, and gazed into empty space. "Your
mother was like you, Millie. She didn't know she was a
witch until a dead witch's energy found her. When the
energy found her, I visited your mother in much the
same way I visited you, and she moved here, to Spellbinder Bay. She enjoyed it here, and she threw herself
into her new lifestyle."

"Unlike me," said Millie.

Henry smiled. "Your mother didn't witness a murder on her first day in the bay, Millie, but that aside — yes, she did take to it better than you have been able to do so far. She seemed less... nervous about finding out what she was."

"She always was tough," said Millie.

"Indeed," said Henry, "and she fitted in here beautifully — until she became pregnant. Which was when she asked to leave the town."

"I'm going to come back to the subject of her pregnancy," warned Millie, with narrowed eyes. "My mother told me that I was conceived during a brief fling, and that she could never find my father to tell him about me. If you've got any answers about that, I'll be wanting them, but right now, carry on — why did she leave when she found out she was pregnant?"

Henry remained silent for a few moments. When he spoke, his eyes had saddened. "When Judith arrived here in Spellbinder Bay with Sergeant Spencer, the story about what had happened — what she'd done to her parents, shocked the paranormal community in the town. Your mother helped them settle in, like the rest of us, but we all struggled to comprehend what that little girl had been through."

"My mother knew Sergeant Spencer and Judith?" said Millie.

"Yes," said Henry. "She helped them adjust. As we all did, to the best of our abilities."

"Okay," said Millie. "So what's that got to do with why my mother left town?"

"When she found out she was pregnant," said Henry. "She did what any expectant mother does — she began worrying about your future. Until Judith came to town, magic had only held good things for your mother. It had never been the cause of tragedy. Your mother panicked, I think. She didn't want her child growing up around magic — if magic had the potential to devastate a child's life, like it had Judith's. She wanted no further involvement in our town, and I honoured her wish. I broke her magical bond with the cottage, and she left."

"So a witch can leave?" said Millie. "If she wants."

"Of course," said Henry. "But your mother hadn't formed a bond with a familiar. She had no other life to worry about apart from the one growing in her stomach."

"Don't worry, Reuben," said Millie, seeing the bird had dropped his head. "I'm not leaving, whatever Henry tells me. You won't be going back to The Chaos."

"I'd rather you live a fulfilled life away from this town, if that's what you'd prefer," said Reuben. "I'd go back to The Chaos if it made you happy, Millie."

Millie patted her shoulder, and the cockatiel fluttered to it, landing gently. Laying a finger on the little bird's chest, Millie turned her head to look at it. "Neither of us is going anywhere," she said. "I happen to like you, and I happen to like the other people in this town. I've committed myself to living here, and I intend to stay." She looked at Henry. "Whatever I learn."

Henry nodded. "That was that," said Henry. "The energy which had found your mother went in search of another witch, and soon she was living in this cottage."

"Esmeralda?" said Reuben.

"Yes," said Henry. "On the day Esmeralda arrived with her camera and her kind heart, Millie's mother left, never to return for three years."

"She returned?" said Millie.

"Yes," said Henry. "She brought you with her."

"So I have been here before?" said Millie. "I knew it! I thought I'd been having déjà vu. Tell me, Henry — have I been to the moon-pool before? I felt like I had when we took Lillieth there after my accident."

"Yes," said Henry. "That's where we tried to tame your magic."

"Tame my magic?" said Millie.

"Your mother brought you back because you'd started to display magic, Millie," said Henry. "Magic your mother was concerned about. You'd begun to make things happen when you became angry."

"She was worried I'd do something like Judith had," said Millie.

"Yes," said Henry. "So I did what she asked. I used the moon-pool to weaken your magic. You had — *you have* strong magic Millie, and I warned your mother that when Esmeralda died there would be a strong chance that her energy would seek you out. After all, you had been conceived in this town, and you were of the same ancestral bloodline as the original coven witches. Your mother ignored my warning and took you back to the normal world, hoping to keep you away from magic."

"My mother kept all that hidden from me?" said Millie. "For ten years."

"Yes," said Henry, "but when she became ill and knew she wouldn't recover, she contacted me. She asked me to keep you safe. So I watched you."

"You watched me?" said Millie. "You used energy to travel to where I was, and spy on me, didn't you?"

Henry gazed at the floor. "Not in an intrusive way, Millie. I needed to ensure that your magic wouldn't cause any problems. You'd lost your mother — that's enough to cause any child to become angry, and with your potential to cast spells in anger, I needed to know you were safe — that the people around you were safe — your Aunty Hannah, Uncle James, and eventually their son."

"All that information you had about me when you came to London," said Millie. "About my ex-boyfriend — that was from spying on me, wasn't it?"

Henry sighed. "Yes," he said. "If you must use the word *spy*. When Esmeralda's energy found you, Millie, I was pleased. I wanted you back in Spellbinder Bay. I knew I could look after you here. So I used the knowledge I had about you to intrigue you. I wanted to ensure you'd be curious enough to come to Spellbinder Bay."

"Why didn't you just tell me I was a witch?" said Millie. "That would have been easier than leaving magical notes and money."

"You'd be surprised how often that doesn't work," said Henry. He smiled. "It's odd, but when you arrive unannounced to tell somebody they're a witch, they often throw you out of their home and telephone the police."

Millie closed her eyes and took a deep breath. "I'm sure I should have a lot more questions for you, Henry, and I'm sure I should be angrier with you, but I'm not. If you were only doing what my mother asked you to do, then I can understand that." She opened her eyes. "I'm angry with her, though. Very angry. I'm angry with my mother."

"I'm sure she knows that on some level, Millie," said Henry.

"How can she? She's dead," spat Millie.

"Her energy lives on," said Henry. "Within this

cavern. Within the cauldron. Every witch who has ever lived here finds their way back when they die. Witches can't become ghosts like non-magical people can, but your energy will return here when you eventually pass over, Millie. Your existence will never fizzle out to nothing."

"I feel her," said Millie, a tear burning her cheek. "I felt her on the first day I arrived here. I remember feeling as safe as a child in the arms of their mother."

"You'll always feel her, Millie," said Henry. "As long as you live in this cottage, you'll feel her."

Millie's shoulders slumped. She looked at the box beneath Henry. "You mentioned a letter from my mother."

Henry stood up. He replaced his glasses on his nose, and opened the box. "Millie," he said, retrieving a white envelope, "you should be prepared before you read this. It contains knowledge I'm not certain you're ready to learn. Your mother was adamant that should you ever find your way to this cavern, I should warn you about something before handing over this letter."

"Warn me about what?" said Millie, holding out an open hand.

Henry handed Millie the envelope. "In that envelope is the name of your father, Millie. Your mother told me who it is, and I must warn you — he still resides in Spellbinder Bay. Your father is here, Millie, and he knows nothing about you."

Chapter 32

*S*itting alone on a bench next to the harbour, Millie gazed out to sea. She licked the honey flavoured ice-cream she held in her left hand, and squeezed the contents of her other hand between two fingers.

"Lovely morning!" came a voice to her side.

Millie looked up at the man standing next to the bench. "Oh, hi, Jim," she said. "Yes, it's a lovely day."

"Admiring the boats?" he asked.

"And the dolphins," said Millie. "They've been jumping like mad. They're having fun today!"

"A bit like me," said Jim. "Having fun. I'm about to set out on a cruise around the Mediterranean. It's always been an ambition of mine, but I've never been able to do it."

"In that little boat of yours," said Millie, shooing a seagull from the bench next to her, its eyes on her ice-cream. "Will it make it that far?"

Jim smiled. He pointed a thick finger out to sea.

"See that yacht moored out there?" he said. "The one too long to bring alongside the harbour?"

Millie nodded. "I've been admiring it."

"Lobster's Gold," said Jim.

Millie raised an eyebrow. "Pardon?"

Jim gave a wide grin. "That's what I've named her — Lobster's Gold. She's second-hand, but she's a beauty!"

"It's yours?" said Millie. "How?"

Jim sat down next to Millie, his old eyes looking young, and his heavy gold watch shining in the sunlight. "Can you keep a secret, young un'?" he said. "I've been dying to tell somebody, and you don't seem like the type of girl who'll get all jealous of another person's good fortune."

Millie turned to face him. "Now I'm intrigued," she said. "Go on. Your secret's safe with me."

"Well, you know when I last saw you down here at the harbour — I was having bad luck with my lobster pots being emptied by some thieving varmint?" said Jim.

Millie did remember, but she wasn't about to tell Jim that she'd found out the culprit had been a mermaid. "Yes," she said. "I remember."

"Well the strangest thing happened," said Jim. "I kept on dropping my pots again every day — the bills weren't paying themselves, and I was desperate for lobsters to sell." He paused. "You'll never guess what happened when I lifted them last Friday!"

"Go on," said Millie, tossing the seagull a sliver of cone. "What happened?"

"Most of them were empty," said Jim. "As I expected, but one of them… it was heavy, young un', so heavy. I thought the tide had pushed a rock in it or something, but guess what was in there?"

"I can't," said Millie. "What was in it?"

Jim's eyes shone. "Gold, young un'! And jewels! And not just any old gold! Treasure it was! Old, old treasure! Rings, coins, chains, and big old slabs of pure gold imprinted with French words. I could hardly lift the pot into the boat, but when I did, I did the responsible thing and told the authorities."

"What did they say?" said Millie, gazing out to sea. *Lillieth*. It had to be. *I'll fix your dress when I learn how to use my cauldron*, she said to herself.

"A man from a museum in London came for it!" said Jim. "They say it's of great historical value — from a Napoleonic shipwreck which has never been found, and as the finder — I get half of its value. They say it's worth over thirty-million quid, young un'! They deposited the first instalment two days ago. I'm rich, young un', rich!"

"That's amazing news!" said Millie. "I'm so happy for you, Jim!"

Jim chortled. "Thanks, young un'," he said. He looked down at Millie's right hand. "What's your news?" he said. "You not going to open it? Maybe it's good news, too."

Millie glanced at the letter from her mother. She looked out to sea. "I don't know," she said. "I've had it for a week. Some news is neither good or bad. Perhaps I'll sleep on it for another night or two."

The End

Read book number 2 in the series HERE

If you'd like to read more of my books, why not sign up
to my newsletter to keep yourself informed of new
releases? I never send spam emails. That's a promise!
You can sign up **HERE**

Also by Sam Short

About the Author

Sam Short loves witches, goats, and narrowboats. He really enjoys writing fiction that makes him laugh — in the hope it will make others laugh too!
You can find him at the places listed below — he'd love to see you there!

www.samshortauthor.com
email — sam@samshortauthor.com

Printed in Great Britain
by Amazon